Love at First Flight

Kristine Lynn

Comfy Cozy Books

Copyright © 2024 by Kristine Lynn

All rights reserved.

This is a work of fiction. All of the names, characters, organizations, places, and events portrayed in this novel are either products of the author's imagination or are used fictitiously. Any resemblance to actual events, locales, or persons, living or dead, is entirely coincidental.

No portion of this book may be reproduced, scanned, or distributed in any printed or electronic form without written permission from the publisher.

Cover image © J Sudnitskay/Shutterstock
Cover design by Book Cover Zone

Printed in the United States of America

For Anna

My writing partner-in-crime.

What a joy to have a dear friend walking this path with me.

One

Flying

"Calling all passengers for Flight 835 to Munich out of Gate 39," the overhead speaker announced.

Sarah Murphy glanced up. She couldn't even see the sign for Gate 39. *Shoot.* How was it possible that even when she flew into the same terminal she was scheduled to depart out of, she was still late? And why did that add to the pervasive fear keeping her up at night that she was showing up late for her own life?

She pressed the phone between her ear and shoulder as she navigated the jog to the gate in her two-inch heels. A paper cup of coffee precariously balanced in one hand while she tried without luck to drag her carry-on with the other at a speed that would break one of her heels, her ankles, or both if she didn't get there soon.

The voice on the other end of the phone just kept on chattering away as if Sarah wasn't playing her own version of *Amazing Race: Airport Edition*. Not that she would have asked her daughter to be quiet for all the money in the world.

"Hey, watch it!" a man yelled as he barreled by, checking her shoulder as if she'd stepped into his path and not the other way around. She was used to the invisibility of her uniform, but it was part of the reason this job was wearing on her by the minute.

Her ponytail swayed with her steps, whipping her in the face each time she had to dodge a traveler that stopped without warning in the middle of the terminal, checking their phones or wrangling kids. *Ugh. Why hadn't she taught herself to do one of those buns the other flight attendants had mastered? It was one more way she felt like a fraud, an outsider, each time she showed up to work.*

21, 22, 23… Good grief. She wasn't even close. It had to be gate 39, all the way at the end. Had to be a military transport as well. She hated those flights. All jacked up young men, testosterone-filled and fueling the crude, often sexist, comments their buddies made with "Huahs" and "Oohrahs."

The sugar-laced voice on the other line asked, "Are you there, Momma?"

"I am, honey. I am. I'm just going pretty fast, and it's so loud here. Can you hear me okay?"

"Yes. Nana gave me 'tella and pancakes for breakfast."

Sarah smiled.

"Is that right? You'd better put Nana on the phone, then, so I can yell at her for giving my princess too much sugar in the morning." Her daughter giggled, but it sounded so far away. Sarah sighed. She missed that little girl. Kora hollered, her mouth so close to the receiver, the scream sounded as if she'd been right next to her daughter.

"Nana, Momma's mad at youuuuu!"

Sarah didn't hear her mom's reply, but Kora giggled again.

"You can't yell at Nana. She says she's your momma and that makes her the boss."

"Well, that's true, little Bug. She is the boss, for now. But when I get back, it's broccoli for breakfast."

"Ewww! No! When *are* you comin' back, Momma? I miss you."

Sarah closed her eyes and inhaled the stale, airport air deep into her lungs. If the pay and benefits weren't so good, she'd walk out of the airport right now and find something—*anything*—closer to home. She'd work at a department store if she had to.

Just three more years. Then, she'd have her degree and could be home more with her daughter while she painted. It didn't guarantee insurance for them both, but she'd figure that out when she had her diploma.

"I miss you, too, Bug. I'll be back on Tuesday, just in time to take you to gymnastics. Does that sound good?"

"Yes! Yes! Will you stay the whole time?"

"I will, and I'll even record it so you can watch it later." Sarah reached Gate 39 and let her carry-on fall to the ground. "Bug," she started, but her daughter was in full-gab mode, talking about all the friends she would see on Tuesday when she got to go to gymnastics, wondering if her teacher would be as nice as her old one, and if Nana would like to come, too. "Kora, Kora, sweetie, I have to go now," she finally got out. Gosh, how it hurt her to say it. Her daughter was only this young, this sweet for so long, and Sarah was missing it. Someday, the sacrifice would be worth it, though. It had to be, or what was she doing?

"Nooooo," Kora wailed.

"Yes, Bean, I'm sorry. Can you put Nana on real quick?"

"Hmph. Nana! Momma wants you."

Sarah bit her lip to stave off tears. "Love you, Bug." She heard her mom rustling the phone away from Kora, always an effort in futility.

"Hey there, Sare-bear. About to head off?"

"Yeah, wheels up in about half an hour. I arrived late from the LA run. How's Kora?"

"Perfect angel, as usual. Don't worry about her, we're fine here. Have a safe flight and drop me an email when you get to Germany."

Sarah was about to reply, add a quip about the Nutella and pancakes, when she was knocked from behind, causing her to drop her phone and fall to her knees.

"Hey! Watch where you're going," she started, scanning the crowded ground for her phone. She sounded like the cranky tourists she served. Another reason she wanted out. The phone was nestled between two flyers' carry-ons and she fumbled getting it back to her ear. She was about to ask if her mom was still on the line, when the person who had bumped into her put a hand down to help her up.

She shook her head, no. All she wanted was to get to work and get this flight over with.

"I've got it, thanks." She stood up and wheeled around to tell whoever it was to pay more attention, that they could really hurt someone, when she froze. In front of her was the most painfully good-looking guy she'd seen in a while. Scratch that. *Ever.*

Holy handsome, Batman.

With broad shoulders and tan, chiseled cheekbones, he looked like the cover of a romance novel come to life. Or, at least the fantasies Sarah'd drummed up after reading one of her mom's stolen Harlequin novels. Her heart rate quickened, and her breath caught in her throat. She composed herself, running her fingers through her ponytail, absently smoothing it.

Get your act together, Sarah Murphy. Is this what four years off of dating did to her ability to communicate with a handsome man? Namely, make it impossible. She swallowed her discomfort as far down her chest as she could manage.

"Mom, I've got to go. I'll get in touch when we land. Love you." She hung up the phone and turned to face the man in front of her. She'd drastically underestimated how tall he was when he'd first bumped into her; he had at least a foot on her, even with the two-inch heels she wore. Though he was dressed in plain clothes, his closely-cropped hair and the tan backpack slung over one shoulder suggested he would be on her flight this morning. She blushed but didn't look away.

Or, *couldn't*.

Suddenly, the lack of someone to gossip about a cute guy with turned into a painful ache in her chest. Because this man deserved to be shared and all she had was her mother, who would probably read way too much into her brief encounter. Sure, her mom was everything else to her—parent, childcare, even an occasional friend—but Sarah couldn't ask her to fill the role of a supportive group of women, too. It wasn't her mom's fault Sarah's life was too broken to cultivate deep friendships.

The ache turned into a stab behind her heart. At one point, she'd *had* friends in her corner, but a year after... after the worst year of her life, they'd tapered off, going back to their families, jobs, growing families. And Sarah'd been stuck in the same rut since.

It was hard to keep up with a world that had left her behind.

"I'm so sorry. I almost got run over by a double jogger and a mom who looked like she meant business."

"Yeah, they can be ruthless. Hell, hath no fury like a mom trying to get to the front of a boarding line."

The man grinned, showing off white, straight teeth and dimples that people wrote home about. Sarah was suddenly self-conscious of the small gap between her front teeth.

"I didn't realize you were on the phone, too. I hope it wasn't too important. I just had a quick question."

"No, no problem at all, I was just hanging up. How can I help you?" She kept his gaze, noting that his eyes were a light brown, almost like the fresh honey she bought at the farmer's market on Sundays. Flecks of gold embedded in the irises caused them to shimmer under the overhead fluorescents.

Sarah fought the way they drew her in, made her want for things she hadn't since Hank had died. Thinking about this man and her husband in the same beat sent her stomach flipping over itself. Well, that was weird. When was the last time she'd felt honest to goodness butterflies? And over a stranger, no less.

"Well, um, my Captain sent me over to the desk to see if we can get a few of us on early, check the plane, set up camp if you will. Except no one's there. Do you work here? I only ask because..." He trailed off, but his gaze trailed down her body. The scrutiny elicited a line of sweat under her arms. What was he looking at? Two seconds from reading him the riot act—because how dare he ogle her like that—his gaze settled on her nametag and uniform-issued ascot.

Oh yeah. The uniform. She was practically a walking advertisement for her airline.

She blushed again but smiled. Why was she letting this stranger get under her skin? She might be out of practice, but she'd done this before, the talking to a cute guy thing.

"My uniform? Yeah, I work here, but not here. I'll be on your flight this morning. I'm a flight attendant." She mentally slapped herself for stating the obvious. Out of practice, indeed; she was acting like a fifteen-year-old girl talking to her school's quarterback crush. "But I can ask someone. Just let me get to the gate and check in. Who should I ask for when I get back?"

"Captain Hoffman. He's the short, angry guy over there yelling at marines." She was disappointed that he hadn't given her his name, but she had no reason to hope that he was as intrigued about this chance interaction as she was. She turned and looked where he pointed and could only laugh. Sure enough, there was a small, balding man, who in any other scenario would be as unformidable as a kitten. Yet somehow, in uniform, he looked like someone she wouldn't want on her bad side.

"I'm Mike. Mendez. Most of the guys call me by my last name—it's how we operate." He chuckled, and she couldn't help the smile that spread across her cheeks, gap between her teeth notwithstanding.

She had a name. *Mike.*

Her brain went a horrifying step further and added her first name to his last. *Sarah Mendez. That didn't sound half bad.*

Mortification immediately followed. Okay, first thing that happened when she got home? She was signing up for a dating site. No way could she be left out in the wild like this. It wasn't safe for anyone.

"Nice to meet you, Mike. I'm Sarah Jean Murphy, but I go by Sarah." They both smiled and ducked each other's gaze at the same time. Yep. It was official. She was regressing back to full awkward teen. She could practically feel the braces and pimples again. She tucked a stray piece of hair behind her ear. "Well, I'd better get to work. See you on the plane." She walked away, fighting the urge to look back.

"Nice to meet you, Murphy. I'm glad it's you that'll be taking care of us."

She waved without turning around. One thing was certain, though. She didn't mind her job half as much as she had on her way to the gate.

Not when it came with complimentary gorgeous men to break up the taste of stale pretzels.

Mike looked down at his feet, his hands in his pockets. If he went back to his guys now, he'd catch endless grief. He just couldn't seem to wipe the dang smile off his face, which wasn't at all appropriate as they headed into an extremely kinetic combat tour.

But he didn't care. He hadn't counted on meeting a woman like Sarah, had he? Those brown eyes, like pools of chocolate staring up at him. Yeah, he was a goner, sunk in those depths without much of a reason to fight his way out. Then, there was the almost-invisible gap between her front teeth he'd spotted when she bit her bottom lip. Adorable.

He ran a hand through his hair. And... he got to spend the next twelve or so hours with the woman.

It wasn't like he had a problem getting dates—partly the uniform's fault—but, it had been years since he'd felt this kind of excitement buzzing through every cell in his body. Which was silly. Because he barely had a name. *Sarah Murphy*. Well, that was a good enough start as any, wasn't it? Maybe he'd seek her out when they were wheels up. Turn that start into some momentum.

Ah, who was he kidding? Of course, he would. He needed as much good tucked away in his thoughts as possible; where he was headed, there wouldn't be anything but loss and fear covered in fine, desert sand for the next seven months.

He turned around to head back but came chest to chest with the new guy to their company, Troy Kint. Mike had shared two words with the guy, and neither of 'em had made him think Kint was a good addition to the team.

"Who was that hottie?" Kint asked.

The quip was exactly enough to wipe the smile off of Mike's face.

"Excuse me, Corporal?" Mike made sure to pull rank. This kid had been a live wire since he got removed from Charlie Company earlier that month and pawned off on them. Why that meant he was good enough to take on a combat tour with a company of damn good Marines was information that eluded Mike.

"Just sayin', she might be worth joining the mile high club for. If you aren't down, mind if I take a swing?"

Mike balled his fists and took a step toward Kint, the noise of the cacophony of voices echoing off the windows mixing with his anger and making him dizzy. "Stand down, Kint."

His breath was rapid, coming out in huffs, no matter how much he tried to control it. Heat built under his skin in a way that had only happened after a firefight in combat, but Kint put his hands up in placation before Mendez could act on his anger.

"Fine, fine, she's all yours, Sarge. I can take a hint." He walked away, his laugh not unlike a cackle and Mike cringed. Times like this, he had no trouble imagining why Kint had been kicked out of his previous command.

Kint had no respect for rank, or women, it seemed. Only one of those was dangerous on deployment, but out there, danger meant injury or worse. He'd need to keep an eye on the guy.

Mike made his way to Captain Hoffman, anxious to see if Sarah would be the one to report back about his earlier request. His anger had dissipated, replaced by a flash of hope. He wanted the opportunity—any opportunity, no matter how small—to interact with her. No such luck, though.

Hoffman was still berating two junior marines about not getting haircuts before the flight. From the looks on their faces, it was the last time they'd make that mistake again. Mendez chuckled.

A blonde woman, taller than Sarah, but wearing the same uniform, approached them and informed the Captain that he and another marine were welcome to board early, if they could bring their military documents and boarding passes to the gate. The Captain looked at Mendez and lifted his chin, a silent question. *Join me?* Mendez nodded back. *Yes, sir.* Yeah, he was bummed Sarah hadn't been the one to deliver the news, but at least he got to be one of the first on the plane, where he'd have close to ten hours of flight time to work up the nerve to talk to her.

"You ready for this push, Sergeant?" Hoffman asked.

Mike shrugged, then nodded. "Feels the same as most, I guess, sir. Ready as we're trained to be, which is to say we're in good shape."

"Your guys nervous?"

"Just the right amount, sir."

Hoffman chuckled. "Good answer, son. Well, keep me posted. I see a few of 'em out there acting like idiots already and we're not even in-country. I wanna stay squared away this go around."

"Yes, sir. I've got my eyes on the issues, and we've got some conversations in the pipe. I'm on top of it."

"I know it, son. Proud to have you on the team. Real proud." To Mendez's surprise, Hoffman patted him on the back. It was such a paternal, unexpected gesture, heat built behind Mike's eyes. Well, heck. The world was set out to make him feel all the things today, wasn't it?

"Thank you, sir." Mike made himself check his boot laces, even though he wasn't wearing his boots yet, and his loafers didn't have any. He just needed to avoid looking his mentor in the eyes in case he saw the same thing he'd wanted from his dad. Respect. Now was not the time to start investigating that particular hole in his life.

Mike strolled down the aisle, taking the pillows and blankets from the seats and throwing them in a garbage bag. No way the guys needed more junk to lug around with them.

It was strange being on a plane with no one on it. It felt wrong, like being behind the scenes of a play where the characters weren't in costume yet. Some of the magic was missing. The only noise besides the purr of the air circulatory system were two flight attendants talking about going home for Christmas.

"Sucks there won't be any sad, lonely single men to pick up on a flight."

"I know, right? I mean, why not give the new girl the day off? She's the one with a kid. I want a stab at those desperate guys heading to Cabo for the holidays." They giggled and winked at him when he passed, then continued their emotionless chatter, both of their voices whiny and shrill. They reminded him of his kid sister and her friends. Boys and cell phones—the modern "intelligent conversation."

Was Sarah the "new girl" they mentioned? If it was, they mentioned a kid, but not a husband to go home to. He wasn't gonna put too much thought into why his pulse spiked at the thought of her going home alone or to a child. The empty place in his chest closed just enough for him to notice, though.

Captain Hoffman stopped to talk to the two women, and suddenly they were the picture of professionalism. Mike smiled. Hoffman could intimidate a male goat into giving milk. Mike had been around the Captain long enough now that he knew how to handle the man. Make him look good, keep the conversation short, and try not to mess up. Especially that last part. So far, it seemed to be working in his favor. He'd earned an atta boy and they weren't even wheels up yet.

Mike waited for him to finish asking them questions—*what is the emergency protocol for my guys, where are the exits, can I handpick who goes in the emergency exit rows*—all stuff that didn't need to be asked, but Hoffman was a man with not just plans A and B, but C, D, E, and F as well. It was what made him so good at his job.

Mike didn't want to stray too far from the Captain, but he strolled further down the aisle, trying to look nonchalant and like his walk was for a purpose other than finding Sarah. He didn't have to walk long, though. She came out from the back galley, and the second her eyes met his, her face lit up.

It made his heart stop, that smile. Her eyes crinkled up but somehow became brighter. He'd never met someone who smiled with their whole face. She walked toward him, and he faltered. What would he say that wouldn't sound stupid?

"Welcome aboard, soldier," she said when she got to him. He smiled.

"Marine. Welcome aboard, *Marine*. Calling us soldiers is the same as insulting our intelligence." Her smile was crooked, one side kicked up just higher than the other, and he found he liked it just as much as the original. Maybe more. The small gap between her teeth wound its way around his heart.

"My mistake, Marine. Mendez, was it?" She winked at him, and he swore his heart touched an actual rib it grew so dang big.

"Yes, ma'am. Now, how can we make this flight an easier one for you?"

She laughed, a throaty laugh that emanated from her belly. "That's supposed to be my line, Mendez." He liked hearing her call him by his last name. It didn't sound at all the same as when his guys said it—she made it playful and sultry at the same time.

His stomach flipped over on itself, a kinda nice surprise considering all his stomach had been good for the past few days was collecting stones of dread that were accumulating every time he thought about his family, the upcoming combat missions, the weighty responsibility of keeping his men alive.

"Yeah, but I know we can be a rough bunch. I'll try to keep them in line for you." This flirty banter somehow also felt natural, like he'd known this woman for longer than half an hour.

"Thank you. I'll try to do the same for my colleagues." She nodded at the two blonde flight attendants up at the front, still talking to Hoffman, still looking as serious as ever. He laughed, and Hoffman looked over at him, a frown on his face.

Mike cleared his throat. "I'd better see what the Captain needs me to do. You've never seen him angry. Annoyed at those junior marines, yes, but when that bald spot glows red, it could be bad for all of us." She chuckled quietly and pointed behind him. He turned and saw Hoffman headed his way. Mike winked, speaking loudly on purpose. "Thanks for the help, I'll be sure to pass that on to the Captain, miss." When he mimed an exaggerated grimace, Sarah blushed and headed toward the back of the plane.

He was giddy, out of control. He only got ahold of himself by remembering Kint's abrupt appraisal of her, which served to wipe the lovestruck idiot look right off his face.

"Getting friendly with the help, Sergeant?" Captain Hoffman asked. Mike stood tall, about to come up with a reply that would save him from any wrath when the Captain smiled. "She's cute, Mendez. Seems to like you, too. But, if she's anything like those flighty bimbos up front, don't waste your time. Now, make yourself useful and go ask her for a club soda, in the can, no ice."

That was it? Just get the Captain a club soda and chat up a pretty girl? Mike didn't know what to say. This day and its good fortune had shocked him stupid from the start, and it looked like it wasn't over yet. Hopefully, this would bode well for the start of his sixth combat tour.

"Yes, sir. You got it." Mendez walked to the back of the plane feeling—*knowing*—that this day, the next few hours, were somehow going to change his life. He just had to make it back from the desert, but he'd worry about that later.

Right now, he had a club soda as an excuse to find out more than just a name.

Two

Trouble in the Air

Sarah listened to Brenda and Brenda-Lyn—the Brendas as she called them; even those names sounded ditzy—discuss how to rope a man. It was all Sarah could do to suppress her groan. If she didn't have Mike a few rows from where she worked in the back galley, turning around to glance her way and wink or make a goofy face every few minutes, she'd go crazy. This was already the longest flight of her career.

Her colleagues pattered on about the Marines, low enough not to be heard by anyone but Sarah. The women openly discussed the men's haircuts, who would be a good kisser, whose butt looked the best in uniform. *Ugh.* It made Sarah ill to listen to the banality of their conversations. They were as deep as the water in the baths she gave her four-year-old.

She glanced at the back of Mike's seat, willing him to turn around and also worried if he did, she'd appear to be stalking him. What she couldn't figure out was why he was so interesting to her. He was cute and all—scratch that, *handsome as heck*—but it was something more. There was something about the way he looked at her that pulled her in and made her feel seen for the first time in years. Maybe ever. Even Hank hadn't totally understood her. Loved her, yes, but he'd never looked deep into her eyes and made her feel as if he got the inner workings of her heart and mind.

It might be a bit too much to pin on a stranger, but it was nice, finally being noticed. Besides, he'd be on his way to whatever mission the U.S. government had lined up for the Marines—not soldiers—and she'd never see him again.

A little harmless flirtation wouldn't hurt either of them.

As if on cue, Mike turned around and tossed a small paper airplane at her. It sailed ten feet down the aisle and she walked forward to meet it, hopefully before the girls noticed. She'd like to stay off their radar, if possible.

She scooped up the airplane, biting back a grin. He'd even taken the care to draw the logo of the airline on the side of it. How freaking sweet. Kora would love this. Sarah made a mental note to share this sweet moment with her daughter on Tuesday. It was rare she had good stories worth sharing; kind and respectful passengers just weren't the norm anymore.

Mike smiled back and mimed opening the airplane. She nodded and tucked it into her blue apron, out of sight. When he turned back around and opened a book, *The Gunslinger* by Stephen King, Sarah swooned. *The man read actual books.*

When Sarah turned around, there was a shorter but extremely broad marine standing in front of her, blocking her way back to the galley.

She smiled at him, ignoring the prickles of warning he sent dancing atop her skin.

"How is your flight, sir?"

When he didn't respond, just sneered up at her, the prickles turned into bells. At least she was surrounded by a couple hundred men who could help if he did anything, but still...

"Can I get you anything?"

"You sure can," he said, his voice notching the bells into warning sirens.

"Okay. Go ahead and sit down, and I'll bring it to your seat. We try not to block the aisle," she tried again.

The look he gave her back chilled her, sent a shiver down her spine. The man's smile was crooked and showed his teeth. By itself this wasn't any different than the other marines who'd smiled at her on the flight so far. But just like Mike exuded something good, wholesome, this man felt *off*.

It was his eyes. They were a deep blue, and narrowed so it gave the impression they were made of ice. She looked away, down at his name tape on his cammies. *Kint*. She didn't know much about the ranking system, but she knew enough to understand that the rocker on the bottom of the teepee on Mike's lapel was higher up than this simple teepee with guns underneath it.

"That won't work. I've got a thing or two you can get me," he told her. "But, none of it's gonna work from my seat."

She frowned. The way his crystal blue eyes took her in head-to-toe as he spoke left no room to misinterpret his words. A glance to her left and right confirmed her fears—he'd cornered her by the two rows that housed gear, not marines who could come to her aid.

"Have a seat, sir. You never know when we might hit some turbulence, and I wouldn't want you to get thrown around." She gave him her most basic customer service smile—lips pursed, no teeth—and held her ground, arms crossed across her chest. Confidence trickled back into her bloodstream, warming her against the icy glare from him. This wasn't the first jerk to hit on her. It was an occupational hazard she'd learned to address the first week on the job, thanks to an older flight attendant named Beverly.

"Give them the impression you care, but make the line you draw beyond that clear and distinct," she'd told Sarah. Boy, did that ever resonate now.

Kint didn't seem to care about the self-imposed lines she'd drawn, however. He didn't move his hand off the two seats on either end of the aisle. With the Brendas' drink cart blocking the galley behind her, the space between seats next to her filled with the guys' gear, Sarah was trapped.

He was one of those, then. The entitled guys who thought because she served them, she owed them something more than just a free soft drink and pretzels. Well, he had another thing coming.

"Excuse me, sir. You need to return to your seat. *Now.*"

"I don't think I do. I'm just stretching my legs. Getting some blood flowing." He moved closer to her now, so that his head was only inches from hers. Her stomach turned to stone, along with whatever courage she'd mustered. "Want to help with that?" He whispered this last part, and goosebumps rose on Sarah's skin, fear blossomed in her chest.

Maybe I could shove the drink cart back? Make it to the empty row without causing a scene?

She'd never felt this vulnerable, this exposed when she was on the job. Most guys who hit on her were put in their place when she stayed firm and professional against their early advances. This guy was different. He wasn't going to make this easy. Someone jumped the bags and closed the small gap between her and the drink cart, pinning her between them and Kint, and her breathing came quicker. There went her exit strategy.

"You heard her, Kint, get your butt to your seat. *Now*. Or, you and I can have a serious talk about your place on our team when we get to Germany." Sarah let out a deep breath and her shoulders relaxed. *Mike*. Just in time, too.

"You serious, Sarge?"

"You really want to find out, Corporal?"

Kint took a fraction of a step closer to them. He was now pressed up against her. She held her breath and closed her eyes.

"*Sit. Down.* I will not ask you again." Mike's breath was warm on her neck, and despite being paralyzed, the heat transferred to her lower abdomen with each word he spoke.

"You're blocking the way now, aren't you?" Kint said, his voice syrupy and smarmy. It grated her nerves like sandpaper on glass.

In one swift move, Mike tossed a few bags out of the way. His hands landed firm on her hips, moved her into an empty space between seats, and pushed himself against her, blocking her from Kint.

"Go. And don't get up again unless it's to relieve your bladder or until I personally come remove you from this plane."

"Yes, sir," Kint spat at Mike as he passed, saluting as he left. Sarah let out her breath slowly, deliberately, and looked up at Mike. The veins in his neck were pulsing, and he smelled of cinnamon and peaches. The juxtaposition of that coiled tension and sweet, enticing aroma was disorienting.

"You 'sir' me again and we'll have more than words, Kint."

She looked around Mike's chest. A jet-black shadow flickered across Kint's face before he broke into a smile, the same one he'd given her earlier, and turned around the rest of the way to his seat. She didn't know why, but an unease settled in her stomach unlike anything she'd felt before, even with Kint a safe distance away.

Mike turned to face her but didn't move back; only inches separated them. She didn't mind one bit. She looked up from under her lashes at him, and he offered a weak smile in return.

"I'm so sorry about that, Sarah. He's an idiot, but hopefully one who'll leave you alone the rest of the flight."

"My hero," she teased, and he frowned. "I'm kidding. Seriously, thank you for your help. He was just getting to the point where I felt super uncomfortable. I don't know what I would have done if you hadn't taken care of him." She meant that, too.

"I hate that he made you feel that way. Is it weird that I felt the need to protect you from the creep?"

She couldn't make words form coherently to answer, and shook her head instead. *Weird? No. Endearing? Um, yes.*

He grinned. "Good. I don't want to come off stronger than Kint. At least, I'm more subtle than those two." He nodded behind her.

She followed his gaze to the Brendas, who were unabashedly staring at them. Sarah shook her head. So much for flying under the radar. The Brendas would be impossible, wanting all the details about Mike.

"Yeah. They're bound to be relentless now. I'd better get back to work. Thank you, again." She blushed when she realized his hands were still on her hips. He must have noticed the flush of her cheeks and the reason for it because he let go of her slowly. Her skin burned where his hands had been.

"Of course. I couldn't stand by and watch you get hurt."

Her heart sped up and sweat formed on her brow. She moved past him in the aisle, straightening her apron as she walked. At the last minute, she turned to look at him again.

The fact was, she wasn't ready to say goodbye yet. She didn't want to give the "why" too much attention, but before she could convince herself not to, she blurted out, "Do you, um, have time in Germany, or do you leave straight away?"

No! Part of the allure of this guy is that you're not going to see him again.

Well, it's not like a coffee in Germany would make that less true. He was deploying and she was going home to a benign life raising a daughter alone. One more hour wouldn't hurt.

That was, if he said yes. Nerves rankled her.

He nodded and at least a little of the fear dissipated.

"I have time. Read the note."

She patted the space in her apron that housed the letter from him. For the second time that morning, she couldn't wipe the smile off her face. She shrugged past the Brendas when they raised their perfectly arched and penciled-in eyebrows at her, and went straight to the bathroom where she could read what Mike wrote without their beady, prying eyes trying to spy on her.

"Hey, where are you heading, Sarah?" she heard one of them, probably Brenda-Lyn, call after her. She waved them off, hoping they believed she just desperately had to use the bathroom.

"That girl is so strange," the other Brenda squawked, and Sarah smiled to herself.

She shut the door behind her, and her hands trembled as she took out the now-crumpled airplane. Good gracious, this man had her acting like an absolute fool. Even though she knew she should be more wary—after all she'd been through, if she never opened up again, no one would blame her—but she wasn't. She could trust Mike. If she knew nothing else about the man, she was certain of that one fact.

With that thought, she carefully undid the folds of the paper plane.

Mike couldn't keep his eyes forward, no matter what he overheard the marines talking about. Some mentioned contraband they were going to have their families ship over, others talked about the two blonde flight attendants and if they might be up for some "fun" when they got to Germany. The words washed over him like he was underwater, making it easy not to let himself get too invested.

They were good men with mostly good intentions, but something shifted when the prospect of combat blocked their view of a future they'd planned for themselves. The feral thread running through each man's heart thrummed a little louder. He wasn't immune, but felt like that thread had snapped after the last deployment. In its place was something that craved something softer, more permanent.

Other marines were watching movies, headphones in, drowning out the world. Mendez envied them that—the ability to put it all away, compartmentalize the flight, the deployment, the combat, the down time. He lived it all at full speed, each aspect of his life informing the rest, until it all bled together.

Including now. He was curious about Sarah, but his world—the harsh tan and brown lethal world he inhabited—careened into the daydreams he tried to drum up of taking her on a real date, finding out who her favorite band was, or kissing her goodnight.

The harsh reality was, something as sweet and innocent as romance didn't compute in the military. Not his military, anyway. However, he couldn't very well ignore the pull she had on him, either. He was only human.

Maybe she wasn't more than an attractive distraction, but why deny himself that when reality was a short thirty-six hours away?

Out of the corner of his eye, he watched her work, feeling both like the biggest creep, and like he couldn't stop himself if he tried. She had such an easy way about her, like she was made up of more bones and muscles than most other humans. Each turn she took started with her hips, and the rest of her effortlessly followed; it was as if the plane was an extension of her, the way she manipulated its corners and edges.

Mike reached into his tan rucksack and pulled out his leather-bound planner and the waterproof pen he'd bought at the PX two deployments ago. He'd fallen for that spiel hook, line, and sinker, paid way too much for a pen to use in the desert, where not so much as a cloud offered shade. Raised voices from a few rows ahead of him stopped him in his tracks, especially when one of them shouted, "Leave my stuff alone, Kint."

What was that kid up to now?

Before he investigated, Mike tossed Sarah another glance. She tucked a loose strand of silky auburn hair behind her ear, and he ignored the itch in his fingers to do the same to another curl on the other side of her cheek. Confusion spread through his limbs as the juxtaposition of her gentle giggle crashed into the sneering laugh from Kint. An urge to protect her from Kint rose up, which was awfully inconvenient. She was enchanting, distractingly gorgeous, but... she wasn't his concern and couldn't be. Not while the next seven months stared down the barrel at him.

Annoyance prickling his skin, Mike got up and walked down the aisle to where the commotion bubbled over.

Kint held a book high in the air, waving it like a lunatic hawking cheap cleaning detergent at the commissary. Another marine not from Mike's squad was leaping in the air trying to get it back from Kint. Kint cackled, the book just out of reach of the shorter marine. He was *trying* to be an a-hole. Mike's eyes narrowed, and his brow set in the way it always seemed to do around Kint. They'd technically only been deployed for six and a half hours now, and already this kid was making his life miserable.

"Give it, Kint. I don't want to lose my place."

"Oh, does the poor, wittle baby want his book back?" Kint's sadistic and satiric impression of a mother's voice was enough to make Mike hope the guy never brought kids into this world.

"Enough." Mike stepped between them in the aisle, one hand bracing himself on the seat, the other gesturing for Kint to hand over the book.

"Come on Sarge, I was just giving him a hard time," Kint whined. It didn't suit him.

"I said, *enough*." Mike was resolute. Sighing, Kint handed the book over to him, but just before it touched Mike's hands, Kint tossed it backwards in the air, over his head.

"Whoops. I slipped," he said, looking up into Mike's now near-slitted eyes. The owner caught the book by its cover, then dove into a recount of the experience for the marines seated on either side of him. They looked over at Kint and Mike, clearly more interested in whether or not they were going to go to blows or not.

"Sit down, Corporal. And if you get up again, I'll have you cleaning the head the first two weeks we're in country. I no longer care if your bladder explodes. I've had enough of your crap. You might find it cute here, but out there it'll get someone killed. Got it?"

Kint smiled that odd half smile, half smirk. "Got it, boss." Mike reeled at Kint's lack of respect. Calling him, boss? Sir? He had an NJP coming, if he wasn't careful. That kind of demerit came with more than a loss of pay–it would stay on his record the rest of his career.

Still, Mike needed to choose his battles.

Kint shoved the two marines on the end of the aisle over so he could fit between them and the seats, before slumping down with a huff. Mike released a sigh of relief, and the other marines around him did the same. He wasn't the only one who saw Kint as a menace, but he didn't want to bring it to the Captain just yet. He'd rather show Hoffman he could handle his own men, and avoid disrupting the man's first-class cabin experience. However, after stealing another look at Kint, who was watching him back through slitted eyes, his lips curled in disgust, Mike hoped that was possible.

When he got back to his seat, the pen and notebook were there, and he smiled. Had Sarah read the note he'd flown her way? He might not have space for more than a casual pen pal relationship with the woman, but that alone was enough to buoy his thoughts about the next seven months. Maybe at the least, he'd get a friend out of the deal.

Patience was usually his strong suit, but as he kept the galley in his peripheral vision waiting for word on if she'd join him for a drink, there wasn't a chance he'd be able to focus on much else.

And therein lay the base of his worries. If the flutter of emotions tearing around in his chest like unsupervised, caffeinated toddlers, was any indication of how this friendship was kicking off, he was in trouble.

Because friend, pen pal, or something... more, he didn't need any distractions when he got to the front lines. Out there, letting emotions override good sense could get someone killed. And like it or not, this chance meeting was drumming up all sorts of emotions that kicked Mike's good sense right out of the cargo door.

Three

Landing

Sarah read the note three times, unable to put it back in her pocket.

Dear Sarah,

I've never felt like the flight to Germany was a short one until today. I know it seems silly, old-fashioned even, but I want time to talk to you. Do you have any time in Germany? We're there for 13 ½ hours, some of that in customs, but I'd love any amount of time I can get with you before I ship out again. Let me know if you can meet up. Coffee shop outside customs (can't remember the name to save my life right now, but it's got a red awning)? Half an hour after we land?

_____ *Yes*

_____ *No (but I'll regret this later, so, yes, I'll meet you there)*

_____ *Get lost, creep*

Each time through, she stifled a laugh, her teeth clamped down on her knuckles. She didn't want any more attention from the Brendas. Her cheeks hurt from smiling, but she didn't care. She had a whole day to kill in Germany, and though she'd been dreading it at takeoff that morning, now she'd never looked forward to a layover as much as this one.

She checked the line marked "yes," and added "Boconero Café. My favorite, but doesn't open till 5 a.m. I'll see you then, Mendez." Walking out of the bathroom, the plane seemed brighter, a soft, gold light reflecting on the seats, on the pins the marines—well, some of them, anyway—had on their lapels. The cramped, cylindrical world she worked in seemed lit from the inside, and she felt it within her as well. It'd been way too long since she'd smiled like she was right now. It started in her lips, and reached all the way to her forehead, crinkling her skin in a way her mother always warned her would permanently age her.

What did she care what her skin looked like if there was even a remote possibility that her life hadn't ended when Hank's had? Even if this was just a brief flirtation—all that seemed possible with their circumstances—hope renewed that romance might still be possible for her.

"So, who's the looker, Sarah?" *Ugh. Brenda-Lyn.* Did this woman not have any tact? The loud smack of her lips as she chewed bright pink gum said probably not.

Sarah put on her best fake smile. "I have absolutely no idea what you're talking about," she cooed in the same half-southern, half-valley girl twang the Brendas used on the customers.

"There's no reason to be so snotty about it," Brenda-Lyn whined. Sarah caught the whisper under Brenda-Lyn's breath, "Who does she think she is, anyway? She's not even pretty."

Any other day, with her limp ponytail and wrinkled uniform, Sarah would have taken offense to the slight. But not today, and not from a woman like Brenda-Lyn. How many times had she told Kora that when school friends teased her for something—a lovely art project, a homemade snack from grandma's—they were just jealous.

Sarah had what the Brendas worked every day for: the attention of a handsome male passenger. She pulled an evasive move past Brenda-Lyn, stopped for another club soda, and walked straight down the aisle toward Mike's seat. She wished she cared more about what those girls thought of her, but she didn't have the time or the energy, frankly. She carefully tucked the note under the soda and placed it down on Mike's open tray table, where his hands held open the book he'd been reading before. They were muscular—if hands could be muscular—and her skin warmed.

He looked up at her and smiled and somehow the light in the small cabin grew brighter still. Her cheeks felt the heat as well and she returned the smile. "Your drink, Mr. Mendez." She'd learned earlier not to call him "sir."

His hand let his book go and when he reached for the drink, his fingers grazed hers. It sent currents running down to the tips of her toes, tingly now in her pantyhose. Well, that hadn't happened to her in a while. Heck, maybe ever. Hank had been calm, steady, which she'd loved about him, but this feeling of excitement? She'd enjoy it while it lasted.

"Thank you, miss." She walked by him and took a special pleasure in knowing that even though she couldn't see him, she still held his gaze. At the front of the aisle, she made herself busy, asking the marines if they had everything they needed. Working her way toward the back of the plane, she kept Mike in the corner of her eye. She sensed by the way his head moved as she did that he was still watching her. It didn't unnerve her the way it usually did when patrons latched onto her.

It also amused her that every other head in the plane was pivoting around Brenda-Lyn and Brenda, the blonde bombshells of flight attendants from the past brought back to life. Why would they care if she took the attention of one of their hundreds of admirers? They had every other Marine's attention with their giddy laughter, bubbly and sweet, their matching southern accents (which Sarah knew from galley talk were as fake as the blonde hair on their heads), and the way they left their hands on the shoulders of the men just a tad too long to be subtle.

Whatever. What they had worked for them, but nothing pleased her more than to observe that Mike hadn't so much as given them a second look. When she got to his seat, his hand reached for hers, on purpose this time. Folds of white paper peeked out from between his fingers and her heart thumped audibly louder and faster. She reached back, taking the note. Good gracious, his hands were as strong as they looked. His fingers closed around hers, swallowing her hand whole.

"Boconero?"

"Yes. Red awning, bad coffee, but a killer crumb cake."

"This flight can't end soon enough," he said, and she nodded in agreement.

"Only two more hours."

"Normally, I'd relish every second we aren't in the airport, one step closer to deployment, but today, those two hours are going to feel like a lifetime."

Sarah thought of her daughter at that moment, of how long these flights usually were—especially the layovers, which meant one more moment, hour, day she wouldn't get to share with Kora. Today, though, she agreed with Mike. She wanted to savor every moment they had together, not wanting to hurry her layover one moment faster. She missed her daughter, missed her like crazy, but this moment was *hers*, and when was the last time she could say that?

No matter what happened, she had Mike to thank for giving her that, at least.

For this one moment of hope, she'd go through all the loss again.

Mike shifted in his seat when the wheels touched down. Instead of the dread that usually accompanied this purgatory-like moment of his combat tours, his stomach flipped when the plane slowed like it did when he was a kid. Excitement and hope buzzed around his chest like a swarm of bees.

Who cared that an hour of organizing his guys, waiting in the customs line, reorganizing the guys and all their gear, and waiting for roll call awaited him? His thoughts lay beyond all that to 5 a.m. to a crummy cup of coffee with the first woman to capture even a shred of his interest since... Well, since Angela.

No need to go there. Just enjoy this fleeting moment—you won't get joy like this for the next seven months, he mentally chastised himself.

It had only been six months since he and Angela had broken up. There'd been some pretty dark depression followed by a three-month field op after the split, so his time to grieve had been limited. Even when he'd gone home on pre-deployment leave, he'd avoided any place he might run into Angela. He'd known for a while he'd need to address those hurt feelings, figure out his role in what broke them up at some point, and he had been. The hard truth was, he'd never imagined her outside the homecomings and send-offs. Not once had the idea of a cozy life chasing down other dreams cropped up with her.

She'd likely felt that and run before her feelings were too invested. Could he really blame her?

Mike shook his head as they taxied toward their gate. Angie didn't matter here. He'd learned that lesson and tucked it away in case he needed to recall it later. Right now, he had other things to occupy his thoughts. Like spending the next few hours with Sarah.

Take it easy, Marine. No need to rush it. His subconscious had a point, but no matter how much he reminded himself to take it slow, to not get wrapped up in the first woman who piqued his interest, he couldn't pull the brakes on this. In his job, he could be as conservative as they come, but when there were moments of hope and normalcy and romance like this? Nah, he'd ride this out and see where it went.

After all, what was he going overseas to fight for if it wasn't the promise of a better future for himself and his country?

Mike packed up his gear, keeping his journal easily accessible. He should probably drop his mother a note, but then again, where would he send it? She wasn't exactly stationary either these days. He didn't begrudge her the happiness she'd found, but it was a little annoying that she reinvented herself every time a new man entered the picture.

Oh, well. He'd jot down a few letters and send them when his mom and her boyfriend landed somewhere longer than a week.

The guys were divided into two camps as the pilots announced they'd reached their gate and could move around the cabin. Half of them were amped, hooting and hollering and tossing the pillows and blankets he hadn't gotten to before the flight at each other, punching each other in the arms with shouts of "oorah, brother, we're gonna get some!" Those same guys were slinging their arms around the two blonde flight attendants in a desperate attempt to have some female contact before facing a desert that was as barren as it could be.

The other half of the guys were sleepily rubbing their eyes, used to this work-up routine already. They gathered their bags wearily, pulled their covers on, but didn't move from their seats. Mike was somewhere in-between. He needed to get off the plane, visible in the way his foot tapped anxiously in the aisle. But being impatient would only make the wait seem longer.

Mike glanced over at Kint. He was up with the others, tossing a pillow around. From here, horsing around *with* the guys instead of against them, Kint looked almost normal. Mike sighed. This was gonna be a long seven months.

A hand rested on his shoulder. The heat emanating from his skin underneath spread out from there, as did a smile. *Sarah*.

"Hi there, Marine."

"Well, hello there, Murphy. How was your flight?"

"Good. More action than I've seen on all my flights this year combined." She winked and it sent goosebumps all down his arms and legs. Thank goodness the Captain had allowed him to be in civilian clothes for the flight and his long-sleeved shirt covered the visceral reaction he had to this woman.

"You're welcome."

She laughed. "Thank you, I think. At least I had a nice guy to keep me company."

"Show me where he is, and I'll have him NJP'd."

Sarah laughed and playfully slugged his shoulder.

"Really, thank you. You made this bearable. All of it."

He stood up and peered down into her eyes, which didn't leave his. There were green flecks in them he hadn't noticed before. What else hadn't he noticed? Not that it mattered, really. After this morning, he'd be wheels up and wouldn't ever see this woman again. A tinge of regret that so much of her would go unexplored by him tickled his skin.

"No, thank *you*. I'll see you at five?" He bit back an urge to tuck an errant lock of hair behind her ear.

She nodded and looked at her watch.

"It's only three thirty in the morning. That seems like hours from now. You won't stand me up? Want to sleep before your next flight?"

He shook his head. "I was going to ask you the same thing."

This time, it was her turn to shake her head. "No. I'll be there. I wouldn't miss it."

He smiled; found he couldn't help it around her. He finally gave into the impulse to tuck the hair off her face, and she smiled, a blush creeping up her skin from where his fingers brushed her cheek. "What are your plans till then, Murphy?"

"Check into the hotel here. Shower. Change. Wash the smelly boy off me. Looks like the Brendas might be thinking the same thing, actually. With company." He followed her eyes and saw the two blondes with their arms around marines, Kint being one of them, on the other side of the plane.

He sighed.

"I hope the guys know they aren't allowed to leave with them right now. I also hope those two girls know what they're getting themselves into. That guy's a jerk. As you're well aware." He nodded toward Kint. What women saw in him, he'd never understand. Though, he didn't know what the guys saw in them, either. The fake-blonde-bimbo act wasn't for him.

"I'll go rein them in. I'll see you later?" She walked away and just like each time she did, he couldn't take his eyes off her.

"I can't wait," he called back at her, and meant that wholeheartedly. As the guys filed out of the plane down both aisles, he realized she'd had her hand on his shoulder the whole time; he was heavier, more weighed down without it there. His gaze followed her to the group of marines and other flight attendants, and though the other marines walked away toward the exit of the plane, the girls in tow, Kint stayed behind, too close to Sarah for Mike to relax. He couldn't hear what Kint was saying to Sarah, but the look on her face changed as quick as if a light had gone out. Her expression got darker, a shadow falling over it.

Before he knew what he was doing, Mike was climbing over the seats and was on top of Kint, his chest tight with anger. "Get away from her, now," he growled. "If you don't get off the plane, Kint, I'll drag you off myself."

"She's not your property, Mendez." At this, Mendez's vision closed in until all he saw was a black circle, Kint's indignant face in its center.

"It's *Sergeant* Mendez, Corporal, and I will not say it again. You are off this squad if you can't respect your seniors." His finger was in Kint's face, practically touching his nose, but Kint didn't even flinch. He didn't breathe, either. Mike turned away and looked at Sarah, who wore a shocked look on her face, most likely at his unexpected anger. "Sarah, leave. *Now.*" He didn't mean to be so abrasive toward her, but he couldn't have her anywhere near Kint.

She might not be more to him than a new friend, but that was enough.

Sarah backed away, her eyes never leaving Mike's, her cheeks flushed and eyes wide. As soon as she was out of harm's way, Mike pushed Kint's chest until he'd backed him into the emergency exit door.

"You need to tone it down, Kint. I don't know what your issue is, or why you have a problem with authority, but the Marines are *not* the place to work those out. Do you understand me? Because make no mistake, there will not be another chance for you."

"No, I get you, Sergeant. What I don't get is why you have to be such a stick-in-the-mud."

"A *what?*" Mike couldn't believe the balls on this kid.

"A bummer, a downer, a guy who can't let loose, let his guys relax, even when they're about to be in the desert for the next seven months with no fun, and definitely no chicks."

At this last word, Kint looked around Mike at Sarah, his eyes moving up and down her body with a lecherous look on his face. That was Kint's fatal flaw. His sick fixation on Sarah made Mike furious. He would hit on anything that moved and was only looking at Sarah to infuriate Mike.

"Get your sorry excuse for a Marine butt off this plane now, Corporal. I'm writing you up when we get in-country."

"Looking forward to it, Sarge." Kint ducked under Mike's arm, grabbed his rucksack, and headed toward the front of the plane at a trot. Mike's breaths were labored, and his fists balled up at his sides, half-moons carved into his palms. He relaxed them, flexing the feeling back into his fingers, and turned back toward the galley. Sarah was there, dumping a coffee pot, her eyes locked on him.

"I'm sorry. I didn't want you to see that." His words were laced with worry. If only he could make her see that this wasn't him. He wasn't the typical marine who flew off the handle every time someone rubbed him the wrong way. It was some feral need to protect something innocent—*her*—from evil incarnate.

"I... I'm not sure what to think right now."

He closed his eyes. *He'd gone and done it now.*

"Sarah, please. I'm sorry. My behavior was..."

She cut him off, her hands reaching out for his, grasping them tight. He opened his eyes, tentatively wrapped his fingers around hers, and found them frigid and trembling.

"It wasn't you at all. That... that *creep* told me he'd make me his number one if I joined him and the other girls back at their hotel room.

When I told him no thank you, he asked me why I thought I had a choice in the matter."

That son of a...

Her whole body shook, and he pulled her into his chest, where she let out a single sob. She pulled away just enough to look up at him, her eyes and cheeks glistening with tears. "I was so scared. I've had some real numbers come on to me in this job, but nothing ever like him. I can't thank you enough for handling him for me."

He pulled her close again, swallowing back his own emotions to help settle hers. But make no mistake—he was taking care of Kint on the next flight. What he'd said was two steps past unacceptable.

"Sarah. I'm so sorry. I knew he was a jerk, but that takes things to another level. I totally get it if you just want to be alone and unwind tonight. Forget the shower, take a bubble bath instead. Why don't you relax in PJs instead of getting coffee, and bad coffee at that?" Her head shook against him.

"No, I still want to talk to you. Unless you need to cancel? Deal with that guy?"

"I don't know what to do with him, but I do need to handle it somehow. Not tonight, though. Tonight, I'm still yours."

Hmmm. The flip his stomach did when he said "yours" had to be from all the drama with Kint, right? Because no way it was wholly wrapped up in this woman he'd just met.

"You mean this morning. It's four a.m. here. Well, almost, anyway."

"That's right. No matter how often I do this, I'll never get used to the time changes."

"How often have you done this?" She'd pulled away from him, and his chest felt the way his shoulder had earlier—heavier without her there. She made him, and the whirlwind of thoughts racing through his head, lighter. Something else he'd appreciate but not attach too much thought to. Not when his mind needed to be laser-focused in less than twenty-four hours with his guys' lives on the line.

"Save the questions for later, missie. We have to save something to talk about." She smiled, vindicating him. He'd intervened between her and the villainous Kint, and made her smile, all in the same five minutes. Meeting her was worth that alone.

"I have a feeling we'll find something to say to each other. You strike me as someone who's got a story there somewhere."

He laughed, a lighthearted chuckle. "You could say that."

"Hey, Mendez, we need you out here. Guys are forming up to grab bags." Mike turned around to see another corporal—not Kint—waiting there. He nodded and turned back to Sarah.

"I've got to run. I'm sorry. Are you okay? Being alone?"

"I'm good. Go. I'll see you soon." She pushed on his chest, and he turned away, following the marine out of the plane. Halfway up the aisle, he looked back again, and she was still watching him. *Go*, she mouthed, and laughed, covering her mouth with her hands. He nodded and kept walking. When he got to his group of guys, they were in a line, bags on their backs.

Mendez was ready to get this over with so he could spend the morning with the flight attendant who'd snuck past any of his worries regarding the opposite sex and made him realize that someday—when he wasn't headed to a desert where the inhabitants would be hellbent on trying to kill him—he might actually be ready for a relationship.

"Let's go, guys. Faster we do this, the faster we get to hit the rack. Move out."

Mike headed to customs, never so motivated to get his job done. Though an uncertain deployment lay in front of him like a portent of doom, he finally had something to look forward to—a breakfast date with a beautiful woman.

If he had that going for him, he could survive anything the war threw his way.

Four

Coffee...

Sarah walked down the stairs from her room feeling like a new person. Flying always made her feel gross—like she'd just done a great workout, yes, but also like she'd traipsed through a humid rainforest.

This flight, however, had left her feeling dirty on the inside as well—and was far harder to get off with the first rinse. She'd been so preoccupied by meeting Mike that she'd let her guard down, subsequently allowing Kint in. He'd rattled her, which was obviously his point. At least, she had her knight in tan camouflage to battle that particular demon for her. When was the last time she'd had someone else to slay giants on her behalf?

If she wasn't careful, she could get used to that again. And then where would she be? Mike was sweet—not to mention handsome as a CK model—but he was leaving. This was just a flirtation with the possibility of friendship, nothing more.

But *still*.

She shivered despite the warm hallway and glanced at her watch, determined to forget about Kint. She had a coffee date with a very handsome marine she needed to concentrate on.

Perfect. She was going to be twenty minutes early to the café so she could sip a cup of tea and calm her nerves before she saw Mike. The last thing she needed was to ramble like an idiot because she'd had no sleep in the past twenty-four hours and couldn't stop shaking after her last run in with Kint.

When she rounded the corner to Boconero, though, she stopped dead in her tracks. Sitting in a corner booth, by himself, was Mike. And, oh my goodness, did he look good. *Like, really good.* He wore a red sweater with a white collared shirt underneath, a pair of snug jeans topping off the "just grabbing some Sunday brunch" look. Why did she long to do just that with—maybe not him, but *someone*—every weekend in the foreseeable future? The ache welled up inside her, deep and all-consuming.

She'd been alone so long now, she almost forgot the simple pleasure of a man across the table from her, someone other than her mom to listen to her.

The only emotion that combated this particular desire was crippling self-consciousness since he looked so handsome and she wore only fleece-lined leggings and a casual sweater dress with a large cowl neck, her hair left to its natural curliness, loose from its previous ponytail.

She glanced at her watch again. Yep. She was a full twenty minutes early for their date, and she hadn't had to go through customs. When had he arrived? The staff was just walking up, rubbing sleep out of their eyes and yawning. They shot Mike a look like he was out of his mind since they'd probably give anything to go home and get more rest.

As she watched him, he moved their silverware close together, then a little further apart, then he'd frown, move it close together again and smile. He repeated this a few times and she giggled quietly. How adorable was that, that he was as nervous as she was? Knowing that somehow took the edge off her nerves, making it hard to wipe the smile off her face as she walked toward him.

"Someone stole my favorite booth." He gazed up at her and grinned ear to ear. A deep sense of satisfaction rolled over her, knowing she was capable of making him do that. "You'd better move before my date gets here." Was she wrong in assuming—out loud, no less—that this was a date? Even an unconventional one with no real hopes of a repeat, it still strolled the edges of a romantic coffee date.

But then, she remembered the way he'd held her hands on the plane, the way they'd felt around her hips... okay, she could put the worry down long enough to enjoy this. She could be herself, her most forward self, around him; after all, what did she have to lose? The guy was deploying to a war zone in a few hours, for crying out loud.

"I'm pretty sure I can take him," Mike replied, patting the seat next to him. She bit back a grin. He'd left the napkin/silverware sets close enough together that she had to cozy up to him, leg-to-leg.

Perfect, indeed.

She slid in and gazed up at him. His eyes were fathomless; it was both unnerving and calming to stare into them and wonder what they hid in their depths. And, he smelled fantastic. Like cinnamon with a hint of soap. How did he manage that after an eleven-and-a-half-hour flight?

"Did you get a chance to clean up?" she asked.

"A PT shower. That's about it. And thank goodness I packed my cover up cologne in my carry on." He winked at her, sending a wave of heat straight to her stomach under his gaze. She looked down at her dress again, picking at a loose thread.

"A PT shower?"

"Yeah, it's basically a two-minute scrub of all the major parts with whatever you've got on you. Baby wipes, dish soap, or in this case, airport hand soap." Imagining him taking a shower, even a PT shower, sent a chill down her spine. "Looks like you got cleaned up, too," he said, looking down at her dress. The heat flushed her cheeks as well, and he must have noticed it, because he lifted his hand and brushed it along her right cheek, causing it to deepen.

Good grief, she was an emotional mess. Maybe this was good to get out of the way so when she made it back home and went on a real date, she'd know a little about how to tame her wild reactions to a sliver of male attention.

"I'd have dressed up a bit if I knew how you were showing up."

He shook his head.

"No way. You look amazing. I don't think I could be the perfect gentleman I plan on being if you'd done anything more." His finger ran along her collar bone until it reached the necklace she wore, a simple one-stone pendant of citrine, her daughter's birthstone. "This is stunning."

Her stomach flipped, and she bit her bottom lip. She didn't want him to be a perfect gentleman, but every fiber in her being told her that's what she needed right now. To slow down, take this easy. Besides, what would that look like if she pursued her overactive emotions and had a one-night stand?

Because that's all this could be. He was leaving this evening for war. The constant reminder of this made her sad.

"I'm sorry. I didn't mean anything by that. I'm an idiot. Especially after what that creep said to you earlier. Please forgive me."

"Of course. No, that's not why I'm frowning. I'd like the chance to know the imperfect gentleman, as well as the sweet one I hope to get to know more about this morning. No, I was just thinking... Well, never mind. It's dumb."

"Nothing you could say would be dumb. What were you thinking?" He looked at her, like *really* looked at her as if he was genuinely interested in what she had to say.

"It's just... there's no place this could go. Even if we wanted to—not saying that you want it to go anywhere other than just a friendship. But still. You leave tonight for a long time." She was rambling, powerless to stop it, though. The floodgates opened with him, and hopefully they wouldn't close back up. They'd been sealed shut for almost six years now. It was time.

"I do. Leave for a while—at least seven months. But, despite that, I do want this to go *somewhere*. I'm just not sure where, if I'm being honest. For all the reasons you mentioned. But that doesn't mean there's not something here that I can't explain, and darn it, something I've been trying to figure out since I met you."

She nodded in agreement, trying not to show her excitement. She wasn't sure what "somewhere" would look like, but they could figure that out together. Together. She hadn't been part of a together kind of thing in so long. Would she even know how to do that?

Her pulse flared, her skin got hot, but she breathed through it. *Later.* She was getting ahead of herself. Right now, the questions formed at what was left at the dam, about to break loose on him. There was so much she wanted to know, and already the time seemed to be ticking by too quickly.

"At the risk of also sounding cliché, I feel like I can trust you. Especially after you saved me twice in one night. Hero stories are written about guys like you." She winked at him, and this time, it was his turn to blush.

"I'm no hero, but it felt good to be there for you."

Sarah suppressed the overwhelming desire she had to look at her watch and count how long he would actually be able to be there for, and with, her.

"So, um, not to change the subject, but back to that question I asked you on the plane. How many times have you done this trip? And where are all your guys? I haven't seen any of them around the terminal."

"They're locked up in customs. Not allowed out with their weapons. I'm part of an advance party so I can come and go as I need to. Do you mean how many combat tours I've done?" She nodded. "This is my fifth. Afghanistan first, two to Iraq, another Afghanistan push, and same for this go around."

"Wow. Are you, what do they call it, at the front?" Five combat tours. She couldn't imagine what he'd seen. *Done*. She suppressed a shiver.

"Yeah, I'm infantry. Didn't start out that way, but that's what the Marines needed me to do, so here I am, five years later, still doing the same thing."

"What did you start out wanting to do? And really, five combat deployments in five years? That seems like so many. I'm sorry for all the questions, by the way. I just don't really know anything about that world, your world."

"Not many people do, really. The news tells you about half a percent about what really goes on, and of that, only about half of what they say is actually true. I don't mind telling you, I just feel like I'm going to bore you to death talking about my job."

She almost laughed at him. Boring? She was fascinated by his courage, his dedication, and wanted to know everything she could about who he was, what he did. She just worried she'd come off like the Brendas if she asked too much about his job, which couldn't be further from the truth.

"It doesn't bore me at all. To be honest, I haven't ever talked to anyone in the military before, probably because I imagined they're all guys like the Kint guy. I haven't ever stopped to think that maybe there are decent men sprinkled in."

"There are, but I can tell you from an insider's perspective, the more-than-decent ones are few and far between." He laughed again, and added, "To what you asked before, though, I used to want to be an intel officer. You know, the kind you see on TV and in movies who always gets the information to his command just seconds before the enemy arrives, saving the day for all the grunts. But, like I said, the Marines needed more grunts and less heroes, so I got taught how to shoot, how to run, and how to hide. Not real exciting, I promise you."

A flash of an image seared the back of her eyelids; she saw him running, weapon at the ready, ducking behind buildings and broken-down cars and debris to avoid the enemy. It sounded plenty exciting to her. And dangerous.

"Would you have had to deploy as often if you were in intelligence? Not a 'grunt?'"

"Yes, but not for as long, and not always to the same places. Those guys get to go to exotic places, like Haiti, Spain, South America... Not desert islands without the water like we grunts get to visit. Plus, the kicker is that they aren't in a third of the danger we are, and they get all the good pay and assignments."

"What kind of danger? I mean, I always assumed that infantry was doing stuff they won't show us on TV, but aren't we done with this war? Isn't that what the President said?"

"Oh no. They made a big move of showing us 'pulling out' from there, sending guys home, that sort of thing, but behind the cameras, they saw that the whole country destabilized and started sending troops back. And what they aren't showing you all back home, is that the fighting is worse than ever. Everyone thinks we've ended the war, so there's no support for vets, who are coming home wounded in bigger numbers than we've ever seen. It's ridiculous."

She sat in rapt concentration, listening with the attention of a star student on the first day of class. She was mesmerized and at the same time, terrified for him and what he would be facing over there. The terror must have been evident on her face, because he stopped talking suddenly, ran his fingers through his hair and looked up at her, a sheepish look on his face.

"I can't believe how chatty I am. Sorry for all those gory details. I've never said word one about my job to anyone, and now I can't shut up." He chuckled nervously.

"Don't apologize. I love hearing it, even though I know the more I hear the less I want you, or any of your men for that matter, to get on the next plane. What do your parents think about what you do?"

"My mom and stepdad know a little of what I do, but... well, they don't want to hear more than that. Anyway, enough about me, Murphy. I've been talking us through the opening of this cafe, and you promised me a crappy cup of coffee. After that, you're on the hot seat." She looked up and was surprised to see a small line forming. There were guests with breakfast sandwiches and coffee mugs on either side of them, and she realized suddenly how good the food smelled. Her stomach rumbled in response. How had she missed all these people milling about around them? Mike had some sort of spell on her, that was for certain.

She smiled and held out her hand to him as she left the booth. His hand engulfing hers replaced the feeling with one of giddiness. She felt all the familiar pangs of a crush forming, and it woke her up more than the drink she'd order when they got to the front of the line.

"One crappy cup of coffee coming up. And, be careful what you wish for. I have to fight to get a word in edgewise at my house, so I'm going to be hard to stop when you get me started."

He led her to the back of the line, where he purposely slid in close behind her. "I'm looking forward to that, Murphy. Now, where's that crumb cake you were talking about?"

Sarah talked their whole way through the line to get coffee and cake, and for the life of him, he couldn't remember all the details she went on about, only that he loved to hear her voice and wished she wouldn't stop talking, ever. He'd bought their drinks and food, despite her pleas to the person at the counter not to accept his card. This was her treat, she'd argued, and the woman behind the counter took his card anyway, with all the enthusiasm of an old lunch lady, looking at them like their energy wasn't much appreciated at this hour, and at this place.

"Danke," he told the woman, who just nodded in response. The unfriendliness of the woman wasn't any deterrent to Sarah, who continued talking through the transaction, through the wait for their food, through the walk back to the table. He was enchanted and amused.

"...and anyway, flights like that are rare, thank goodness. I don't know if I could keep it up for much longer if they were all that long."

She stopped and gazed up at him, and her face flashed beet red. "I'm so sorry. I do this when I'm nervous. I talk and talk and like I said, I never get the chance to at home, or at work, so, yeah. Sorry." She wasn't even breathless. He didn't know how she did it, but he liked it. A lot.

"Don't apologize. Ever. I love listening to you. How long have you been a flight attendant?" He wanted to egg her on, have her keep talking to him. It was the most relaxed he'd been in months. She took the bait.

"For three years now. Some days it feels like I just started, and other days, like today," she playfully punched him in the shoulder at this, "it feels like I'm getting ready to retire after forty years in."

"I get that. It's the same in the Marines. Some days, it's everything I got into it for, and others, it's all I can do to get by."

"Same. I wonder if that's all jobs, or just the ones where you're in constant go-mode?"

"I dunno, but I think you're onto something there. On that note, why'd you pick being a flight attendant? Travel? The handsome guests?" He took a sip of the coffee, which stuck in his throat. "You're right. This is awful."

She laughed. "To be fair, I warned you."

"You did. So, the flight attendant thing?"

"Well, it had the best benefits for my family. For my daughter." She paused, gazing up at him with wide, expectant eyes.

Whoa. She had a family. A daughter. He let that sink in for a bit, even though he'd caught a hint of that from the Brendas on the plane. Hearing it from Sarah made it real.

Her gaze was pleading with him not to run, and he wished he could convey that he wasn't going anywhere, but he sat there, frozen, taking sip after sip of coffee he'd have rather dumped in the trash. When her hands fidgeted, he reached for them.

"Talk about burying the lead," he said, and when she opened her mouth to protest, he laughed. "I want to hear about her, if you don't mind telling me. I'm not scared, Sarah." Not really, anyway. He had a hard time imagining that she would have led him on if she had a husband, but the way she'd said "family" had thrown him for a loop.

Sarah's shoulders relaxed, which meant he could fully release the breath he'd been holding. He had a feeling, the way she could revert back to the closed-off woman he'd first seen on the phone, that she'd been through a lot. He didn't want to ever add to that for her.

"Her name is Kora, and she's almost five. She's the best and worst of me, wrapped up in the cutest package. All my mom's sass, of course. Would you like to see a picture?"

He nodded. "Please."

Sarah pulled out her phone and as soon as she unlocked it, a mini version of her popped up on the screen. Kora was her mom's clone, down to the glint in her eyes and the squinty-eyed smile on her face. The only difference was the pinchable cheeks on the little girl. Well, that and the ringlets tumbling down around her face. Next to her was another version of Sarah, this one older.

"She's too cute. Looks just like you. Is that your mom?"

"For better or worse, she does. And yeah, my crazy mother."

"For better. Definitely. The three of you are clones." When Sarah looked down, he realized he'd maybe gone too far. "Sorry. Am I being too forward?"

"Not at all. It's just been awhile since anyone has noticed me. That way, I mean."

"I can't imagine that's true. What about Kora's dad? Is that an okay question?" Mendez was nervous. He didn't want to ignore the obvious, that Kora's dad had to have been in the picture at one point, might still be, but he had to know.

"Hank. He never met her. He died when I'd just found out I was pregnant with her. We'd only been married a year. It's why I took on this job. Nothing else offered the benefits that would take care of me. Of us."

Mendez's heart sank. She was a single mom, worked full time traveling and taking care of other people's needs, had endured the loss of a husband, and still didn't seem to know how amazing she was. He squeezed her hand.

"I'm so sorry, Sarah. What happened? To him, I mean."

"Cancer. Sarcoma. He got it later than most people. Usually it affects kids, but Hank was just one of the unfortunate ones, I guess."

"I can't imagine what that must have been like for you. To go through that. And to have a baby on the way when you lost your husband? You're amazingly strong, Sarah."

"Not really. I was a mess back then. Was until I had Kora. Then I had no choice but to be strong. Gosh. That makes me sound like a bit of a downer, huh? Really, I'm fine now. It's been a long time since all that. But I understand if she, Kora, changes everything between us. Whatever this is..." Mendez didn't waste any time answering her so she wouldn't read into the pause.

"You aren't a downer at all. I wasn't expecting to meet anyone until I was long out of the Marines, but none of it changes me wanting to get to know more about you. If that's okay with you?" She nodded and Mendez felt *happy*. There was no other word to describe this feeling, this serendipitous event that led him to her.

"It's absolutely okay with me. But only if we can switch back to you."

"I'm fine with that but know you can't just drop a child on the metaphoric table and run, right? We're coming back to her?"

"Okay. That's fair."

He sipped his coffee again and screwed up his face in disgust.

"But we're definitely not coming back to this coffee."

"No, we're not. But try the crumb cake. It's everything you've ever wanted and never knew you did."

He looked at her, stared deep into her eyes, and relished each second she looked back.

"It will be. I believe you," he said, before pulling her hand to his lips and kissing it.

Five

And...Dinner...

Sarah took a small bite of the crumb cake, scrunched her eyes, and pursed her lips. "Sometimes I think I take these Munich flights just so I can stop here on my layovers. I always have one or two for myself, and then sneak one back in my bag for my mom. My mom..." She trailed off, dropping her fork suddenly, and it clattered to the ground. People looked up from their pre-coffee dazes at the surrounding tables, but she barely noticed them.

"Oh no. My mom!" Sarah leapt up out of her chair, knocking it over.

"Are you okay?" he asked.

She shook her head. Worry surged through her veins, a byproduct of being a mom.

"No. I'm not. I promised my mom I'd call and let her know I made it. I totally forgot. She's going to be so worried." She gathered her purse, cleaning up her napkins, and wouldn't look at him. If she did, she'd see the disappointment in his eyes. She was being irrational, she knew it. But it was her family, all she had left of it, anyway.

"I'm sure she knows you're okay. Do you call her after every flight?" She finally looked up and relief at the softness in his eyes pushed away the worry.

"No, I mean yes. I do, but only because she watches Kora when I fly. I tuck her in wherever I am in the world. *Snug as a bug in a rug.* She'll have been in bed for hours now. Ugh. Do you remember seeing an international pay phone?"

"Take mine. I keep international calling on my cell since I'm in-country so much. Makes it easier to call the folks, especially during the holidays."

"Are you sure?" All this craziness would probably make him want to ship out as soon as possible.

He reached in his pocket and pulled out his phone. He handed it over to her. "Please. Take it. I would never keep you from tucking your daughter in."

"Thank you," she told him, dialing even as she spoke to him. "You have no idea how much this means to me." She placed her hand on her heart, and mouthed, *thank you,* again. He nodded back at her as she heard the phone pick up.

"Hello? Sarah?"

"Hi, Mom. I'm so, so sorry for calling late. You wouldn't believe the day, and night, actually, I've had so far."

"Were you delayed out of LA? Those fires have been outrageous."

"No, actually. The flight was on time. I'll fill you in more tomorrow before I fly out. There's so much to tell you."

"What's his name?"

Sarah smiled. Her mother knew her so well. She moved away from Mike, certain he could see the red flush that came back to her cheeks for the millionth time.

"Mom. I'll tell you everything tomorrow. I promise."

"At least tell me if he's cute." Sarah turned back to look at Mike, his broad shoulders and chest that she'd been curled up against not hours before. She sighed.

"Yes, Mom. Now, can you tell me if my tiny Bug is by some small chance still awake?"

"She's not, hun, but I'll have her call you tomorrow. Is this number okay to reach you at?"

Sarah mouthed to Mike, *Can she call back here?* He nodded back at her, enthusiastically.

"Sure, Mom. Call anytime. I'll be up."

"Be good, hun, and I expect to hear *every last detail*."

"You bet. Love you, Mom. Thank you, again, for everything."

"Of course. You know it's my favorite thing, spending time with that girl. She's special, you know."

"I do, Mom. Gosh, I do. Talk to you soon."

"G'night." Sarah hung up the phone and handed it back to Mike. "Thanks for that."

"You feel better? Did you get to talk to Kora?"

"No, she was sleeping, but my mom guessed I was late because of a boy."

Mike raised his eyebrows at her, a playful grin playing on his lips.

"Oh, yeah? You do this kind of thing a lot?"

"Um, no. Not even remotely. She knows me, though, through and through. We got really close after I lost Hank, and she lost my dad."

"Wow. When?"

"My dad two years before Hank. Heart attack. But I'm not going there now, mister. Now, it's your turn. Tell me about your family."

He sank into his chair more, motioned for her to come sit again next to him. She slid back in, until her knee was touching his. She pretended not to notice that he slid his arm along the back of her seat.

"There's not much to say about my family. Mom and Dad are still together. Thirty-four years this March. Sister just got married last year, and is a few months away from having their first baby. A boy. Milo. They have a dog, Chester, and we just lost the cat from my childhood, Eegee."

"That's quite the family. I'm sorry about your cat, though."

"Don't be. He was an idiot."

Sarah laughed and kept on laughing until tears formed in her eyes.

"I'm sorry," she choked out between gasps for air and fits of giggles. "I get giggly when I'm tired."

"This is good to know. I'll just have to keep you up all night before we hang out again so I actually seem funny." She had her head on the table now and was convulsing with laughter. He laughed, too, and this sent her over the edge.

"Okay, tell me something sad. Something that will stop this, or I'll still be here when you get back from deployment," she wheezed. She'd give anything to stop this laughing fit, but she was at the mercy of her overtired emotions. This would hammer the nail in her coffin with Mike. He'd surely want nothing to do with her now.

"Okay. Let's see. My cat died last week?" She shook her head and howled louder. "My favorite Halloween candy is candy corn?"

"Mine. Too." she said, and the tears kept streaming down.

"You've left me no choice then. I'm pulling out the big guns. My next flight takes off in four hours. After that, it's seven months till I get to see your face again."

She sat up straight, wiped her damp cheeks with the cuffs of her sweater, and looked down.

"That *is* sad."

"Sorry. It's the best I could do on short notice. It seemed to work, though." He winked.

"Yeah. That's pretty heavy. And, I feel like we're barely scratching the surface of getting to know each other. We're either making an absolutely horrible decision to keep talking when we know what's about to happen, or—"

"I pick '*or*'."

She smiled so deeply, she felt it in her chest. This man sure said all the right things.

"So, shoot. Not literally but ask away. I'm an open book, Murphy."

"You asked for it. Let's start with sports, school. The safe subjects."

"Safe, huh? Well, clearly you didn't grow up in a football family. There's nothing safe about sports, especially on Sundays."

"Who's your team?"

"Green Bay, all the way."

She groaned.

"Don't tell me you're a Bears fan?" he asked.

"Worse. Vikings. My dad was from Minnesota and raised us in purple and gold."

"That *is* worse. Did you play anything in school?"

"I did. Tennis for six years, cross country through high school." She took a sip of her coffee and gagged. "Ugh. It's cold."

"It should be—there's no way anyone likes that coffee enough to drink it warm. Should we go somewhere else? Get some real food?"

Sarah glanced at her watch. *Whoa.* They'd been sitting and talking for over six hours now, about everything and nothing. Time hadn't flown this fast since she'd first had Kora. One moment she was in labor, and the next Sarah and her mom were celebrating Kora's first birthday.

"Yes, let's. I know a decent pasta place in the terminal if you're interested. Except, I just realized I don't know if you eat meat. Or dairy. Or gluten. Or any of those other diet fads."

"I eat everything. You?" They got up out of the booth and began walking. She led the way, pointing out places he should or should definitely not visit if he came back through this airport.

"Me, too. I don't understand people who can't appreciate a good steak. Or better yet, a good French bread with the steak. And, of course, a glass of wine to top it all off..." She trailed off and looked at him. "I'm starving. Can you tell?"

"I can, and I second that. How about we switch that pasta place to a steak joint. Do they have any of those here?"

"Follow me, Mendez. I know just the place." He grabbed her hand, and she felt the same jolt she'd felt earlier, but with more of a sense of peace with it now. Like, this was how it was supposed to be, so long as she didn't think about the next few months.

It was just so odd that she'd only met him less than twenty-four hours earlier. Weirder still that she knew without a doubt that he was going to be in her life—or at least in her memories—for a very long time, and that none of it bothered her a single bit.

⚜

Watching her order her steak—medium rare, change the sides to be double mashed potatoes because no one orders veggies in Munich, not especially when there are potatoes as an option, side salad with light dressing, glass of house red since she didn't have to fly for another six hours—made him feel at home. It was all he could do not to chuckle and sit back in his chair, amusement splashed across his face.

His mom used to say you could learn a lot about a person by watching not only how they order at a restaurant, but what they order. Sarah was a woman who had taken care of herself for years now, who knew *exactly* what she wanted, and wasn't afraid to ask for it.

Darn if that wasn't more attractive than her soft curls and small gap between her two front teeth.

He seconded the order for himself, trading in the wine for a draft Hofbrau lager. When the drinks came, they toasted to a safe deployment for him, and a safe flight home for her. She didn't waste any time in firing away with the questions once they sat down, and he answered all about his high school football career, his dreams of playing college ball that were dashed when he found out he wasn't any good. She'd laughed at this, and it made him want to say anything, do anything to keep that sound and that smile on her, especially after her interactions with Kint.

He'd told her about his sister and her husband, how they'd just gotten married, how he'd been worried for her at first, but now that their first child was on the way, he'd never been more sure of true love. He went on and on about his past, her questions never ending. He'd never talked so much in his life, and with a chatty daughter at home, he guessed Sarah hadn't, either. He'd talked all the way through a shared appetizer of calamari, and a pint but rather than exhaustion from being the center of her focus, he felt *seen*. No one in his life had been that passionately curious about him.

"So, that's pretty much it. Not much more to tell. Unless you get my mom involved. Then, the baby books and embarrassing stories will come out, and I'll never see you again."

"Careful, I'll call her if I have to, to get the full story."

"I'll give you her number. I'm not afraid of you, or her, Murphy." Sarah laughed again. It was contagious, a spring of hope and joy before the barren desert just hours away. He shoved the dread beneath the compartment where he kept all things war-related. "In all seriousness, I'd like you to have her number. That way, if you need to know anything while I'm gone, and you haven't heard from me in a while, you can call her."

"You'd like to exchange numbers? Talk while you're gone?" Surprise showed in her parted lips.

"Of course. Don't you?" He grabbed her hand. "There's something amazing here, and even if it's just a friendship in the end, I'd like to see it through."

"That's exactly what I want. But, how does that work? Do we write, or call, or send pigeons? I don't have a clue how to communicate with someone at war."

"Well, I'll write and call when I can, so we can keep the pigeons at home, safe from RPGs."

"RPGs?"

"Rocket-propelled grenades."

The space between her lips widened, as did her eyes.

"You have those over there? Gosh, I wish you didn't have to go. Any of you."

He'd never agreed with that sentiment—if he didn't go, someone else's son would have to take his place. Until today, that was. Each second he spent with Sarah made it infinitesimally harder to want to do his duty.

"I know. But having a pen pal will help."

"Oooh. I've never had a pen pal before. This is exciting. Have you?"

He thought for a minute. About Angela. About how when she'd stopped writing, when she'd sent one, final, *Dear John* letter on his last deployment, how he didn't think he would ever get over that. Was he strong enough to open himself up to that again?

I was lost the minute I met Sarah. From that moment on, there was never a chance that he wasn't going to follow this through to the end, even if that was the moment they both walked off the plane to separate lives in separate places. Not that he'd tell her all that. A man was entitled to keep a few cards close to his chest.

"No, nothing like this. I already can't wait to be over there so I can get the mail call."

"Hey, watch it. Don't be so ready to leave yet. We still have a killer steak coming our way. You'll miss that when you're over there, won't you?"

"That and about a million other things." He squeezed her hand. "Steak, yes, but sushi, a good beer," at this he held his up and clinked glasses with her, "a real shower, a crappy drive-through burger, my mattress at home, sand not being in everything I own... The list goes on. It's actually kinda depressing how different life is over there."

"Can I send you stuff besides letters to make it more homey? Like a care package?"

"You can send everything you want and still the only thing that'll make my camp homey is if we nuke it and start over. But I would love packages from you. Just don't feel obligated. I feel like I've put too much pressure on you, and you've got enough going on. Besides, we just met."

"Does that bother you?"

"Not as much as it should, to be honest."

"Well, I'd be happy to send you things. It'll help to have something that's just for me, you know?"

He nodded.

"So, you mentioned your mattress at home, but where is home? When you aren't deployed."

"I share an apartment in 29 Palms." When she looked at him, head tilted to the side, he realized that she, along with the rest of the world, had no idea where that was. "It's about two hours inland from Temecula, in the middle of the desert. Believe me, you're better off not knowing where it is."

"Who do you share the apartment with?" He knew the subtext to her question. She was really asking, *Is there anyone else who is going to be sending you letters while you're gone?* At least now, he could answer her honestly, no matter who he used to share the place with. He smiled.

"Another sergeant in a different battalion. We sort of trade off deployments, so it's like living alone most of the time. Not a bad deal, if you don't count the small town it's in. How about you?"

She smiled sheepishly, and he knew she was pleased with his answer. There would be plenty of time to get into Angela and him, and this first date—if you could call it that—wasn't it. He didn't want to hide anything from her, but he did want to concentrate on her, not a ghost from the past.

"I live with my mom and Kora outside of Long Beach. Kora and I went at it alone for a while, but then, when my mom was going to sell my childhood house because she couldn't take care of it, I offered to help. It turns out it was the best move for both of us, and now Kora has a second parent. A win-win-win. So, why the Marines?"

"That's a change in tack. Um, well, I'm not sure, really." A server arrived with their steaks, and refills of drinks for both of them. "Wow," he said, "this feels indulgent. I've never had a deployment send off like this."

"This is perfect. Thanks for talking me out of spaghetti." She dug in, taking big bites of steak and mashed potatoes, switching between the two back and forth. A bite of one, then the other, then back to the first. She had so many quirks.

He surprised himself by wanting to know all the stories, all the reasons why she was the way she was. How long she'd had those crazy laughing fits, why she had to order calamari at any restaurant that had it on the menu, why she talked in circles that he somehow could follow with ease.

His phone rang, though, and he saw it was the number she'd dialed earlier. He handed it to her, and the way she smiled when she answered spoke volumes about what an amazing mother she must be. He tried to look like he wasn't listening in, but he could tell her daughter was mad about Sarah not calling to tuck her in the way Sarah was negotiating with her. It wasn't unlike the way his command negotiated with suspected terrorists.

Her voice was an octave higher when she talked to Kora, "I know, and I'm sorry. How about I bring you a snow globe from Munich?" Then, a pause as she waited to hear if that was enough, followed by, "and sure, I can bring some crumb cake for you this time, too." He could only imagine what the precocious little girl on the other end was demanding of her. She eventually hung up, after what he assumed was a full-on peace treaty where Sarah gave up all her assets to keep the peace. She exhaled deeply, handing the phone back to him.

"Thank you."

"She sounded upset," he noted.

"Oh, she was. Anyone who complains about how to make their boss happy at work clearly has never been a parent. It's lose-lose, usually. Sorry. So, anyway, the Marines?"

"Yeah," he said, his mouth full. She barely skipped a beat, even though his own head filled with questions about Sarah, her daughter, and what it was like moving on from such grief as she must have done.

But hopefully, there'd be time. "I knew I was going join the service, but thought I'd be in the Air Force, in intelligence. When I went to enlist, they weren't looking for anyone in my MOS, my job description." He took a long pull from his beer. "So, I went down the list until I got to the Marines. They wanted me, paid a decent signing bonus, and promised me the world. Then, a year later, they closed out my MOS and moved me to infantry. Been here ever since."

"Did you ever think about leaving? Doing something in intelligence out of the military?"

"No, not really. I got used to infantry, and honestly, ended up loving the pace. Intel was a lot of hurry up and wait, and this, the fighting side of things, is much quicker. Plus, I feel like I am doing more in this job, leading the men, than I ever did as a POG."

"POG?"

"Position other than grunt. People who stay behind, do the cushy stuff."

"Thanks. There's so many acronyms, huh?"

"So many. The Marines, and well, the military in general, pride themselves in making things their own. Including a language that no one outside the military can understand, and the Marines, they want to speak it."

"Was anyone in your family in the military?"

Mendez took a bite of steak and chewed slowly. This was another can of worms that he wasn't sure he could get into tonight. He played it safe.

"My dad. He did ten years in the Army."

"That makes sense then. Following in the family footsteps."

"Yeah. Exactly." He exhaled.

Just as he was thinking of a way to move the conversation to something less potentially volatile, the server came back with a tray of desserts.

"Mmmmmm," Sarah said. "Will you share one with me?" He laughed. He didn't know where she put all this food. She was just over five feet tall and couldn't have weighed more than a hundred pounds. She'd polished off her steak, mashed potatoes, over half the calamari, her salad, and then the last two bites of his mashed potatoes he was too full to touch ("you don't waste food, Mendez. Especially not these mashed potatoes."). Not to mention the two crumb cakes she'd delicately made disappear earlier. It was kinda nice that she wasn't shy around him, especially with food.

Not that he was comparing, but Angie hadn't ever eaten more than a salad in front of Mike. This kind of openness was refreshing, that's all.

"You bet. What looks good?"

"Well, that depends. Are you more a cake and brownie guy, or a pie and pastry guy?"

"I'm all of the above. You pick." He watched her face light up when he said this, like she was a proverbial kid in a candy store. The way she tentatively bit her lip and scrunched her eyes in concentration made Mendez wonder if she'd ever been given free rein to just indulge herself without thought for the money she'd spend, or what her daughter needed, or what having fun would do to her daily checklist she'd told him about when they were in line for coffee.

"I'd love the brownie a la mode. No, the key lime pie. Ooh, ooh, ooh. The berry tart. No, the brownie. I'll stick with a classic." She was beaming.

"Is that your final answer?" He teased. She clapped her hands together.

"Yes. Yes, the brownie." The server didn't look near as impressed with Sarah's indecisiveness as Mendez was. It must be a Munich thing, he thought, the stoic, emotionless customer service business plan.

The server gave them two spoons, and Sarah dove right in, talking about how she didn't bake, because she didn't trust herself around all that baked stuff, and how she didn't like cooking either, so he should see what she and Kora ate when her mom wasn't around. Well, he shouldn't actually, because then he'd run for sure.

They were a couple bachelorettes, she told him, and he had a weird flash forward to him cooking for them, making sure they never ate frozen meals again.

Don't go there, man. It's too soon on so many counts.

His subconscious was right, but then, how could he stop the barrage of emotions slamming like a tank against his heart?

"What are your favorites?"

"Favorites?" Sarah looked confused, and he laughed.

"You know, flowers, candy, dessert, meal, vacation spot, your favorites list."

"Oh, hmmm. I haven't thought about any of that in a while. Favorite flowers have to be daisies. They're so simple. Otherwise, gosh. Candy? I could no sooner pick a favorite. It totally depends on the mood I'm in."

"Yeah? Give me some examples." It was adorable how serious she was taking this.

"Well, candy corn in fall, duh. Sour Patch Kids in the car, long trips only—it helps keep me awake."

"Of course. What about movie nights, though?"

"That's easy. Plain M&Ms. It's only a bummer that most movie nights are in the dark, though."

He chuckled. "Oh yeah, why's that?"

"Because then I can't see them to eat them in color order. Brown first, then the oranges and greens, then blues and yellows, and I save the reds for last." They looked at each other for a few seconds, and then both broke out into loud, raucous laughter.

"I know, it sounds crazy. It's just something I've done since I was a kid."

"No, it's charming. I've seen my share of crazy, and eating M&Ms by color isn't even close." Sarah mimed wiping her forehead in relief, and they both laughed again, drawing the eyes of the customers closest to them. She went on about her favorite dinner (spaghetti), time of year (summer—she hated to be cold), and vacation (anything by the beach). He listened and took mental notes of each detail of everything she loved. It was just more proof that this woman knew exactly what she wanted out of life, and who she was.

If only he was as sure of things.

After a few obligatory bites, Mendez slowly pushed the brownie closer to her side of the table and though she didn't notice, she didn't stop eating and talking between bites until the last of the melted ice cream and brownie were gone. She set her spoon down, and sighed, a faint smile on her face. She looked sated, content. And also, the most relaxed he'd seen her since they met. The server came and dropped the check, and Mendez didn't let her near the bill, slipping it back to the server with his card on top, and telling Sarah her money was no good there. It came back and he signed as Sarah sipped at the last of her wine.

"Thank you so much. This was the nicest—" She paused, glancing down at her hands.

"Go ahead, you can say it." He tossed her a wink and she blushed. Coiled heat gathered in his stomach, tight and warm.

"*Date*. It's the nicest date I've ever been on."

"We need to get you out more, I think." But then he looked at his watch and cringed.

"What is it?" she asked.

"It's time."

"Oh. Already?"

"Yeah. I guess."

"Wow. That went fast."

"Too fast."

A tear formed in the corner of her eye, and the smile was far from her face at this point. A small pit of dread built in his chest until it wasn't a pit anymore, but something that felt like it was consuming him. Even after six years of dating and Angela leaving, he hadn't felt like this.

This... this emptiness that consumed him. It was too soon, too much, but he was also powerless to stop it. This one chance encounter had changed his life, no matter where it led next, if anywhere.

He cupped Sarah's chin in his hands and tilted her face toward his.

"It'll be okay. I promise. I'll write and call, and you'll write, and the seven months will fly by."

"I know I must look like an idiot, crying after only knowing you a day. You're going to combat and aren't being this much of a baby."

"Not on the outside, but trust me, I'm not taking this any better than you, and it has nothing to do with combat." She looked up at him, her eyes sparkling. "Sarah, I am not going to let you down. Meeting you is the best thing to happen to me in as long as I can remember, and I can't help but think this is just the start of something wonderful." She sniffled and nodded. "Will you walk me to the gate?"

She nodded again. When she took her bottom lip between her teeth and her glance dipped to his lips, the warmth in his stomach grew outwards to his limbs.

He kept her chin in her hands. "Sarah, can I kiss you?"

She nodded a third time, and he barely let her head move once before his lips were on hers. It was a soft kiss, both tender and tentative in equal measure. Her lips were as soft as they appeared but that only meant the longer he stayed here, the taste of chocolate on her lips tempting him, the harder it would be to walk away.

And no matter what version of the future happened for them, him walking away from her in the next five minutes was the only guarantee. So, if he knew it was coming, why did it hurt as badly as it did?

He pulled away, but left his forehead on hers, his fingers laced behind her head.

"At the risk of sounding forward, Sarah, can I have your phone number?" She laughed and nodded again.

He tucked her laugh away in his chest where he could draw from it as he needed the next few months. They traded information, including his mother's phone number—just in case, he told her. She waited outside the restroom for him to change into his cammies, and they walked together to the gate.

The energy there was much different from the plane, even though it was the same guys. He could tell who was a boot—a marine who hadn't seen combat—by the quiet way they watched the other marines interact. It was real to them now. This was the last time they would be in relative civilization, and what they were heading to was as formidable as anything they'd ever seen. He remembered vividly the way he felt when he was in the same position they were. He'd just started a new relationship, had never been in more than a fist fight in high school, and was terrified about what might happen to him.

Or worse, what he would be asked to do.

"Mike? This is going to sound stupid, but can we get a picture together? I don't want to forget this, no matter what happens."

He pulled out his phone. "Of course, but I wish you'd believe me when I tell you to be optimistic. There's nothing, nothing that could make me forget this." He held the phone above them both and took a photo. Then, he leaned in and kissed her, snapping another picture, surprising her.

"Well, at least this will help you from confusing me with all the others." She smiled, but it didn't reach her eyes.

"There aren't any others."

She looked up at him, and he snapped a final photo.

"Let me see it! I wasn't ready!" she squealed, laughing. He showed her, and she gasped.

"Oh. It's perfect." In the photo, she was gazing up at him, a look not unlike the one her daughter gave her in the photo she had shown Mendez.

She looked, if not happy, at peace.

"I agree. Like you." She playfully swung at his shoulder again, and he caught her hand, pulled her around the corner, bringing her in for another kiss, this one more passionate, filled with all the things he would have told her face-to-face if he'd met her on the way back, rather than on the way to combat.

When he pulled away, he glanced over her shoulder, and saw Kint, there, watching them, the corners of his mouth pulled back in a sneer, his arms crossed tightly across his chest. Mendez stared back with an intensity that he hoped would convey what a nightmare Kint would be walking into should he choose to challenge him.

Mendez looked back down at Sarah, whose head was nestled in the crook of his shoulder. He kissed the top of her head, and when he looked back, Kint was gone.

"I'll send these to you when I get on the plane, and hopefully when you have service again in the good ol' US of A, you'll get them."

"Thank you." He could barely hear her over his heart thumping.

"I have to go," he whispered. She nodded, silent again. "I'll miss you, you know."

She pulled away from him. "I know."

"I'll call you when we get to base. But, look out for a letter sooner." He patted his pocket, where she saw a blank envelope sticking out. She grinned.

This wouldn't be so bad. He could write to her almost every day, and call, hopefully, at least once a week.

"Take care of yourself, Mendez. Come home safe."

"I will. I've got something I want to come home to. Bet your salary I won't let anything mess that up."

Captain Hoffman called out to the men to form up in squads, looking very much like he was annoyed they hadn't just read his mind and done it already. He was a man who didn't like to waste his words.

"That's my cue. Bye, Sarah. I'll talk to you soon."

"I can't wait. Thank you, Mike."

"No, thank you for the most perfect first day of a deployment ever."

"You're welcome, Mendez. I had a pretty good time, myself. For spending the day in a Munich airport with a stranger, that is." She winked, and this time, the smile reached all the way to her eyes.

He reached down and kissed her on the cheek, and walked away. He understood now that whatever he'd felt when Angela had left him wasn't anything resembling true heartbreak. It didn't come close to this unnamable thing that had wrapped around his heart and squeezed ever since he met Sarah in the most opportune way at the most inopportune time.

He took a deep breath, one more look back, and waved at the woman standing behind him, closing in on herself. He walked through the doors to the gate, and when they closed behind him, it took the last of his courage not to break down.

Instead, he walked onto the plane where he was greeted by another faceless, blonde flight attendant that wasn't Sarah.

Oh, well, he thought as he sat down, *at least I'll sleep on this flight*. Well, after he did one last thing. With that, he pulled out the blank envelope, ripped a piece of paper out of his journal and began to write.

Dear Sarah...

Six

Pen Pals

The kitchen counter was littered with bills and crayons, many of the envelopes covered in unique drawings that made them look less formidable. Oh, Kora, the little artist. Only she could turn a dreaded affair—paying bills that barely kept them afloat—into one Sarah didn't mind so much.

Sarah inhaled and smiled. She loved that her home smelled like cinnamon. Though she couldn't quite figure out why, it would always be the smell of home to her. Sarah's mom, Luise, sat across the counter from her, a cup of coffee between her hands, and an amused look on her face.

"So, you're telling me you stayed up for twenty-four hours to talk to this guy? He must be great. You love your sleep."

"You tease, but he's pretty great. I haven't felt this way since...since—well, in a while."

"Since Hank?" her mom asked. Sarah looked down at her lap. "It's okay to be happy, Sare-bear. You deserve to have someone who loves you, who takes care of you."

"I just met him, Mom. Don't say the 'L' word yet."

Luise laughed.

"Well, you can call it whatever you want, but I see a man who saved you from some creep, not once, but twice, and who sat and talked to you for hours, while paying for all your meals. If he doesn't love you, then it's only a matter of time." Sarah put her hands to her cheeks and felt the heat coming from them. She'd woken up after a much-needed full night's sleep, feeling like she must have imagined her Germany trip and the incredible events that had transpired. Recapping it for her mom made it seem even less realistic, like something out of the romance books her mom not-so-stealthily hid behind her cookbooks in the den. Certainly nothing that happened to *her*. Maybe the Brendas, but not Sarah Murphy, single mom and widow.

"Mooooom. Stop. My hopes are already so high. I want to take my time with this. What if he forgets about me while I'm here and he's off fighting the bad guys?"

"I doubt that'll happen, hun. He didn't spend the whole day with you just to pass the time. From what you've told me, he feels the same way you do. Trust me."

Sarah sipped her tea, lost in thought.

Her mom was right. Every time she remembered their first kiss, Sarah was reminded there was something special about Mike. She also knew that he felt the same, at least until they'd said goodbye. It was something in the way he'd looked at her, especially the times he didn't think she could see him watching, like on the plane.

She shook her head. It was just… it was too short a time together before too long a separation. Half of her wanted to cut and run now that the magic had worn off and she was back home, back to her regular flight schedule. Who knew what he was doing, where he was—she assumed he was in the Middle East, though that could have changed—or if he even thought of her after he got on the plane.

Sarah was snapped out of her spiral by the doorbell. Her mom looked at her and nodded to the door.

"Don't worry, Mom, I've got it." She left the kitchen, calling out behind her, "It's not like I just got back from twenty-three hours of flying or anything." She was shaking her head at her mom when she opened the door to a face full of daisies.

"I'm looking for Sarah Murphy?" said a voice from behind the massive bulk of white.

"That's me." A small face appeared and produced a clipboard from somewhere beneath the large glass vase.

"Sign this, and they're yours." She took a pen from the clipboard, scribbled her name, and handed it back to the delivery person, who she could barely see. He pushed the flowers forward and she grasped at the vase, getting hit in the face with aromatic, silky smooth flowers. She inhaled deeply and smiled. They were gorgeous. Ostentatious, sure, but gorgeous, nonetheless.

She brought them into the kitchen, navigating blind, and her mom, from somewhere near the fridge, laughed. Sarah joined in, put the flowers down where she hoped the counter was, and stepped away. There were probably forty-five long-stemmed daisies, all emanating from the center of a thin, round glass vase. Sarah put her hands on her hips, surveying the floral delivery through wary but wide eyes.

"Tell me again how this stranger you met yesterday isn't in love with you?" Luise said, snatching the note from a small, plastic stick in the center of the flowers before Sarah could.

"The evidence is against him, sure, assuming these are actually from Mike." Sarah gestured for the note, but her mom ignored her, reading it out loud instead:

Murphy, There aren't enough daisies in the world for me to thank you for such an amazing day yesterday. I hope these find you safe, home with your family, and thinking of me, wink, wink. You'll be on my mind the next seven months. I miss you already. XOXO Mike (Mendez) P.S. Tell Kora hi from me. Your mom, too.

Heat welled up behind Sarah's eyes and on her cheeks simultaneously. She felt like she could both cry and take off in spontaneous flight at the same time. Maybe she wasn't crazy. Maybe yesterday really had happened, and exactly like she remembered it.

Maybe this was real.

Her mom came over and wrapped her arms around Sarah, squeezing her shoulders and giving her the card.

"Like I said, darling, you deserve this. Enjoy it." Sarah nodded, drawing a deep breath of the floral scent filling the kitchen. The cinnamon was masked by the daisies, but she didn't mind.

"Okay, all this is great," Sarah said, waving her arm at the flowers, tucking the note in the back pocket of her jeans, "but you still haven't told me how Kora was for you this weekend."

"Ah, good job, Sare. You know the only thing that will make me switch the subject off my only daughter's happiness is that precious little thing."

"I do. Glad to see it worked."

"She was fantastic. She drew you a picture. Hold on, I'll grab it from the office." Her mom walked out, and Sarah snuck out the note, rereading it until she heard her mom's footsteps padding down the wooden hallway.

She wondered about what her mom had said. Was it possible to love someone this soon, or was that an old wives' tale—the whole idea of love-at-first-sight? Did she love him? She wasn't sure, only that she was more excited than she'd even been with Hank, though they'd had a more traditional courtship. She'd also noticed the "XOXO" at the end of the note, rather than the riskier "Love."

Oh well, she was probably overthinking it.

"Here," her mom said, coming into the room with a large, 11x16 piece of drawing paper, covered from border to border with color. She turned it around to reveal three stick figures, all with big, brown eyes, long, brown, curly hair, and pink or purple dresses. The only difference between them was their relative size. Sarah pointed to the tall one, and her mom laughed.

"Yep, that's me. Because I'm 'old, like Santa,' Kora said." The two women laughed. "The only thing she said her family was missing, was a daddy." Sarah frowned at her mom. "Hey, her words, not mine, Sare-Bear. She's starting to notice she's different from the other kids in her class. She was bound to say something sometime."

"She wouldn't happen to have been coached, would she, Mom?"

"Not at all, Sare. I'm being serious here. I'm happy to help, in fact it's one of the greatest joys of my life, caring for that little girl, and don't get me wrong, I'm proud as heck of you for all you've done for her, for me, but no matter how much you give her, there'll always be one thing you can't..." She grabbed her daughter's hand and Sarah knew what she was going to say before she did.

"You can't give her the love of a father. You can't show her what a healthy relationship should look like."

"No, Mom, but I can tell her, and so can you. We've both known love, great love, in our lives. Don't you think that's enough for her, to know that it's possible?" Sarah was getting frustrated now. She'd worked so hard to give Kora a life that meant her only child wouldn't want for anything, and now her own mother was telling her why it wouldn't ever be enough. It's not like she left her husband and ran off with their daughter.

She'd had every intention of loving Hank forever, and did love him for *his* forever, but that was so much shorter than either of them had expected. And now Kora was paying for that. Sarah felt like it was better to have had an amazing partner and lost him, than to share her time with one who hadn't wanted the gig in the first place, as so many of her friends were doing with their kids.

But would her daughter feel the same when her friends' dads came to recitals and ballgames and hers never would?

"I want her to have it all, but that means risking so much."

"I know, hun, I know. Just don't think that because you've known love, even a great love, that it's all you get in your life. You deserve to be happy forever, not just a few years of your life. Just think about it, that's all I ask."

Luise pointed to the flowers, and left Sarah there, with her thoughts and the most beautiful bouquet of flowers she'd ever seen.

She pulled a daisy from the rest and brought it to her nose, drawing in her favorite smell—the wildflowers in Alaska in the summer—and images of the man who'd been amazing enough to give them to her. All she could wonder was what the right thing to do for Kora was.

And more pressing, what was the right thing to do for herself?

She didn't have any answers, nor did any seem like they were on the horizon, but she did have a short-term plan. She was going to send a thank you note like her mom had taught her when she was little, hopefully before her daughter woke up so she would be free to smother her little bug with kisses.

Plus, while she was writing Mike, she had some more questions for him that she might as well throw in.

"Take cover," Mendez yelled. "Sandstorm from your three o'clock!"

The fine, tan dust swirled around them like they were caught in a snowstorm, and the new guys, the boots, fumbled with their scarves, trying to get them over their mouths while holding onto their rifles.

Mendez wanted to laugh, but nothing was funny about any of this. The sand, if not protected against, would worm its way into not just their bags, their gear, their weapons, but their bodies as well, and it was deadly if too much was inhaled.

At the same time, if the men dropped their weapons, even for a moment, they were at risk from the other, more unpredictable, enemy in the war-torn country.

Mendez was used to this. There weren't many differences between the countries he'd been sent on his deployments, at least not from his perspective. All of them were filled with people trying to kill him and each mission so far had been the same.

Get established on a base, go on small operations, eat bagged meals, sleep in small, four-hour shifts, and start the whole thing over. It was more mundane than scary, but when the scary moments did happen, it was nothing like he'd read about or seen on TV.

Time didn't stand still so much as speed up, so that at the same time, he would hear a shot, yell for his guys to grab cover, find a safe spot to hunker down, and return fire. It would seem like milliseconds would pass and afterwards, he would wonder how so much had happened so fast. That was actually the hardest part about coming home, the fact that everyday life moved at a "normal" speed, which for him, meant that it crawled at a snail's pace. He found himself bored by civilian life, or at least he had been until two weeks ago.

Even though he knew thinking about Sarah would make the time between firefights pass excruciatingly slowly, he couldn't help it. She'd been the only thing on his mind besides the missions, which was new for him. His other times on deployment had been spent reading books, borrowing magazines, playing his rackmate's X-Box—anything to get his mind off the world he'd left behind. Mostly, because of what had happened with Angela during his first deployment, he'd tried anything to avoid picturing what she might be doing at any particular moment.

Now, though, it was different. Picturing what Sarah was doing was *all* he could do. If he wasn't careful, all this distracted thinking would get him in trouble.

"Sergeant Mendez? Yo, Mendez. You in there?" Mendez saw a hand wave in front of his face and shook his head clear.

"Yeah?"

"What's up? You okay, man?"

"Of course, I'm great. Livin' the dream. Why?"

"Oh, only that I was callin' your name the last minute and a half, and you were somewhere else entirely. I still don't know how you can do that out here. It's like a gift, man."

"Yeah, Lopez. A real gift. Sorry. Just thinking about stuff. What's going on?"

"Nothing too serious, just that the captain radioed in from HQ and wanted to know when we'd be there."

Mendez took a look around out of the five-ton tarp and assessed the surroundings. The low mountains to the left meant they were getting close to Haqleniah. Probably thirty minutes out.

"Looks like thirty. Make sure the guys in the other two trucks know. Tell 'em to keep a good lookout. This is enemy territory."

"You got it, Sarge." Mendez could hear the corporal calling up the convoy to "watch their six," and telling them their ETA.

Considering where they were, and what they were there to do, Mendez knew he should be more concerned—and he was, up to a point—but he trusted in his men to do the right thing. After all, he had trained them well. The road was bumpy, and Mendez was thankful for their helmets as they were rattled around the inside of the five-ton truck.

He pulled out his phone and opened it to his most recent photos. Sarah's face beamed back at him, and the smile on his face wasn't like anything he saw when he looked in a mirror. He looked genuinely happy, and he vowed to make sure he kept his promise not to forget her, so neither of them lost those smiles. He flipped to the kissing photo and the look of utter surprise and delight on her face brought out a grin, even as his head bounced for the umpteenth time on the steel post holding the canvas's shape.

He sighed. This was going to be a long seven months. For once, he wished for a bit of action, if only so that time would pass quicker.

The rest of the convoy went relatively smoothly, if he didn't count the potholed roads. There wasn't any contact from the enemy, and the citizens on the dirt streets milled about as usual, something experience told him wouldn't be true if anything was about to happen. Typically, the townspeople were warned if there was going to be an attack on the "infidels"—the Americans—and stayed clear of any place the humvees were. Mendez learned pretty quickly that there wasn't a world more dangerous than an enemy country without an enemy.

When they were safely back on base, he hopped out of the truck and was met by Captain Hoffman, who held out his hand. Mendez shook it and was reminded of the short man's strength.

"How was the rest of the trip out, Sergeant? Everything go okay?"

Mendez nodded. "So far, so good, Captain. The town looked normal, the baseline activity looked good, too. Thankfully, nothing to report."

Captain Hoffman, a superstitious man, knocked jokingly on his helmet. "I'll take that for now. It won't stay that way, but for now, it'll give us time to get the guys set up and base switched over."

"Where do you want me and my guys?"

"Let them unpack. For now, I want you with me. Follow me."

Mendez followed Captain Hoffman down the center road of base, a small, dirt path with semi-permanent tents lining both sides. Marines in various stages of dress walked in pairs in all directions, some quickly heading somewhere that seemed important, others strolling, but each of them had a buddy, part of the safety system here.

A couple guys like him and his guys, in full battle rattle, either headed from or to a mission, while others were in their cammie trousers and a tan shirt, boots, and cover. They were the ones mostly strolling, either on a rare day off, or just heading between chow and the head. All the tan, including the tents and gear and landscape, made for a bland picture of how Mendez would be spending his next few months. He longed for the color of Sarah's red lips and flushed cheeks.

They got to a large tent with "Command" posted on a sign out front, the flaps of the doors shut. The Captain held open one of the sides for him, and when he stepped in, Mendez saw a completely different story than the one on the footpath. In here was all movement and color on screens, on maps, and on the marines themselves. There was an urgency in here that betrayed what looked like an otherwise calm base.

"Captain, good to see you. Look here," a marine Mendez hadn't seen before said, ushering them both over to a table where a map was spread out on a table.

"Colonel, this is Sergeant Mendez, one of my most capable marines. I've brought him in on this since he'll be leading many of these missions."

"Of course. Nice to meet you, Sergeant. I've heard good things. Okay, so here's what we've got." The three men bent over the map and spent the next thirty minutes going back and forth over the approach to guarding the bridge, a major medical supply route.

Mendez cleared his throat. "Sir," he said, addressing the Colonel, "I have an idea that may be unorthodox, but that I think could gain us some clout with the locals and get the job done."

The Colonel looked amused and gestured to Mendez to continue.

"I think we could get the local Citizen's Army to guard the bridge—under our direction, of course—and have them be responsible for the checkpoints on either end as well. We would be there on radio, and in a small outpost here," Mendez pointed to a small shack on the map, right at the mouth of the river, fifty yards from the bridge. "That way, the enemy gets used to not seeing us as much. Maybe they get lazy, and we can catch some big fish on a slow day."

Mendez detailed some of the smaller components of his plan, surprised at how responsive the Colonel was. Captain Hoffman just stood there with his arms crossed over his expansive chest, a smile on his face. After answering some questions and showing some of his ideas in pencil on the map itself, Mendez stood up.

"Impressive, Sergeant. I think this looks good, and after I submit this up stream, I'll get back to you on the details, Captain. For now, though, this is our best bet. Sergeant Mendez, a word with you privately please?" Captain Hoffman nodded to him and left the tent. Mendez's heart rate sped up. He didn't spend a lot of time with the brass, and being in this tent, though familiar in an odd way, was intimidating.

"Yes, sir?"

"I've been keeping tabs on you through Captain Hoffman. You're not only an exemplary marine, but you've got the brains and vision to be in here, working for command. Have you thought about your future, son?"

Mendez took a deep breath. He had thought about this—until it'd been ripped from him after his first year. The part of him that had wanted to pursue intel burgeoned with hope, a part of him that hadn't ever disappeared, no matter how much dare he say "fun" he had with the infantry.

"I have, sir. In fact, I used to be an 0231."

"Intel, huh? Why'd you give it up, son? You seem to have a natural talent for it. Could have gone to college on their dime and had a quick rise through the officer ranks, if you ask me."

"I have a degree, sir. Computer Engineering, with a minor in Military Tactics."

"That's not so bad." The Colonel chuckled, patting Mendez on his back. "Why didn't you go the officer route, then?"

"Sir, no offense, sir, but I thought I could do more good on the ground. With the men."

"No offense taken. I started out that way. Not sure if the Captain told you." Mendez shook his head. Before today, Mendez hadn't a clue who this man was, or that Captain Hoffman was talking to him on Mendez's behalf. "That's neither here nor there. The important thing is that we get you squared away on a path that will take you somewhere. You got a girl back home, son, a family?"

Mendez blushed, thinking of Sarah, wishing he could share this with her. Whether they were to that point in their "relationship" or not didn't matter.

He nodded, trying unsuccessfully to hide a smile. "Sort of, sir."

"Well, good luck with that, Sergeant." The Colonel chuckled. "But think about her, about what'll be best for the both of you if you plan to continue your career in the Marines. You do plan to continue with the Marines, don't you, Sergeant?"

Mendez nodded.

"Okay, then. Think about this, talk to your girl, and let your Captain know what you decide. I can put the paperwork in whenever you're ready."

"Yes, sir." Mendez started to leave and then came abruptly back. "Thank you, sir."

"No, thank you. It was nice to finally meet you, Sergeant Mendez." Mendez nodded, and left the tent, hearing the Colonel barking out orders after he left. He certainly had a lot to think about. When he got to the footpath, however, Captain Hoffman was there, waiting for him.

"How did it go, Sergeant?" Captain Hoffman's smile was more of a smirk, and Mendez smiled back.

"Very well, sir. Thank you for talking to the Colonel for me."

"I only did what I think is best for the company and battalion, and you rising out of the stinky depths of infantry duty seems like the best move for you and me both."

"I don't mind the infantry, sir."

"I know you don't, Sergeant, and that's part of what makes you a good leader, but another part of leadership is knowing when you aren't fully using your God-given talents and seeking out a way to do that. I just figured I could help you along."

"Thank you, sir. I get it, I do. And, I think now might actually be the right time for all this. Can I take a minute and think about it? Run it by some people?"

"Of course. I'd be worried if you didn't. Now, you wouldn't be talking about a particular lady I saw you talking to most of the flight to Germany, would you?"

Mendez looked down at the path, trying to hide the heat on his cheeks that even on this hot day, flushed more than usual.

"It might, sir."

"Ah, I thought so. She seemed like a nice girl. Did you agree to keep in touch?"

"We did, sir." Mendez filled the Captain in on the flight, careful not to tell him too much about Kint, and then about the coffee date that had eventually led to dinner.

"Well, Sergeant. It certainly sounds like a good thing. Just go in with your eyes wide open, make sure she knows what a military man does, and what it means to wait for him."

"Yes, sir." Mendez agreed with the Captain, but he knew Sarah was different.

Angela had been exactly the type of woman Captain Hoffman was alluding to—the kind who thought it sounded good to be able to tell her friends her boyfriend was a marine, until it came time to watch him leave, when she would pout, refuse to write, and get otherwise restless while he was on training ops or on deployment. Once, only once that he knew about, he'd even found out that she'd kissed someone else while he was gone. Since that moment, he'd known something wasn't right, and though he'd stuck it out—they did have some good times—he'd been wary of trusting her too much.

The Captain wished him well, told him to get some rest before the missions kicked off, and reminded him to talk to him the minute he knew what he wanted to do. Mendez assured him he would and slipped inside his bunk tent. His mind was operating on overdrive. There were so many things he was thinking about, from what the

Colonel had told him, to his and the Captain's talk, but most of all, wishing he could just run to the phone to call Sarah.

Unfortunately, his base was in River City, or "reduced communications," something that happened after an incident. They had taken contact earlier in the week and still hadn't notified the families of the marines involved, which meant no comms.

He took his boots off standing up and then walked over to his rack and placed them underneath the cot. A small, yellow envelope with cursive scrawl caught his attention on his pillow, and he sat down on top of his sleeping system and grabbed it. The return address read "Murphy," and his heart sped up faster than it had in the Command tent.

He was careful to open the envelope so as not to rip any of its contents, using a knife to slit only the top. He pulled out a card with daisies on the front and smiled. Two sheets of paper fell out, and though they were folded in quarters, he could tell they were completely written on, front to back, in small script.

Instead of being daunted, he was excited to see what she had to tell him, and dove into the card first, which simply said, "*Thank you. The flowers are stunning, and the smile they brought to my face is probably still there as you are reading this. Kora was jealous, so I gave her a few in a small cup. You did good, Mendez.*"

There was a winking smiley face and heart, with a comma, then her name. A heart. To match his XOXO, hopefully. He'd wanted to sign off his card that accompanied the flowers with "Love," but that had seemed too forward. For now.

The Colonel's words echoed in his mind, though. *Do you have a girl back home?*

Gosh, I hope I do.

When he unfolded the letter, a small photo slid out, face down. He turned it over and saw that she had printed the surprise kissing selfie they'd taken. He stared at it, marveling at how that photo seemed so long ago, and like yesterday all at once. He also realized, with some surprise, that he felt stronger for Sarah now than he had in the picture, that somehow, writing two letters to her, and waiting for her responses, had made their relationship less of a fleeting, incredible meeting, but one of hope and the beginnings of actual friendship.

He couldn't wait for her to get his letters. He'd been more open in them than he ever had been with Angela. Whether or not that had added to her leaving him in the end, Mendez wasn't sure, but either way, it had felt forced with her in a way it didn't with Sarah.

He put the photo aside, still in view, and started in on the letter.

"Dear Mike," it began, *"Forgive me if this letter rambles, but I feel like I have so much to tell you, even if you don't find it interesting. I thought you might like to know what my day-to-day looks like. Like I said, it might ramble..."*

He read the note slowly and with great care, and when he got to the end, he laid down on his rack, put the picture on his chest, and reread it. She told him of the rest of her trip, the return flight from Germany, how her mom had picked her up at the airport with a sleeping Kora in the backseat who lightly and adorably snored. She talked about her mom's reaction to the flowers, to him in general, and he'd smiled ear-to-ear when she wrote to him that her mom supported this budding relationship fully, that she hadn't seen her daughter this happy in a long time.

It was exactly what he'd needed to hear, and he devoured the rest of the letter two more times, soaking in small details about her life, memorizing her phrases of speech. She was incredibly intelligent, he realized, and he made a mental note to ask her about what she'd gotten her degree in.

He lingered on the small moments of her day, imagining being there for each one. Namely, picking up Kora at school, and the bribes she had to offer her (right now a dollar cone at McDonald's) to get her to not walk around her preschool classroom and do the other students' work when they were "so slow, Mommy." He'd laughed at that, and pictured the three of them going out for ice cream, talking about school and hearing the five-year-old's account of the classroom goings-on. He'd also pictured himself there when Sarah'd written about some rainy weather that had pushed through southern California ("good for the fires," she'd written), making it easy for her to put on her comfy sweats and curl up with a cup of tea and her favorite book, a book that coincidentally she'd read almost a dozen times. He wondered if there was anything he loved enough to reread or rewatch it, and nothing came to mind, causing him to be jealous of her passion for not the first time. It was horribly infectious and made him want to read what she was reading. He made another mental note to ask her for the names of the books so he could order them next time he was in Leatherneck.

The part of the letter that he kept reading and rereading, making way too much of the meaning, was the way she signed the letter. This time, it read, "Love, Sarah." He rubbed the part of the paper that had her signature, picturing her pen scrawling the word that had been tumbling around in his head for a couple weeks now.

He put the letter in his pillowcase just as the flap to the tent opened, and Kint walked in.

"Did you see that yellow envelope I put on your bed, Sergeant? Looks like somebody was a good kisser. I wonder if Jodi will help keep her company while you're gone. You don't leave a girl like that behind, not if you want to keep her."

Kint passed Mendez, whistling to himself, strutting until he reached his rack, two down from Mendez's. "Jodi" was a nickname for the guy back home who preyed on women who waited for military men to come home, seducing them in their loneliest moments.

Mendez ignored Kint, not giving him the pleasure of a retort, even though he wanted to pin him up against the wall and tell him how he really felt. The crummy thing was, Kint had voiced the one thing Mendez was most afraid of—Sarah being swept up by someone who could be there for her, for her daughter, and give them both what he couldn't.

Time.

He shook his head, ridding himself of thoughts that wouldn't get him anywhere. All he could do from here was write her often, do his best to get to know her, and court her from afar. It definitely made him think about what the Colonel had said earlier. Should he stay in, and stick with his MOS, or move up in the ranks, making more money to take care of a family, and more of a strategic career move, but enjoy his job a little less? Or, should he get out altogether, finding a job that would let him be around for Sarah and Kora on a daily basis? He mentally slapped himself out of his spiral, noting that he was reading a lot into a couple week relationship, if he could even call it a relationship.

Mendez made sure Kint wasn't watching and put the picture of Sarah and him in his pillowcase as well, careful to make sure it didn't bend. He snuck a piece of paper out from his trunk, grabbed his waterproof pen, and laid back on his rack. Regardless of everything going on in his head, he was excited to put it all aside and write Sarah back.

He had so much to tell her, from his ride into Haqleniah, to his conversations with the Colonel and Captain, to getting her letter. And, he had to be sure to remember to ask her about the books.

He settled in and got to the work he actually enjoyed.

Seven

Falling Slowly

When Sarah got home from the gym one Friday afternoon, she found a smaller, but equally beautiful bouquet of flowers, this one a mix of daisies in all the colors of the rainbow, on the kitchen counter. Her mom was unloading the groceries, and Sarah grabbed some of them and pull out what she needed for dinner, trying to be nonchalant. When all the groceries were put away, and her mom still hadn't said anything, Sarah broke down with a groan.

"Fine, I give in," she said, shredding carrots and squash. "Another one? Where's the card? And yes, before you say anything, I did notice they were smaller, but that's fine. The last bouquet was too big. He couldn't possibly keep that up."

"They aren't for you, as a matter of fact." Luise had a smirk on her face that rivaled any Sarah'd ever seen. Sarah frowned.

"Oh, yeah? Well, then, who are they for?" She'd put down the potato peeler and walked over to the flowers, inspecting them. "Seriously, where is the card?" She tried not to show her frustration, but there was no other way she could feel right now. She'd been dying to hear something, anything, from Mike since the first bouquet of daisies had arrived.

"Well, Miss Everything-Is-About-Me, they were for Kora. She has the card in her bedroom, fawning over it still, I'd imagine."

Still frowning, Sarah walked back to Kora's room, ignoring her mother's chuckles from the kitchen. Sure enough, when she got back there, she saw Kora holding a small sheet of cardstock in her bean bag chair, her dolls lined up in front of her, like an audience, and her black-and-white kitten, Princess, curled up on her lap. Sarah had balked about adding a pet to the mix, when she wouldn't be there to help take care of it, but her mother said it would help Kora not feel so lonely when Sarah was away. Sarah listened to Kora read the card from the bouquet from what must have been memory, since she was still learning her sight words in kindergarten.

"These are for you, Kora. May they brighten your room like your momma brightens my day."

Tears formed in the corner of her eyes, picturing him thinking of this, of him arranging for her daughter to have the attention all on her, for once, not as a byproduct of her mom's. Sarah felt an arm slink around her shoulders and squeezed her mom's hand in the doorway, as they watched Kora tell her dolls that she had a boy who liked her, that she got flowers that weren't for Nana or her Momma.

"It's sweet, isn't it?" Luise asked.

Sarah nodded, lost for words. She swallowed the heat at the back of her throat, afraid that a few tears would turn into a flood.

"He's a keeper, Sarah." Again, Sarah nodded. "Now, make yourself useful and go make us dinner."

Sarah laughed and headed back out to the kitchen, lost in thought.

Later, after seconds and thirds had been had by all ("This was so good, Momma. Not like the other stuff you cook"), Sarah heard Kora's voice singing in the shower, loud enough to be heard over the water in the bathroom, and the clanking and sloshing of her mother doing dishes in the sink. The rule was whoever cooked got to relax after dinner while the other did the dishes, and secretly, Sarah loved the nights she pulled cooking duty, despite not liking to cook.

She got to curl up in the nook of the couch and read while she waited for Kora to get out of the shower, and then got to snuggle her little girl when she came out dripping, in just a towel with a hood. Those were her favorite nights, the three of them separate, but together in the same room. On nights when her mom worked, it felt like something was missing, and Sarah never cooked, preferring instead the easy frozen meals from the grocer. Thankfully, at least to some degree, her mom didn't work much anymore.

Sarah tried to place the song Kora sang, but realized after a bit that it was made up, the lyrics consisting of a unicorn that brought her candy and stayed to live with her as a pet forever. She was a girly-girl, through and through.

"Whatcha reading?" Luise asked from the kitchen. "Anything good?"

"*The Poisonwood Bible.*"

"Again? Haven't you read that a bunch of times already?"

"So? It's so good. The way she does each of the characters so distinctly? They just don't write 'em like that anymore."

"Well, that's nice and all, but I have something else you might be more interested in reading."

Sarah didn't even look up from her book. "Yeah?" she replied absently. She yelled back to Kora to hurry up, which Kora seemed to take as a cue to sing louder, stopping only to yell back, "Momma, I am *not*.

Done. Singing!" Sarah chuckled to herself. She'd forgotten about the brief conversation with her mom until something dropped into her lap. Two white envelopes with red and blue-striped borders. A man's scrawl, trying hard to be neat, but mostly failing. The only difference between the two were numbers in the upper left-hand corner. A number one and and number two. She bent her neck back and saw her mom's smirking face lurking over her.

"When did these get here?!" she yelled.

"Sare-Bear. I'm right here. You don't have to yell." Her mom's smirk got more playful, the corners of her mouth starting to resemble the Joker's.

Sarah turned around to face Luise. "I have every right to yell! When did these get here?" Despite her volume, Sarah was smiling. How could she really be mad, when there were two letters from Mike in her hands? She playfully wacked her mother on the shoulder with them.

"Before the flowers. In today's mail. I wanted to wait until Kora went to bed so we could gush over them properly, but now it doesn't look like that'll happen before she graduates. Let her karaoke a little longer and read those out loud. And enunciate, please. It's hard to hear by the sink."

Sarah whacked her mom on the shoulder again.

"Nice try, Mom. You get the second viewing. Now, scram. I want some privacy."

Her mom smiled and went back to washing the dishes. Sarah scooted back into the corner of the couch, so that only the top of her head was visible. She tore open the top of the first envelope, almost ripping the letter. Her hands were shaking.

Dear Sarah,

Hey there, lovely lady. I hope you got the flowers I sent. I couldn't wait on the slow military post to get this letter to you with any sort of speed, and I needed you to know how much today meant to me. Well, yesterday, by the time I get to Camp Leatherneck to send this. I figured if I sent it on the first day from Leatherneck, and then the next letter the first day I got to our base (sorry, but I can't put that location in here in case it gets intercepted by the enemy), you can gauge how long the letters will take to get to you. Sorry if this one took a while. The mail here is as reliable as the weather is (more on that later). On that note, I've numbered the letters so you'll know if you're missing one. Do you mind doing the same thing? I totally forgot to tell you about that when we were in Germany. I think I was a little distracted by the idea of kissing you. In hindsight, I would have just kissed you right away, on the plane, so I could concentrate more when we got coffee, and more coffee, and dinner. Wink, wink.

When we get to the base, we'll be at for the next seven months, things should even out a bit, get on somewhat of a schedule. I'll send you as many letters as I can, but it'll be a few weeks yet till I can call. I'm sorry about that. We just have to establish base before we can get the comms up and running.

That guy, Kint, is on my watchlist. In addition to the crap he pulled with you (which is unforgivable), he was giving some of the other guys some grief as well. I'm not sure what to do about him, and if I am being 100% truthful, I don't trust him. Not one bit. I'll keep you updated.

On a lighter note, how was your flight home? Hopefully you didn't meet any horribly gorgeous men with an equal combination of wit and wisdom on your way home like you did on the way out. Just sayin'. ;) How's Kora? Your mom? Tell them both hi from me. I saw a little girl in Germany right after you left that had to be Kora's age, and she was head-to-toe dressed in pink frills. It made me laugh, especially since you said Kora can be a diva. This girl's dad had her on his shoulders, the biggest smile on his face. It made me so happy for some reason.

Anyway, it's only been like an hour since I last saw you, and I already miss the heck out of talking to you. The flight attendants on this flight aren't near as friendly as they were on my last, which I have to say is a good thing. I could use some sleep, haha.

You take care of yourself and know that our day together was one of the best I've had in a while. Here's to a few more of them, with you, in a few months. It'll go by faster than you think, I promise. I've got a few surprises up my sleeve.

Mendez (Mike)

Sarah reread the note again, and even though it didn't have anything new in it, nothing substantial, it was the part with the little girl on her father's shoulders that got to her. It reminded her of what her mom had said a couple weeks earlier about Kora needing a father figure in her life.

Maybe—and she would never tell her this—maybe her mom was right. Sarah loved how the image of a father and daughter made him happy. She wondered if he wanted kids, to get married and do the whole thing. Maybe she'd feel him out in her next letter, ask him the personal stuff straight away so she knew where she stood. She wasn't sure she wanted to ever get married again, but she wasn't as scared of the prospect as she had been a few years ago.

She heard the shower shut off—a mere fifteen minutes after Kora had started the water—and put the letters on the coffee table under her book, out of sight. On cue, thirty seconds later, a wholly soaked Kora came screaming into the living room, leaving a trail of water behind her, the hooded towel wrapped completely around her like a robe. She jumped, mid-run, onto the sofa, into Sarah's outstretched arms.

"Momma! It's your little bugaboo!"

"It is, isn't it?" Sarah asked, her face nuzzled in Kora's wet hair. "I love you, little bugaboo. Now go dry off and put your pjs on, okay?"

"Um, um. Not until you make me a dry-as-a-bone bugaboo!"

Sarah laughed. She loved this routine and got sad every time she imagined the day that it would end. She played along, rubbing Kora's arms with the towel, then, like she always did, she dug her fingers into Kora's armpits, tickling them relentlessly, Kora squealing with laughter the whole time.

During a break in the tickle fight, Kora looked up at her mom and asked, "Momma, who are those flowers from? Nana told me they were from a boy, but when I asked her which boy she said I had to talk to you."

"Well, Bug, they're from a friend of mine that I met at the airport."

"Why did he send me flowers if he's your friend?"

"He sent me those beautiful daisies and knew how much you might want some of your own, so he sent you some colorful ones. Boy, does he know you, doesn't he, Bug?"

"He doesn't know me, Momma. He knows you."

Sarah laughed and rubbed Kora's head of wet hair. "True, baby girl, true. Well, you enjoy those flowers, and I'll enjoy tickling you silly." Kora screamed again.

Luise came into the room and immediately joined in, tickling Kora's belly until she was breathless with laughter. She then picked Kora up, tickling her the whole way back down the hallway toward Kora's room, and Sarah heard her mom tell Kora she would help her pick out the perfect bugaboo pajamas.

Kora squealed "Yay! Thanks, Nana!" Luise winked at Sarah and pointed to the book, miming reading it, but Sarah got the hint and smiled.

Nice pick, Mom, she thought.

She reached under her book and pulled out the unopened letter, being more careful opening it this time around. This one had three sheets, the last two stapled together, and at a glance, she saw that the stapled pages were a list, and the other was a letter, like the first. She started with the letter.

Dear Sarah,

Thank you for the letter. It was amazing getting to hear about your days and nights and what you do in-between flights. How often do you fly, by the way? Is it always an international flight? Those seem so long and like they'd throw off your whole routine, especially sleep. I know a bit about that in this gig, since I sleep any time I'm able, night or day. It's taught me how to fall asleep anywhere, which I think is cool, but makes me a bit of a freak, especially when I'm on a plane next to a stranger. They can be mid-introduction, and I'll already be out like a light, ha ha.

I was thinking the other day, you said you were a flight attendant because it had good benefits, but what would you do if you didn't have to worry about money? Not skip town and head to the Bahamas, but what would you do for a job? It's nice to be able to ask this in a letter, because I genuinely want to know the answer, but if we were on the phone, I'd have to answer it, too, and honestly, I don't know what I would do if I won the lotto. I'd like to think I'd stay in the Marines, but as I hear the mortars going off in the distance, and I picture you, sitting there reading on your cozy couch, I can't help but think I'd find anything closer to home. And, speaking of your cozy couch, can you give me a list of books I should read? I'm especially interested in the ones you've read a bazillion times, since they seem like they're worth your time.

On the job side of things, though, I had a couple interesting conversations with my boss, and his boss's boss today...

Sarah read on about how Mike was offered a promotion—she only sort of understood the logistics of the deal, especially the differences between being enlisted and an officer—and got excited for him. His passion for his job came through his words clear as day, the way he talked about his superiors and the respect he obviously had for them, for what he did. She did understand his reluctance to go the officer route, as it would take him away from his guys, and she remembered the way he'd talked about them—like they were his brothers.

She also gave thought to his question, about what she would do for work if she didn't have to worry about money. It had been so long since she'd thought about what she wanted to do, what would make her happy. The answer came to her in an instant, though.

She would be an art teacher.

She'd always loved to paint and imagined having a space of her own where she could spread out, spend time making something beautiful, and teaching that to others. How amazing, she thought, that a perfect stranger, and a chance meeting, could make her think about something she'd not thought about in years. To top it all off, he'd also signed this letter, "Love, Mike," meaning he'd seen hers and matched it.

Her heartbeat sped up, and her palms got sweaty holding the paper.

Putting the letter aside for the moment, Sarah brought out the list, laughing when she saw the title. "The Favorites List." After that, she saw a list of everything from Mike's favorite colors, to songs, to books, to places he'd love to visit.

Two things in particular surprised her. First, how many of the same things they had in common, especially foods and places they'd like to visit. Second, she was surprised at how many of the songs and movies she hadn't heard of. He had eclectic taste, and she was intrigued. At the bottom of his list, which spread over the front and back of the page, was an arrow pointing to the back page. She flipped it over and laughed, eliciting a "What is it, honey?" from her mom in the back room.

"Nothing, Mom," she shouted back.

The second page was titled "Murphy's Favorites List." There was the same list of categories, but instead of the corresponding answers, there were blanks for her to fill in. At the bottom of the back page, instead of an arrow, was a note to her.

"*Homework: Sarah, send this one back to me. <u>No blanks allowed</u>.*" This was amazing. She felt like a kid whose crush had slipped her a note in class. She couldn't wait to head to bed tonight to fill out her answers. It would give her a chance to listen to his choices of songs on her phone as well.

Padded footsteps raced down the hall so Sarah slipped the list under her book with the letters. Her daughter came running toward her full speed, sliding on the tile floor in her footsie pjs, laughing the whole way.

"Nana let me brush my teeth *and* hair in her bathroom."

"Did she, now?" Sarah picked Kora up and walked her back down the way she'd come from, tickling her sides as she went.

"Mammmmaaaa! Stop!" Kora cried, giggling.

"Can't hear you, bugaboo."

"MAMMMMAAA!" That was all Kora could get out before exploding into a fit of uncontrollable giggles and gasps for air.

"What is going on out here? This is utter chaos! I should send you both to bed without supper," Luise said, coming out from her bedroom.

"But, Nana, we already ate dinner. And, I brushed my teeth for the whole two minutes."

"You're right. Hmmm. Maybe just bed for the little bug."

"Awwwww. I don't wanna."

Luise and Sarah tucked Kora in, making sure her nightlight and music were on, and that the door was opened just the right amount. It was the same schedule every night, just like the bath routine, the morning routine, the drop off and pick up from school routines—all of it something Sarah treasured being able to be there for.

When they got out to the kitchen again, Luise went to the cabinet above the dishwasher.

"Wine?"

"Yes. Thanks for taking bedtime duty tonight."

"Umm hmm. I assure you it was wholly selfish. I wanted you to have a chance to read those letters so you can fill me in. Now, dish." Luise handed her a more-than-full glass of red wine, which Sarah raised her eyebrows to. Her mom waved her off, taking a long sip from hers, which was just as full. "C'mon. Out with it, Sare-Bear."

"You're relentless, aren't you?"

"Kora gets it from somewhere, doesn't she?"

"That's for certain. I don't know where she gets all her energy, though."

"That's why you have kids young, so you have some hope of keeping up with them."

Sarah laughed. "I don't know, Mom, you're doing okay holding your own."

"Oooh, you're a sassy one, aren't you?" They both laughed. Her mom cleared her throat and her hands gave a "give it here" gesture.

Sarah went to her book, pulled out the letters, and handed them to her mom, who pulled the reading glasses from her shirt pocket and put them on.

"Here, read them yourself. And hold the commentary till you're done, please," Sarah instructed.

For ten minutes, Sarah sat there, oscillating back and forth between biting her nails and sipping her wine with rapidly fraying nerves. She was sorry for telling her mom to be quiet until she was done, because this silence was killing her. She had no idea what her mom was thinking.

Was the letter too much, too fast? Was he ridiculous? Was she? *Ugh.* She wished her mom would read faster. After what seemed like an eternity, Luise set down the letter, took off her glasses, and wiped at her eyes.

"Are you crying?" she asked her mom. Of all the reactions she'd expected from her mom, tears weren't on the list.

"It's just lovely, Sarah. This is what I've always wanted for you." She sniffled, wiping more at her eyes. Sarah sniffled, too, choked up at her mom's rare display of emotion. She'd always been Sarah's rock, keeping things light, giving advice when it was warranted, but she hardly ever cried.

"I know. I'm glad you agree."

"I do have one question, though."

"What's that?" Sarah frowned.

"Who the heck are the Trampled Turtles?"

Sarah laughed a loud guffaw, sloshing some of her wine on her lap and the table. This was the mom she was used to. "Shoot!" She grabbed a napkin and dabbed at the wine, still laughing. "It's *Trampled by Turtles*, not the Trampled Turtles. They're a band."

"That's a stupid name." Luise sat there, shaking her head, and refilling her and Sarah's wine. "When do you leave tomorrow?"

"I'll head to the airport around 4. I can pick Kora up from school and drop her here on my way."

"That would be great, hun, thanks." Luise refilled her glass one more time, adding some to Sarah's as well, and faked a yawn so poorly that it set Sarah off laughing again. "What? I'm tired. So, I'm gonna head to bed, since it seems like your night is pretty planned out." Luise pointed to the letters in Sarah's hands, and she blushed, hiding herself behind them.

"I do, don't I? Okay, I'm gonna head to bed, too, then. I love you, Momma. Thank you. For everything." Sarah hugged her mom and jogged happily to her room, her letters from Mike in one hand, her half-empty wine in the other, carefully balanced.

Sitting on her bed, an hour and a half later, the letters and lists laid out in front of her, the phone playing *Trampled by Turtles*' song "Alone," Sarah had an idea of exactly what she would do in her next letter to Mike. She went to her bookshelf and tore down books, carefully tossing them on her bed. Many of them were held together with tape, and she doubted fully that they would survive the trip there and back, but she didn't care. Not if it meant sharing such an intimate part of her with him.

She dug around her closet until she found a box filled with old bills and receipts, and dumped the contents on the floor. It looked like a robbery had occurred when she was done another hour after she'd started, but she was thrilled with the results. She carefully taped the box shut, put his address on the top, and brushed the remnants of her project off her bed and onto the floor, before falling down on top of the comforter. She was asleep within minutes, where she dreamed of fields of daisies and books, her daughter skipping between the rows of each, and Mike, standing at the edge, watching her.

In her dream, at least, she got to have it all.

The shot hit barely two feet from Mendez's left ear, sending shards of concrete flying toward him.

That was close. Too close.

"Everybody down!" he shouted. "Watch your six!"

Chaos erupted, but everything was in freeze-framed slow motion for Mendez, whose pulse spiked into the red zone. Only flashes of what he was doing registered.

Whipping his gun from his holster and aiming it...

Throwing Owens out of the line of fire...

Dialing in on where the shots were coming from...

And then it sped up, like time was trying to even itself out.

He dove for cover, rolling on the dirt floor before coming up in a kneeling position, his rifle at the ready. All his training converged into muscle memory.

He laid down heavy fire in the direction he heard the bullets coming from, but the shooter had moved. They were somewhere in the three-story building across the marketplace, but the way the light hit him and shaded the south end of the shooters' hiding spot made keeping them in his sights almost impossible.

What the hell do I do next?

Sooner or later he and his team would run out of ammo, and who knew how prepared the enemy was.

"Eddie, we need air support, like NOW!" he called down the hall to his Comm guy.

"You got it, Sarge." Mendez heard the crackle of the radio and someone in the Command tent back at base responded to Eddie's request. "It'll be fifteen till they can get here, Sarge!"

"Not happening, Eddie. This'll be over in one way or another in less than ten. Let 'em know we need that support five minutes ago."

"Will do."

The radio crackled to life again, and Eddie yelled louder over the comm equipment. "No go, Sarge. They're inbound from Leatherneck. Had to do a casualty drop."

"You're freaking kidding me. Okay, gents. This one's on us, then. Let's get it done."

He pointed to the fractured doorway, where a beam blocked part of the entrance since the firefight. Corporal Evans nodded back at him and took three marines through it to provide cover for Mendez and his team. They crouched down in a low squat until they made it out of the back door and around the left side of the dilapidated structure. Mendez gestured to Jones and Robbins, motioning them forward to provide additional cover for him, Kint, and Sanchez. The bullets from the yet-to-be-seen enemy rained down over them, making any forward movement almost impossible, despite the cover from both sides of Mendez's team.

"Keep it coming, Evans. Move north ten meters, till you get to the wall. Give 'em hell."

Evans nodded and moved his men to behind the wall, where they had a better vantage point. Mendez noticed the drop in fire headed his way, thanks to Evans' team, and with two fingers as his pointer, guided his men to behind an abandoned truck.

The air smelled like burnt hair and week-old trash. It singed his nostrils but didn't cut through his focus.

"Kint, I want you here, covering us from this angle. Between you, Evans, and Jones, Sanchez and I should be able to get to the building. When we're in, follow us, and Jones and Evans will watch your six. Come around back and listen for my call." Kint didn't say anything, didn't even nod, but checked that his rifle was fully loaded.

"You got it, Kint?" Kint nodded once.

Kint never gave an affirmative response as was dictated by protocol for everyone's safety, but Mendez would fix that in the debriefing—if they made it that far. Now was not the time.

He turned to Sanchez to fill him in on his plan for once they got into the building, who would flank which side, when out of the corner of his eye saw Kint stand up.

He was completely without cover.

"Get down, Kint," Mendez shouted. "Get behind the truck now."

Kint kept walking forward, shooting toward the building as he walked.

Mendez's heart and mind raced. What the heck was Kint doing? He was going to get himself, and probably others in his team, killed.

"Get back here, Kint." Nothing. He kept walking. "You're gonna get shot, you crazy schmuck. GET. DOWN." When Kint nonchalantly kept moving and shooting toward the building, Mendez gestured to Sanchez. "Let's go save him."

Sanchez looked as angry as Mendez was but nodded his agreement.

They got up, still crouched, Sanchez with his back to Mendez's, checking to make sure they were clear from behind. They were moving slower than Kint at this point, doing their best to stay out of the way of Evans and Jones in their fighting positions as well. Before Mendez could do anything, he saw Kint disappear into the building.

"You've got to be... Ugh. Let's go. He's in." With that, Sanchez whipped around to Mendez's three o'clock, and they ran at a full sprint toward the building, bullets landing on either side of them, barely missing.

The shooter must be spraying blind. That was the only explanation for why they were still standing.

They got to the front entrance to the building, and though Mendez wanted to call in, find out where Kint was to make sure they didn't shoot him thinking he was the enemy, he also didn't want to alert the enemy to Kint's presence if he—or they—didn't know he was there yet.

They moved silently through the building, clearing each room on the first floor one by one to make sure they weren't ambushed. When Mendez got the all-clear signal from Sanchez, he nodded in the direction of the stairs to the second floor and Sanchez nodded back. Before they'd each gone more than three steps, however, they heard yelling coming from the third floor.

Mendez couldn't tell if it was in English or Pashto, only that it was heated. Before they could react, the yelling was cut off by the sound of semi-automatic fire, and with a shared look, the two men raced to the top of the stairs, rounded the corner, and without clearing any rooms on the second floor, continued taking the stairs to the third floor two at a time.

Only one thought made it through the focus and fear: *Sarah*.

With something to live for, every danger held more risk, less reward.

It was carnage when they got to the third story, an open floor with no rooms other than a great, open expanse. Three men in full robes and turbans lay spread out, blood pooled beneath them, their rifles awkwardly angled from their fallen bodies. Mendez scoured the room until his gaze landed on Kint lighting a cigarette in the corner, standing against the wall with one leg crossed over the other, seeming totally at peace, despite having just shot three enemy combatants in a matter of seconds.

Mendez was there in less than three seconds. He pushed Kint up against the wall, his hands shaking with fury.

"What were you trying to pull, Kint? You could've gotten yourself killed."

"Yeah, but I didn't. And I didn't *try* to pull anything. I completed the mission. Cleared the building. Your plan was too slow."

"But it was *my* plan, Kint, and I'm the one in command on this mission, and any others we get assigned. You understand?" His hand pressed against Kint's chest, and he so badly wanted to deck the guy for his insolence—insolence that could have killed the squad—but at that moment, he pictured Sarah's face, angelic and watching how he would react.

He released Kint.

"It was a stupid move, Kint, whether or not you actually pulled it off. I'm having you brought up in front of the Captain."

"Fine. Whatever. A simple, 'thank you' would have been sufficient." With that, Kint pushed off the wall as casually as he'd sauntered into the building, and Mendez followed behind him with Sanchez, short-wave radioing to Jones and Evans to subdue fire, that the enemy was eliminated, they were headed back to base.

When they got back to Haqleniah, Mendez sent the guys to shower and change into clean cammies before their debriefing, but he waved over Kint.

"You're with me." Kint's brows were furrowed, his smirk wiped clean, but he obeyed quietly for maybe the first time since they'd arrived in country a month ago. They both walked into the Captain's tent, and Mendez delivered the day's events free of the emotion that surged through his veins.

It was almost an hour later that Kint was released, sulking over his two weeks of latrine duty, and Mendez stayed behind.

"What's his deal, Sergeant? He's new to your team, isn't he?"

Mendez nodded. "I'm not sure, Captain, but it's been an ongoing problem I thought I could fix in-country, but now I'm not so sure."

"What do you mean? When did it start?"

Mendez finally filled Captain Hoffman in on the plane ride over, and the multiple negative interactions he'd had with Kint, including some of his troubling insubordination since.

"Hmmm. Do you think he's a danger to anyone other than himself?"

"I'm not sure. Today says yes. He was successful, but he directly disobeyed an order, one that was part of a multi-team plan of attack. He could have been hit by friendlies who weren't in on his internal decision-making."

"I see that. Let's keep an eye on him, see how he does on limited duty."

"Yes, sir."

"And next time, bring these issues to me sooner. I won't see it as a weakness in your leadership, unless you think you can solve it yourself." The Captain smiled and placed a hand on Mendez's shoulder. "Got it, Sergeant?"

"I do. And, thank you, Captain."

"Any time. Now, go get some rest, and tell the rest of your team I'll see them at 0400."

"Yes, sir." Mendez walked out of the tent and hurried back to his own. He didn't want to run into any of his men, didn't want to respond to any answers about Kint, didn't want to think about the corporal anymore that night.

When he got to his rack, he laid down on it, dirty cammies and all, and was almost asleep when he heard the tent flap open. He lifted his head, annoyed. A marine from Alpha Company poked his head in.

"Mail call, Sergeant Mendez."

Mendez sat all the way up, suddenly more alert than he'd been during the firefight. The marine handed him a bundle of letters and a large box. Mendez grunted under the weight of the box, put the stack on his rack, and thanked the marine.

He sifted through the letters and was overjoyed to find that three of the four were from Sarah, the fourth from his mom. Just her name in the return address spot, not his dad's. He sighed and put that letter off to the side, looking at the package. It, too, was from Sarah, and he couldn't help but forget all about the day's events as he turned the box over in his hands.

It was abnormally heavy given its size, and packed to the brim so that no matter which way he turned it, nothing shifted inside. He was beyond curious but put it next to the letter from his mom since it bore a "3" in the corner, and he saw that the letters were numbered 2, 4, and 5, just as he'd requested.

He read them in order and was pleased to see that the first was another letter about her recent flights to New York and back, then to Nashville and back, as well as Kora's progress in gymnastics, and her mom's recent trip to the doctor to assess some numbing in her arm. In answer to her trip to Germany, it was for a friend, she told him. She never did international flights because they took her away from Kora for too long. She'd been asked by one of the only flight attendants she liked—a man named Jeffrey, who was as gay and funny as the day was long, in her words—if she could cover for him so he could meet up with a guy he'd met on the internet in Boca.

"I accepted, but it took a lot of cajoling since it was a military flight—not my favorite transport, or at least it wasn't ;) Anyway, I sent him a bottle of wine last week, along with a note explaining why the trade was the best thing since Chris Harrison was kicked off The Bachelor."

Mendez chuckled, especially when she added that Jeffrey was curious about him, about his intentions for her, and said he'd be sending a letter for Sarah to forward to Mike one of these days.

Mendez leaned back, a gentle smile on his face. He pictured Sarah and Jeffrey dishing like two good girlfriends about their crushes. A flush of heat warmed his chest as he realized Sarah'd been willing to tell a good friend about him.

The last part of the letter responded to what she would do if she didn't have to work. There wasn't any doubt in his mind that her answer—an art teacher—was perfect for her. He thought how lucky the students would be who got her to teach them about art.

That letter also had her reply to his Favorites List, and he pored over her choices, noting that she'd written in red pen what they shared in common, and was overjoyed to find that over half the responses were crimson. Those that weren't were the most intriguing to him, though. When he'd described Kora as a princess, he'd assumed that Sarah would have similar tastes, but he was more than pleasantly surprised to discover that she liked indie music and movies, some even he'd never heard of. In fact, when he got to the bottom of the list, he chuckled out loud.

She'd actually written, *"I hadn't heard of any of your music or movies, but I've spent the past night and a half staying up and listening to all of them before I thought I'd do the same for you—give you homework to complete that will hopefully give you the super cool experience I had in discovering not just your music, but a little bit about you."*

He loved that idea—homework shared, back and forth. It was like interactive letters, not just explaining, but asking the other to play along.

There was a final asterisk at the bottom of the list, which told him to open the package, if he had it already. He wasted no time in abiding by that request, tearing open the box with an abandon he normally lacked.

The inside panels of the box were littered with quotes from people he didn't know, and at first, his brows furrowed in confusion, until he saw one by "Alice" reading "I sometimes believe in six impossible things before breakfast."

It's from *Alice in Wonderland,* he realized.

Skimming over the other quotes, he saw they were all from characters in books.

Clever. Curious, he took the tissue paper covering from the box, and discovered seven novels tucked inside. The urge to giggle like a kid welled up from his stomach, but he stopped himself when he noticed their worn covers and dog-eared pages. The first one had underlined passages and notes in the margins in the same handwriting as the letters.

Hers. These were the books she'd read and reread, and she'd trusted him with them. His hands were sweating, and he wiped them on his dusty trousers, then his sleeping bag.

Shutting the book, he traced the cover, knowing her hands had likely done the same. *The Poisonwood Bible,* by Barbara Kingsolver. He'd never heard of it. Heck, he'd never been much of a reader mostly because he'd been too intimidated to ask, as a grown man, what he should read. Now, though, his whole body buzzed with anticipation in seeing what the pages in front of him had in store for him, including the notes from Sarah herself.

He was almost more excited to see what she found to be important enough to underline and make notes about.

The other books were more titles he was unfamiliar with. *One Hundred Years of Solitude, A Prayer for Owen Meany, Written on the Body, Alice in Wonderland, Beach Music,* and *The Alchemist.* They were various lengths and had different bindings, but they all bore the trademark red pen scrawls and underlining. It was like a mystery he couldn't wait to unfold. But first, he had to get through her other two letters, a task that was as much pleasurable as maddening since he now had thousands of pages of her thoughts—through someone else's words, though—to pore over. Not to mention find the songs and movies she listed as her favorites next time he was at Leatherneck. It was like an early Christmas for him.

He opened the envelope numbered "4," and pulled out another letter, and what looked like another list behind it. Though he was more curious than ever, he forced himself to read the letter first. The handwriting was different, like Sarah was in a rush when she wrote it. He'd never seen anything but impeccable handwriting and grammar from her, but when he started reading, it wasn't just the handwriting that seemed off.

Dear Mike,

This is letter number three, if you don't count the box of books. I want to apologize for sending over so many. I was sleep deprived and giddy from your flowers and letter, and got a little out of hand. Please don't feel like you have to read them all, or any of them for that matter. I woke up the next morning after packaging them up, and my mom had shipped them off to you before I could slap myself out of it. Sorry in advance!

In other news, though, I FINALLY got Kora to ride a bike without training wheels! She was so adamant about getting it right that we spent four of the longest hours of my life out on the road, going up and down, weaving in-between parked cars, and then, after falling a few times, she could turn all the way around without stopping. I'm so dang proud of her. You should see it. I'll take some video and email it to you. Also, she loved her flowers. Like, loved them. Thank you. So much. There are a few that she snuck out as I was preparing to toss them (when they died—I'm not a monster), so who knows when I'll find them. That girl.

Not to be the queen of awkward transitions, but on that note, are you able to check your email? Or call? It may sound needy, but I miss your voice. I miss your laugh, and at the risk of sounding not just needy, but cheesy, I miss your face. Your flowers have passed on, and I feel like you may be fading. Sooooo.... On that melodramatic note, maybe now is a good time to tell you I have had about a bottle of wine. To myself. And I don't normally have more than a glass. You have my mom to thank for that one. In fact, there is a strong chance that you won't see this letter because I'll wake up tomorrow, see it sitting on my desk, and rip it into the million pieces it deserves.

But since this is my letter, and right now I get to ask you anything without consequence (I am an immediate satisfaction girl when I drink), I am curious about why your dad didn't want you to join the Marines. Was it because he was an army guy? Also, on that note, do you have a college degree? I was looking up the difference between the enlisted and officer jobs you were talking about, and the officer one said you need a degree. What did you study? I hope this doesn't make you like me any less (assuming pretty heavily at this point that you like me at all), but I actually don't have a degree. I married Hank early into my undergraduate, and he got sick not that much longer after that. Sometimes I wish I would have stuck it out, but then, I'm not sure how I would pull it off. Someone to watch Kora while I went to classes, a flexible schedule so I could fly—it all seems so impossible now.

You want to know the kicker to that situation, the Hank situation? I got off birth control when he got sick. They said it wasn't "necessary" since he was "sick," and "sterile." Turns out he was just sick, but that it was *necessary*, and he wasn't *sterile*. Hence Kora. I like the word hence, by the way, but man, do I love my little girl. No matter what else sucked about losing my husband so young (a lot of things suck in that situation, let me tell you), I have her, and that decidedly didn't suck. It still doesn't. It's a lot of work, and I don't even know who I am anymore, besides her mom, but she is the number one best thing about me. So, you might be thinking I was cute, or that I had a nice butt, but the best thing I'll ever be is her mom.

Mike, Michael, Mendez, Michael Mendez, I think you're pretty great. Thank you for being pretty great. Stay safe, you hear? I wanna kiss that face again.

Love (cause why not, huh?),

Sarah Murphy

P.S. This is Luise, Sarah's mom. I've also had some wine, so I apologize in advance for doing what I am about to do, which is send this letter. It may be the ramblings of a drunk, overworked, overtired woman, but she's never been as honest as she just was, so I think we need to not rip this letter up, as it seems she plans to do. You stay safe, and it was nice to unofficially meet you. Chow. Or is it spelled Ciao? Anyway, bye, Felecia. Haha, we just watched Friday *the other night. It's one of my favorites. Don't judge my daughter for my bad taste.*

Mike didn't know what to do besides laugh. Here he was, in the same smelly, dusty, sweaty cammies he'd been in since yesterday when he'd been sent out of the wire to shut down sniper fire in the market bordering the bridge, having almost been shot to heck earlier, laughing harder than he had in a long time. He found Sarah, and her mom for that matter, hopelessly endearing, hysterical, and adorable. These three women were going to be a force to be reckoned with in Mendez's life, that was certain.

Now he had to know what the list was behind the letter. He pulled it out, still wiping tears from his eyes and shaking off the laughter, only to find a "Top 5 Of..." list. On it, she had listed her top five of everything, from song lyrics, to movie quotes, to main character sidekicks, to R&B pop artists of the eighties. His favorite was the top five hair band ballads.

Who is this woman? And, how did he get lucky enough to meet her when all likelihood said they shouldn't have? She surprised him in such wonderful ways each time he was let into her world.

Copying his protocol, she'd left a blank page for him to fill out his top fives. Some of the categories she'd chosen for him to fill out, while the others were left for him to decide for himself. Also like he'd done, she requested that he send these back to her.

Well, dang. This was going to take some time. His brain was on overload, and all he really wanted was to divide himself in two, and have one work on the list, coming up with new homework to send her in response, and the other start in on the novels she'd sent. Neither were conducive to his work schedule, but he'd make the time. It was important.

One book his mother had required him to read was *Sophie's Choice*, and Mendez had found it to be bleak, unrealistic, and melodramatic, but now, faced with a far easier task, he couldn't decide what to do and empathized with the main character.

As he got up to grab one of the books, the third and final envelope, marked "5," fell to his feet. Crap. He'd forgotten about that. After all she'd sent so far, what more could she do to win him over? He stood there, beside his rack, boots and cover still on, and gingerly opened the last letter. It was a single page, and there was only one paragraph, perfectly spaced and written on the page.

Dear Mike,

Well, dang. How to follow up that last one. My mom is getting the major silent treatment right now, I can tell you that. Found the flowers Kora hid—they were in her pillowcase. Just wanted you to feel like you solved the mystery too, especially since I probably won't be hearing from you again after that last letter. Ugh. Wine. I'd say I will never drink again, but that is an impossibility since I now have to drink away the memory of the shortest pen pal (well, the only pen pal, actually) I've ever had.

I hope this finds you well, and again, I am sorry.

Best,

Sarah

Mike was flabbergasted. She actually believed he wouldn't be head-over-heels in love with her after that last letter? He dropped the sheet of paper in the pile on his bed and ran out of the tent, desperate to find Captain Hoffman before the debriefing.

He was breathless when he reached the Captain's tent, Hoffman looking at him like there was imminent danger afoot that he needed to quelch. Mendez shook his head as he caught his breath.

"Captain," he got out in more than the necessary syllables, "I need to ask you for a favor. It's important."

"For the girl?"

Mendez nodded, and the Captain smiled.

"What can I do?"

Mendez came the rest of the way into the tent and explained his plan.

"It's kinda simple, but it has to happen just right..."

Eight

Surprises

Sarah dialed her mom as she walked off the plane.

"Hey there, baby girl. Make it safe?"

"I did. It was a boring flight, actually."

"The best kind."

"Gosh, yes. How's Kora?"

"She passed out on the couch while we were watching *Frozen*. I left her there, I hope you don't mind. I just worried moving her would wake her up and she was missing you pretty bad tonight."

"Oh no," Sarah said, pinching the bridge of her nose. She hated when her daughter had tough days and she was nowhere close enough to offer comfort. Helplessness crept inside each of her cells, suffocating the idea that she was doing this for her daughter. But, how could it be worth it if she couldn't be there for Kora now? "What happened?"

"She got a little upset when I found a bunch more of those dead flowers under her stuffed animals when I was cleaning sheets. I told her I had to toss 'em, and she lost her mind. I think it was the perfect storm of tired, hungry, and missing you. So, we went to Anna and Elsa to calm her down, and it seemed to work."

"I'm sorry, Mom. Ugh. I wish I could find something closer that didn't need a degree. Maybe I'll apply at the school again as an aide."

"Don't you worry about it, hun. She's fine, just a normal five-year-old who misses her momma. You keep doing what you're doing. I'm proud of you. When it's time to change things up, you'll know."

"Yeah, you're probably right. Thanks."

"I love you, Sare-Bear. Call us tomorrow before you take off. I promised Kora she could stay home with me tomorrow and help me with some chores around the house."

"Oh, yeah, what are you two up to?"

"Nothing much. Don't you worry about either of us. We've got plenty to keep us busy and help distract her until you get home."

"Hmmmm... Okay, then. Hug her for me, please."

"Always. Be safe. Goodnight, hun."

Sarah hung up and her shoulders sagged, followed by her heart. In moments like these, she thought about giving it all up, and those moments were coming more and more often. Nausea rolled around in her stomach.

Wanting to calm down before she caught a cab, Sarah went to the bathroom to wash her face. Looking in the mirror, she took deep breaths.

What am I going to do? She sighed out a flood of anxiety. Nothing was going to be solved tonight, so she might as well get to the hotel and rest. She could think about next steps tomorrow. She walked outside and cold air assaulted her cheeks, waking her up.

So did another, different, worry than how to help Kora.

Unease about walking around New York at night fluttered in her chest. Getting a cab and heading to a hotel in a city she wasn't from never sat well with her, which was why she preferred the out-and-back schedule. Plus, it got her back to Kora and her mom quicker.

Unfortunately, those weren't the cards she was dealt this time around, so she found herself outside JFK airport at two in the morning on a Tuesday, waiting for a cab, wishing more than ever she was already home. The air was chillier away from the baggage doors, and she pulled her coat tight around her. It didn't help much. Gosh, where was everyone? Her flight in had been full, but those people had long ago caught other rides or flights. Now, JFK was a ghost town. Being alone in the city that never sleeps was a weird feeling. Ominous.

A man in a black trench coat and beanie stood creepily close to Sarah, despite the rest of the sidewalk being open. She didn't want to look directly at him, but from what she could see in her peripheral vision, she didn't recognize him. He wasn't on her flight, and now that she thought of it, where was his luggage? She put her hand around her keys just in case, something she'd seen done in a movie, though she wasn't sure she could swing them around to hurt anyone if the need ever arose.

The man moved closer to her, and panic rose like bile in her throat. She couldn't see his hands, which were shoved deep in his pockets. Anything could be hidden there, and her imagination went straight to the worst-case scenario. Gun? Knife? Rope?

Only an occasional bus to the rental car lot drove past. She thought about calling her mom but didn't want to take her focus from the man in case he took advantage of her distraction.

When he moved closer again, Sarah put one key in between each finger, making her hand into a Wolverine-looking contraption. Her breath was trapped in her throat. She thought of Kora, of what would happen to her daughter if something horrible happened here tonight. Her mom would raise her, but how long would her mom be okay? She'd barely made it through the last stroke, the one that had made Sarah move back home.

God, oh God, where can I go to be safe? Back inside the terminal? There were hardly any people in there, either. Her hands shook inside her jacket, jingling her keys.

As the man stepped one final step closer, Sarah pulled the hand holding her keys out of her pocket, fully prepared at this point to use them. Her arm raised, and as it did, the phone in her pocket rang. She didn't remember turning her ringer on but was delighted when the man abruptly turned around and jogged the other way.

Sarah exhaled, not realizing she was holding her breath until her lungs no longer burned. In her pocket, the phone continued to ring. She was so relieved that she was—at least temporarily—safe, that she'd forgotten about the phone. She fumbled trying to get it and answer it, her hands still shaking. The incoming call was 00-00000-000, which she didn't trust, but she wanted to keep whoever it was, even a solicitor, on the line until a cab came along.

"H-hello?" There was silence for five seconds and she pulled the phone away from her ear to shake it. She had full-service bars, so she had no idea what was wrong. She tried again. "Hello?"

"Hi! Sarah?"

"Who is this?" The voice on the other end sounded far away and like he was speaking through a pillow. It sounded familiar, but the distance made it hard to place.

"It's me, Mike. Mendez?"

She lit up, the long flight and day's events sliding off her.

"Wow! Can you hear me okay? You seem so far away." Again, there was a pause.

"Yeah, I'm on a satellite phone, so there may be pauses and some static. How are you?"

"Um, well..." She couldn't think about how to answer that. She thought she wasn't ever going to hear from him again, and that, combined with the stranger who she'd been certain was going to attack her, was too much for her.

She let out a sob and tears streamed down her cheeks.

"Sarah? What's wrong? Talk to me."

"I just didn't think I'd ever be hearing from you. Not after my mom sent that horrible letter; ugh, I could kill her. And then there was this guy just a minute ago. He ran away when the phone rang, but..."

"What guy?"

She took three deep breaths, trying to calm herself down.

"Sarah? What guy?"

"There was a guy here on the sidewalk. It was just us waiting for a cab, and he kept getting closer and closer, and I had out my keys in case I needed to use them, you know, for self-defense, but then you called."

"I'm so sorry. I hate that I am this far away and can't be there for you. But at least I can hear your voice. I'm sorry it took so long to call. We don't have anything but a sat phone at our FOB, the small base we're on."

"Why did you call? I don't mean to be rude, but did you get my letter?"

"The one that drunk Sarah and drunk Luise wrote?"

Sarah nodded and sniffled before she realized she had to verbally respond. "Yes. That one."

She heard him laugh heartily on the other line. "Oh, boy. I'm sorry if you felt like you had to be embarrassed about that. Truthfully, I loved it. And, I wish I could have told you that sooner. This lack of comm out here has been the bane of my existence. All I've wanted to do since I got here was to call you. I've missed your voice. And your face."

She groaned.

"I'm teasing you. But, I do, miss your face, that is."

"I miss you, too. I'm sorry I got so emotional. I haven't been that scared in all the flying I've done, in all the places I've traveled to. There was something so sinister about that guy. But then—hey, guess what?"

"What?"

"You saved me from yet another creep. I'm starting to think you really are my hero, Mike." Again, she heard him chuckle.

"Glad to be of service. You have no idea how relieved I am that you're safe, though, seriously. Are there any taxis yet?"

"Nothing. It's empty."

"So, talk to me, tell me how you've been. I don't want the guy to come back. Tell me all the details. I can't believe it's been almost two months since I've heard your voice."

"Not much has been going on here, honestly. Besides Kora learning to ride a bike. That's the biggest news here."

"I do believe drunk Sarah wanted me to know that information. And that she can make full turns now. Tell her congratulations for me."

"Of course, drunk Sarah would tell you all that. What else did she tell you, and I'll fill in the blanks."

"Well, she wanted to know if I have a degree, which I do, and what I studied. Tell her I have a degree in computer engineering and a minor in military tactics."

"I'll pass that on, but I don't know that drunk Sarah will be joining us much anymore. She and hangover Sarah don't get along very well. Plus, she's rather embarrassing when it comes to talking to cute guys."

"Oh, she visits that often, does she?" He stifled a laugh, and it made her giggle. "Ah, there it is. That laugh I miss almost more than that face."

She laughed harder. "Very funny, mister. Before we move on from drunk Sarah, did she tell you anything else? She can be awfully chatty."

"She did tell me you don't have a degree. That you started one, but then Hank got sick, and you weren't able to finish it. She, you, didn't mention what you were studying, though."

"Oh, um, I hadn't settled on a degree yet, but I was leaning toward art. At the time, I probably would have gone into art history, but now I don't know. I would honestly love to teach, like I mentioned in the first letter. I could be around for Kora more, and be off when she's off, especially since she's heading into the first-grade next year, and my mom isn't getting any better."

"Your mom? What's wrong?"

"Oh, sorry, nothing really, right now. She had a stroke a few years back, and that's why Kora and I moved in. She needed round-the-clock help for almost a year."

"I thought you moved in because she was selling the house?"

"Yeah, I mean, part of that is true. She was going to sell the house because she couldn't take care of it anymore. She's okay now, but I can tell there are moments when it's just too much for her. I'm sorry. I don't want you to think I lied to you, but I'd just told you about Hank, and my dad. I just didn't want to get into it with my mom, too. Especially not when she's okay."

"I get that, I do, but I hope you feel like you can come to me when things are hard. I really like the laughing, happy Sarah, and I'm pretty fond of drunk Sarah, too, but sad and frustrating things are going to happen, and I want to be there for you for those, too."

Sarah closed her eyes and smiled, and when she opened them, she saw headlights and a yellow "In Service" light heading towards her. *Finally.*

"Thank you, that means so much to me, you don't even know. But hey, give me just a second. A cab finally showed up."

"Thank God you can get out of there. Head straight to the hotel. No strangers."

"You got it." She flagged the cab down and gave him the address of the Sheraton she was staying in until her flight tomorrow, which thankfully, took off mid-afternoon. "I'm back. Thanks. And Mike, I do feel that way, but it's hard, pouring my darkest secrets into a letter, sending it into the abyss, hoping you'll get it."

"I understand. Luckily, there's a good chance my Captain, who you met, will let me use his sat phone until we get one established on base, or head back to Leatherneck for some reason."

"That's good. Because I love sending and getting letters from you, but it's pretty one-sided."

"Say no more. I agree. I promise I'll get better at calling you. And, we have wifi, oddly enough. We need it for comms. I can send more emails, too."

There was a pause, and Sarah said. "Not to...," right as Mike started to speak again.

"Actually..." he began. "Oh, sorry, I didn't mean to cut you off. The time delay here is awful. Go ahead."

"Thanks. I was just going to say, not to change the subject, but how are things there? I know there's so much you can't tell me, but are you okay? Are your guys okay?"

He filled her in on what happened with Kint, and she wished she were surprised. He was an accident waiting to happen with his attitude, and she told Mike as much. Her cab pulled up in front of the Sheraton, and she paid the driver, waving off the need for any change.

"I agree. We've got eyes on him, and he pulled limited duty for a while, so we'll see what happens."

"What will happen if he pulls another stunt like that?" she asked. She walked in the glass doors to the hotel lobby and blinked in the bright lights. She finally felt safe. She was inside a well-staffed hotel and talking to Mike. He had the ability to make her feel like everything would work out, even from thousands of miles away.

"If no one is hurt, it could just be a page eleven, which is a disciplinary thing that could dock him in pay or cost him rank."

"And if someone does get hurt?"

"Then, it's a different story. He could go in front of a board and lose his rank, maybe get kicked out of the Corps, or if it's grievous enough, he could go to the Brig."

"The Brig?"

"It's a military jail. It's rare guys get sent there, but something big like that—disobeying an order multiple times, resulting in casualties on our side—that could do it. Let's just hope that doesn't happen, for a bunch of reasons."

"Wow, yeah. So, um, changing tack again, I'm assuming if you got the letters that you got the books I sent?"

"I did."

"And?" She was nervous he'd tell her they weren't really his thing, or worse, be blase about them, brushing off some of her favorite authors and novels. These pauses in conversation while the phone struggled to keep up were killing her.

"They are amazing. I'm already halfway through *Beach Music*. I stayed up half the night reading it, and I hope you don't mind, but I added parts I enjoyed to the margins—in pencil, of course."

Sarah giggled and covered the receiver on the phone so he couldn't hear her. It was in vain, though. She was overjoyed that he enjoyed the book so much that he felt the need to write in it. Plus, her heart skipped a beat imagining getting to read his responses when the books were returned to her.

"Is that a laugh I just heard? Are you laughing at me?" he teased.

"No, I mean, yes. I am laughing, but not at you. I am just happy, that's all. You don't need to use a pencil. I've already trashed them pretty badly."

"Then, the jury rules. We'll allow happy laughing," he teased again. "Anyway, Conroy's writing is incredible. The way he does detail, and the way you can imagine each character saying exactly what they do… Man, he's so good. I'm surprised I hadn't heard of him until now."

"He's a little out of the mainstream now. My mom is the one who turned me on to him, and yeah, he's fantastic. Just wait though. Every book I sent will have you feeling the same way."

"I really can't wait. I wanted to dive into them right away when I got them, but I had to do a couple things first."

"Work?"

"No, actually. I have homework for you, while I get through these novels you sent. Though I am going to warn you, you'd better have a backup set of books the way I'm getting through these."

"I already have a list forming." Sarah walked over to the front desk and mouthed to the woman manning the desk this late, "Pencil? Paper?" and mimed writing a note. She wrote down ideas for other books that Mike would like, even as he was telling her his plan for what order to read the rest that she'd just sent in. She heard him mention *Written on the Body* by Jeanette Winterson and stopped him.

"Wait. Read that last. The Winterson book."

"Okay," he said. "I can do that. Oh, and I meant to tell you, I love your list, but no one I know has heard of that movie, *Once*. Do you know if I can rent it online?"

"I'm not sure. Hold off on it for now, though, especially with those books you've got piled up."

"Haha, that's a good plan. Now, on to your homework. Do you have something to take notes with?"

"As a matter of fact, I do. Go ahead." She sat on one of the lobby couches, pen at the ready. Was she tired a moment ago? She was so wired, she couldn't remember a time she'd been otherwise.

"Alright. Here's the plan, and there is no backing out. I've checked all the angles, and there is no way you can talk your way out of any of it, okay?"

She nodded again. "Yes."

"So here goes. I sent you a package yesterday, but it's from Amazon, so it should be there much faster than the ones I send. I'm hoping tomorrow at the latest, when you get home."

"How do you know when I get home?" she asked, her curiosity piqued.

"After you get the package," he started, ignoring her question, "you need to ask your mom what to do with it before you open it. That's a very important part of the plan, okay?"

She laughed. "Okay. But my mom? When did you talk to her? Wait. *How* did you talk to her?" Sarah had so many questions, but loved not only that he'd sent her a package—her mind raced with ideas about what it could be—but that he'd collaborated with her mom to make it happen.

"All that will be answered in due course, I promise. But, for now, make sure to call your mom to pick you up at LAX. No cab. She'll explain more when you see her. Until then, check in, sleep tight, and I'll try and call you in a couple of days, okay?"

"Okay. Thank you."

"Well, wait until you get the package to say thanks."

She laughed. "True. Either way, thank you for calling. I have a feeling you literally saved me from a bad night."

"You're welcome. Sleep tight, Sarah, and trust me, it'll all be okay." She believed him, more than she had anything before. "I miss you."

"I miss you, too. So much."

"Good night."

"Good night, Mike." She hung up the phone, put it back in her pocket, and walked to the desk to check in.

Up in her room, she was still energized from the conversation with Mike. Despite it being three in the morning, Sarah didn't feel like she could possibly go to bed now. She paced the floor of her room, walking up and down, her mind turning over and over, ruminating on what Mike had up his sleeve.

Finally, she decided to put her energy to good use and went to the coffee table, looking for stationary. Finding some, she laid down on her stomach on the bed, feet up like the sixteen-year-old she felt like, and got to work thinking about what to write Mike. She might only have letters and the occasional phone call to get to know him, but she wasn't going to use that as an excuse for letting such an amazing man slip from her life.

So, with that, she put pen to paper and started anew. This time things were going to be different.

This time, it was going to be amazing.

It was the hottest day of the deployment so far, and all across base the marines were in various stages of undress. Most of them were in skivvies, the small green PT shorts they wore for workouts, if they were off duty. The others wore tan dry wick shirts tucked into cammie trousers if they were working.

The air was heavy, and everyone was restless. It was too hot in the tents, where even though there wasn't any sun, there was no air flow, either. So, they were all outside. Even Command, with the exception of the poor schmuck who pulled duty, was outside the tent, making calls on sat phones, and writing up mission orders. Each square inch of shade by the barrack tents was taken by groups of marines playing cards, napping, or in Mendez's case, working out. He figured if he was going to be sweaty and miserable, he might as well be earning it.

"Can I get a spot?" he asked Jones, who was playing cards next to the weight benches.

"Ugh. I can't believe you're working out in this. Aren't you freaking hot?" Jones got up anyway, and headed over to where Mendez was loading forty-five-pound plates on his bar.

"Aren't you?"

"Good point. This sucks, man."

"It does, but it's not much different than the rest of deployment. It's not Cancun, no matter which way the weather shakes out."

Jones laughed. "Another good point. Hey, I've been meaning to ask you about that book you've been carrying around. *Bible* something or other?"

"Yeah? What about it?"

"It's long, bro."

This time Mendez laughed. "It is. Good observation, Jones. What's your point?"

"Well, I dunno. Why are you reading it? We got those magazines in the tent."

"True, but they're mostly pictures. And, I don't really have anything better to do out here, do I?" Mendez placed the bar back on the rack, too exhausted to move. "Besides, it's good—a heckuva lot better than a car and truck magazine."

"Yeah, I guess. But where'd you get it? You have a lot of those big books, right?"

"Sarah sent them. A whole box full. Why are you so interested, Jones?"

"Well, actually, I was wondering if you might have something I could borrow. I sorta finished the magazines and I'm bored as hell, man."

Mendez laughed again. "Sure. But, I'm gonna start you off on something simple. Come on by the tent later, and I'll hook you up with something that'll interest you."

"Thanks, bro."

"You bet." Mendez sat up from the bench and wiped the sweat from his brow. The closer the sun got to the top of the sky, the more the shade disappeared. His benches were now under direct sunlight and the heat had to have been close to 110 in the sun.

He was done lifting. He turned to the guys playing cards.

"Mind if I join you for a hand?"

"Nah, bro. Grab a seat." Mendez turned the workout bench around, taking the last square of shade around the table. "7-Card Stud."

"Sounds good. What're we playing for?"

"Desserts from MREs. You still in?" Everyone chuckled.

"I dunno, Jones, that might be too rich for my blood."

"Ah, you know they're all melted anyway in this heat. You won't be losing much."

"Who says I'll be losing?" Mendez challenged. The group erupted into laughter and hollering, all of them reaching out for fist bumps with Mendez.

"So," said Robbins, "what's this I hear about you having a girlfriend, Sergeant?"

"Oh, yeah? What exactly did you hear?" Mendez knew it was only a matter of time until his guys wanted to talk to him about Sarah, but he'd keep the details to himself. Deployments brought the guys closer, but that sometimes came at a cost, the good times and bad both infectious amongst the men. If one of them was going through a divorce, or found out their girl was cheating, he'd try and convince the rest that their women needed to go as well.

Mendez meant to keep Sarah as far from that as possible.

"Just that you met on the way out here and been writing ever since."

"That's about right. It's nothing, really, just a nice way to pass the time." He hated lying but keeping it casual to his men was the only way to protect what he had.

Someone across the table called for cards to be laid down, and Mendez saw that he'd won. *Nice.* He gathered his winnings—brownies and M&Ms that were both probably worse for the wear in this heat, but he didn't care. It was just nice to relax with his guys on one of their rare days off.

They'd had a rough mission a few days ago, and Eddie had been shot in the arm. He'd be fine, but probably wouldn't be back this deployment. Lucky guy. But the men had all been granted a slight reprieve from being outside the wire until the paperwork from Eddie could be processed, and his family notified that he'd be heading back to Balboa Medical in San Diego.

As Jones dealt a new hand, a shadow passed over the table, blocking the sun that had crept in. Mendez looked up to see Kint standing there, his arms crossed over his chest like usual. The air was sucked out from around the table as the other guys looked down, or right at Kint with utter contempt.

He'd been responsible for watching Eddie's six on the mission, and the marines felt it was his fault Eddie had been shot. Mendez also knew it was probably negligent behavior that had led to the injury on Kint's part, but he couldn't prove anything. He'd said as much on the drive back to base, and Kint told him he was right—Mendez couldn't prove a thing.

"What do you want, Kint?" Mendez asked. The sneer Kint gave him sent chills down his spine, despite the heat.

"I heard you talking about that hot piece you met on the plane, and that she was only a distraction while you were here. Thought I'd find out a little more."

"That's not how I put it, Kint." Mendez was seething. Sarah had been Kint's obsession since the plane. Where had he even been that he heard Mendez say anything?

"That's how I heard it. For a girl who sends you letters almost every day, I don't think she'd like to hear how you really feel about her."

"Back off, Kint. This ain't none of your business," Jones chimed in.

"I dunno. I met her, and I think if she knew Mendez was just using her while he was on deployment, she'd appreciate a real man coming to her rescue when we get back. Someone who wouldn't let her even consider Jodi."

Mendez stood up. "You mention her again and I'll find a way to fry your chances of leaving here the Corporal you somehow still are. You'll be pulling latrine duty the rest of deployment, and I'll guarantee that the only MREs we order are Chicken Vindaloo. It'll make the last two weeks seem like paradise."

Kint put his hands up, conceding, the sneer even more pronounced. "I see. Well, my mistake. I'm sure you really do care about her. Oh, and you have another package on your rack, Sergeant. Pretty little hearts on a certain return address. I've always wanted to visit Long Beach. You all take care, now."

When he walked away, the table buzzed.

"What a tool," Jones said.

"That dude could never hold down a girl. Too creepy," added Robbins.

Mendez looked down at his palms and saw that he'd been clenching them so tightly, trying to resist the urge to punch Kint, that he'd dug small half-moon shapes into his skin. His hands shook. He chastised himself mentally for letting Kint get to him like that, but there was no way he would tolerate anyone talking about Sarah like that. And he'd been so prepared to strangle Kint when he'd told him he'd gotten close enough to the package Sarah sent to see her address, that he hadn't fully appreciated the fact that he had a package waiting for him.

"Sergeant? Hey, Sarge?"

Mendez finally snapped out of it and looked up.

"Yeah? What'd I miss?"

"You want in on this round?"

"Nah. Thanks, though, guys. I've gotta take care of some stuff. Here," he said, handing over the brownies and other desserts in their bland, tan packaging.

"Thanks, bro. And hey," Jones started. Mendez looked back. "Ignore that jerk. He's just jealous, man."

"Yep. See you at chow." Mendez jogged as quickly as he could in the stifling heat to his tent, where he only went in long enough to grab the package, stop to make sure Kint wasn't there, and head out. It was a rather large box, and as curious as he was about its contents, he still fumed about Kint.

Mendez hightailed it to the chow hall, where he snuck into the back of the tent. He waved at the marines working in the abysmal heat, miming wiping the sweat from his forehead. They laughed and he nodded toward the large fan in the back.

"May I?" he yelled over to them.

"You got it, Sarge," one of them called back.

Even though it was only a degree or two cooler in front of the fan, the airflow felt amazing. He took out his pocket knife and sliced the tape from the package, noting the hearts in the space where Sarah'd put her address. They were small, almost impossible to see, and Mendez got angry all over again, until the paper at the top of the package slid off and revealed what was beneath it.

Suddenly, it was like Kint didn't exist. Mendez's face lit up like it was Christmas. Inside the box was everything you'd find at a movie theater in order to enjoy a night out. There was his favorite candy, Sour Patch Kids, in a giant bag that would last him a few movies at least. Underneath those was a bag of Harkins movie popcorn, already popped.

He was laughing now. *How cool is this?*

He thought it would be four more months until he got to have any of this again. He pulled out the popcorn and resisted the urge to tear into it right away. An envelope fell to the bottom of the box, with

"Open first" written on the front. It must have slipped down during shipping. He put it aside, curious about what was left in the box.

Mendez discovered an old school portable DVD player that looked like it had seen better days. What the heck, he wondered. What was all this? Next came a comfy pair of socks that made Mendez laugh. There was no way he'd be wearing those any time soon, but he loved the sentiment. He was putting things together now, but there were still four things left in the box. There was a homemade CD in a case, no label on it, a small bag of Doritos, and a tin of nacho cheese. The last item was an older, also slightly beat up iPad. The smile on his face was impossible to erase.

This girl, he thought. *She's amazing.*

Wanting to know what she was thinking when she packed all this, Mendez tore open the letter, letting the envelope fall back into the box. There was one paragraph and then a set of instructions.

Dear Mike,

So, what you'll find in this box is everything (except me) needed for a proper first date. There's a movie (you'll have to wait to see which), popcorn (movie popcorn no less, and though it may be sort of stale by the time it reaches you, I am sure it beats the heck out of those packaged meals you talked about), candy (yes, I listened when you told me your favorite wasn't candy corn anymore, though I still can't see why not), a DVD player to watch it on, and finally, some Doritos and fake nacho cheese. Like I said, the only thing missing is me. Buuuuuttttt.... You can have me, too, if you follow the instructions below.

    1. *Have your DVD player (Kora's if we're being technical) set up and ready to go, with the DVD I sent queued up.*

    2. *Get cozy somewhere semi-private. Bring the candy.*

    3. *Log in with the iPad to your wifi.*

4. *Call me Friday the third of July on Facetime (Kora's old iPad). I've added my mom's contact info so you can reach me on her computer. If that date doesn't work, any Friday after will, until August 21st.*

5. *Any time after 2 am your time (I've done the math—I'll be home).*

6. *Push play at the same time as me.*

7. *Voila. Date night.*

Miss you, Mike. So much. I can't wait to see you... Hugs. And kisses ...xoxoxoxo
Love, Sarah

This woman was the best thing he'd ever had happen to him. How did she barely know him, and yet know so much about him at the same time? He looked at his watch. It was only June 29th. Dang. He had so long to wait and next to no patience to do it. He tapped his foot. Unless he got called out on a fluke mission, he should be on base this Friday.

Yes. He didn't care about the candy or the movie, though the popcorn he had to admit made him salivate. He cared about getting to see her face again. About talking to her and seeing that illustrious smile that made him giddy.

He packaged everything back up, taking care to put it back in the order he'd found it in so it would close. He walked back to his tent, no longer thinking or caring about Kint, or the heat, or the last mission that had gone so spectacularly wrong.

He had a date on Friday, and he couldn't be happier.

Nine

Change

Sarah put the final touches on the canvas and stepped back to appraise the work. It was the first time she'd touched a brush to canvas in four years and it felt... fantastic. Inspiring. Lovely.

She was happier than she'd been in her adult life. Life had been hard, loss shaping her like water settling in the cracks of her heart, only to shatter her when it froze. But for three weeks, she'd worked on reclaiming the broken parts and melding them back together.

And, she had Mike to thank for it. Literally, as it had turned out. She thought back to when it had all turned around.

The day she'd arrived home after Mike's first call to her, she'd found the package he'd sent on her bed. She'd also found Kora's small, single bed in her already-small room, setting off alarm bells in her head.

Hmmm, she'd thought, *what meltdown precipitated this move?* But she'd listened to Mike's directions and waited for her mom to get back from picking Kora up at school to ask what to do next, hoping that her taking a cab home hadn't ruined everything. Her fingers had itched to rip the package open, until she eventually sat on her hands to keep them from overriding the voice in her head that kept telling her, "Wait for Mom, wait for Mom, wait for Mom..."

It was Kora who reached her first, though, bounding through the door from the garage, jumping on the bed. She'd wrapped her tiny arms around Sarah's neck, screaming, "We're going to be roommates! Yayyyyyyy!"

Sarah could only laugh and hug her daughter back.

Kora had gone on, a mile a minute, Sarah laughing the whole time, so happy to finally be home, and surprisingly delighted to have a shared room with Kora. "Do you see my bed, Momma?" She pointed to her bed where Princess was curled up in a ball. "We get to sleep every night together! But Nana says only if I am good and go right to bed, or she will put me outside on the porch. I don't wanna sleep on the porch, so I'm gonna be so good. Just watch. Did you bring me anything from New York? Did Nana tell you this package is from your friend, Mike? He seems like a nice boy. Not like the boy at school who pulls my ponytail. Ugh. He's a jerk."

"Hey there, little lady. We don't say that in our house."

"Sorry, Momma."

"It's okay. So hey, where's Nana? I have some questions for her. Starting with how she moved this huge, big girl bed into my room all by herself." Sarah pinched Kora's nose until she squirmed away.

"Nana didn't. It was these guys that came by in matching hats and brown clothes. They did it for us!" Sarah had looked at her, puzzled, until Kora gasped. "Oops! I wasn't supposed to tell you that. I'll go find Nana. Don't tell her I told you!" Kora yelled on her way out the door.

Sarah met up with her mom in the kitchen, unloading groceries.

"Hey there, Sare-Bear. We missed you. How was your flight back?"

"Good. Hey, Kora, why don't you go set up your stuffed animals on your bed? I need to talk to Nana for a minute." Luise looked at her daughter, concerned. When Kora was out of the room, Sarah filled her mom in on the scary situation she'd found herself in the previous night.

Luise had her hand over her mouth, and when Sarah finished her story, explaining how the man had only bugged off when Mike had called, Luise shook her head.

"I swear that man was put on this earth to save you, hun. What a story. I'm glad you're okay," she'd said, coming over to hug Sarah.

"If he's some sort of guardian angel, why did it take so long for him to find me, and why did he have to leave as soon as I met him?"

"We don't always know why the timing of things are the way they are. We just wait for the plan to fully lay itself out for us. Maybe you weren't ready for him until now."

Sarah frowned. "Really, Mom? More of this 'have faith' stuff?"

"Like it or not, it's the way things are. You've had to learn how to do it on your own so when the right person came along—and I'm not saying that's Mike, but be open to the possibility—you'll be the person they need you to be."

"Yeah, okay, Mom. I love you and your hippy, dippy stuff. Now, spill everything about this box on my bed, and why Kora is now my bunkmate."

Luise had smiled and used her finger to beckon Sarah to Kora's room, whose door was shut. "Okay, so look first, and then I'll explain."

Sarah narrowed her eyes at her mom, but had nodded, and opened the door.

And that's when everything had shifted. Her world was no longer the pale beige and gray landscape it'd been before. Now, it was in vibrant color. Again, literally.

She'd gasped, her hand covering her mouth, tears forming in her eyes. What was once her daughter's room was now an artist's studio, from floor to ceiling. There was an easel in the corner of the room by the window, and the light, Sarah had realized, was perfect for painting.

Next to that, were a plethora of paints on Kora's old toy shelf, from acrylics to oils to watercolors. Beside those were a jar of various brushes, and a pile of rags for cleaning up. Sarah had walked around the room for a good half an hour, marveling at the detail that had gone into making this the perfect space.

In the corner opposite the window was an oversized chair with throw pillows—throw pillows!—and a lamp behind it. On Kora's old bookshelf, now painted a light blue, sat not all, but most, of Sarah's novels that had been stuck in the garage for the past five years. Last but certainly not least, was a smaller version of both the easel and chair in the corner by the door.

Kora. He thought of Kora. He'd thought of everything.

She'd sobbed, tears of joy streaming down her face until her mom came in and put her arm around Sarah, drawing her close.

"You deserve this, hun. Start believing it."

Sarah nodded, unable to talk through her tears. When she'd calmed down, she walked out of the room and went to the living room, collapsing in a heap.

"How?" was all she could get out.

"Well, he called the house phone a few days ago," Luise began. The house phone. Of course. Sarah had given him all the ways to contact her, just in case. "You were on your San Francisco flight, but I think he knew that, because he went over what he wanted to do, assuming you weren't listening in."

Sarah laughed. "Sneaky, huh?"

"I was amazed he'd thought of everything, down to the details. Most of the stuff he got second hand, but the paints and brushes he had some marines pick up. They sent Kora and me out for the day and when we came back, it was all done. Even the painting of the bookshelves. I think it turned out marvelous."

"It's beautiful. But, why did you agree? How'd you get Kora to give up her own room?"

"Ha! That part was easy," Luise had told her. "I explained that if she was a big girl, and listened to you about bedtime, that you two could be roommates. I also showed her the private space she has to read and paint now, and she was delighted. Wait till you see what she's painted you."

"But, why did you want to do this?"

"Oh, baby girl, that was the easiest part of all of this. Because you deserve the world, and finally someone agrees with me."

"Okay, I hear you, and I am so, so grateful, but why the studio? Why not just an easel in the corner of my room? And what's with the box?"

"Ah, yes. The most important part of all of this. Go grab it."

Sarah sprinted back to her room and ran in carrying the large box, noting that it was particularly heavy. She looked quizzically at her mom.

"Just open it, Sare-Bear."

Sarah cut the box open with a knife from the kitchen and threw the packing material to the ground like a kid at Christmas. She stopped when she saw what the box contained, and looked up at her mom, who was holding a sheet of paper out to her. Sarah took it and started crying again. Inside the box were textbooks—four of them—and the paper listed four corresponding art and intro to teaching courses Sarah was enrolled in at the local community college.

"What the—?" she cried. "You guys are killing me, Mom. This is too much."

"Is it, though?" Luise replied. "Are you interested?"

"Am I? I've been thinking about this so much since Hank died. How I want to quit flying and teach, but I need a degree first. Oh, this is just wonderful. I don't know what to say, Mom."

"It's not me, hun. This was all Mike."

"Yes, but the room, and watching Kora while I go to class. It's both of you. I couldn't do any of it without you, either. Thank you."

Luise smiled. "You're welcome, hun. Now, what classes did he register you for? I'm dying to know what you'll be studying."

"It looks like art history, watercolor, light and shadow, and how to teach paint mixing."

"Wow. Can you handle all that?"

"I think so. I can paint when Kora heads to bed, and study in the mornings when she goes to school." Sarah had collected everything to bring back to the studio. "At this rate, I think I can even graduate in three semesters. I'll have to contact the school and have my transcripts sent over to make sure, but it shouldn't be too hard." She was almost out of the room when she stopped, turned around, and ran back to her mom, falling into her arms, box and books and all.

"Thank you, Mom."

"Oh, hun, it's my pleasure. Now, go set that all up so I can take my two girls out to lunch to celebrate our college student."

Sarah had practically skipped back to her studio, too excited to put the books down for too long, her fingers itching to paint again. Suddenly, it was as if a dam had broken, and all the ideas and desires to paint had come back to her at once.

Now, three weeks later, she was still just as happy, if not more. She had two in-person classes, and two more online each week, and they were all extremely flexible with her flying schedule, allowing for early or late submissions, and giving her partners who also needed more mobility.

Her favorite class so far was definitely her watercolors.

She found it to be the most peaceful, the most natural. Thoughts found their way to her canvas through the medium without much urging on her end, and within an hour, a vibrant colorscape took shape on what had been a blank canvas just moments before.

All of that was inside her, waiting to get out. All she'd needed was the nudge from Mike and her mom and it had a way to do just that.

Speaking of the man who occupied the lion's share of her thoughts—she wrote to Mike about some of the work she was doing, along with a gushing thank you note a week ago.

Now, though, she had even more to tell him, and was giddy at the prospect of showing him her work. She thought more and more about him returning from deployment, and what that might look like.

She considered what it could look like if he joined her family, but she had no idea if that's what he wanted. One thing she knew for certain now, though, was that she was in love with him. There was no way around that, and she didn't think she wanted there to be. Yes, it might be complicated, but she knew now it was worth it.

Plus, to make matters more exciting, tonight was the night of their first real date. Mike had called earlier in the week to let her know he'd received her package in the mail, that he'd loved it, and was thrilled she was enjoying her classes. He didn't have much time that night to talk but promised her a date that would leave them plenty of room to catch up. He'd also told her to be around the house at 7 her time.

She came home from her night class and sprinted inside, kissed Kora, who was asleep in her bed, and jumped in the shower. She was covered in paint, and her hair was a disaster—certainly not befitting of a first date outfit for a man you were in love with.

"You're running late," her mom chided her from the living room, *Lost* on in the background.

"I know."

It was 6:35. *Shoot*. She brushed and blow dried her hair, and threw on a quick bit of mascara and blush.

"You'd better hurry," from the peanut gallery.

"I *know*."

6:49. *Ugh*.

It was the outfit she was most worried about. She didn't want to look like she was trying too hard, or that she didn't care at all, but what was the happy medium? She settled on a pair of fitted but comfortable black jeans and a loose-fitting red tank top that accentuated her arms.

Checking herself in the mirror, she approved. Nerves fluttered over every square inch of her skin, through her veins, before finally landing in her stomach.

What if... Her heart gave voice to her concern. *What if it doesn't feel the same? What if that was a fluke?*

"He's going to call any minute."

There wasn't any way to answer that other than to give it a try. So, that's what she'd do.

"I know," Sarah repeated. "I love you, Mom. But you're not allowed on this date with me."

"I'll be in my room."

Sarah smiled.

6:58. Two minutes to spare. She got her computer, loaded up the movie, and made sure she was available to Facetime.

In a last-minute shift, she decided on the oversized sofa chair in the studio so she would have privacy and not wake Kora, as well as to show Mike the gorgeous room he was responsible for.

Right at seven, the computer chimed, and she took a deep breath. *This is it.* She answered it, and Mike came on the screen looking tan and rugged, the slight hint of a beard growing. Her stomach flipped and she felt her limbs warming. She'd forgotten how handsome he was.

Um, never mind. It wasn't a fluke.

She blushed, feeling like he could see right through her and hear what she was thinking.

"Hi there, stranger," he said, a huge smile on his face.

"Hi. Glad you could make it to the theater on time."

He laughed. "Me, too. What a great idea, Sarah. Thank you so much."

"Not at all. I actually felt like it wasn't near enough after your home renovation project here."

"How is that working out, by the way?"

"It's incredible, Mike. There really aren't words. Do you want to see it?"

"Yes, please. That way if anything is off, I can call and chew out the RBE."

"Who're the RBE? Are those the guys who came and put this all together? I've been meaning to ask you about that."

"The remain behind element. They're the guys who stay behind and make sure all the barracks are ready for the men when we get home, that all the battalion paperwork gets filed okay. Basically, the marines we thought were too worthless to take with us, we let screw things up at home." She laughed. "I'm kidding. Some of them are close to retirement or too new to join us. But dang, they seemed to do okay over there, didn't they?" he asked, as she scanned the span of the room for him.

"Yes, they did. I couldn't ask for anything more. Well, except maybe one thing."

"What's that? Let me know, and I'll make it happen."

"You. It needs you." He smiled, and redness creeped into his cheeks.

"Sarah, at the risk of sounding absolutely crazy, can I tell you something?"

She nodded. "Of course."

"I've fallen in love with you, and I know it seems sudden, and that we still have so much to learn about each other, and we do, but I also know that I can do that—we can do that, and I can still love you..."

She cut him off. "I love you, too, Mike. I think I've known for a while, but it took coming home to the studio that made me realize it."

Mike was laughing and wiping the tears from his eyes at the same time.

"This is turning out to be a pretty great first date," he teased.

She laughed. "Just wait till you see the movie. It'll change your life."

"I can't wait. Shall we?"

She nodded, and they both made a show of pushing the play button so that *Once* started at precisely the same time on both their devices. She saw him alternating between eating his popcorn and the Sour Patch Kids, and was finally, after years of getting close, at peace with her life.

She had everything she needed, and at this point, nothing could change that.

The date with Sarah was the best he'd ever had. Even Kora had snuck in, claiming to need water. Though, when Sarah went to get it, Kora had introduced herself, three of her animals, and then proceeded to tell him all about her life. It was freaking adorable.

The only thing Mendez would have changed was Sarah curled up next to him on a couch and getting to share his snacks with Kora. More and more he'd been thinking about finding a home big enough for him, Sarah, Luise, and Kora when he got home. When he had spare moments between missions, sleep, chow, reading Sarah's books, and writing the woman he loved, he looked at homes in the Long Beach area near good schools for Kora, and hopefully, if all went well for Sarah, her teaching prospects as well.

When he'd been with Angela, none of this had ever even crossed his mind. More and more he wondered if he was ever even in love with her, and why he'd let her absence wreck him so badly. He'd wasted so much time on her, when *this* was out there for him. He wished he'd met Sarah years ago, when Kora was a baby, and their whole lives were in front of them.

Now, though, it was like getting a taste of the good life, and all he really wanted was to leave this place and get back to it. It was going to make the deployment seem even longer, that was for sure. The one thing last night solidified, though, was that he wanted to take the Colonel and Captain up on their offer to switch MOSs to Intel. He wanted a job that was safer, where even if he had to leave for some time, he wouldn't be adding extra stress and worry to Sarah's full slate. He wasn't even thinking about how it might feel to leave the infantry—it was a foregone conclusion at this point.

Mendez sighed and looked out over the tan and brown hellscape just outside his tent. His glance fell to the item in his hands, a token of his intentions.

Gathering up the small rope ring he'd braided the night before, he kissed it.

"I love you, Sarah." He stuck it in an envelope with a letter explaining his plan, as well as his plan for the three of them. He wanted to marry her, if she would have him. He told her he'd never been more sure of anything as he was of everything he'd put into that letter, and that once they got to know one another better, and it was okay with Kora, he would be open to adoption, to giving her a father she could count on every day. He asked her to hold onto the ring until he got home and could give her the one she deserved. The last paragraph hoped she didn't find the gesture cheap.

He loved her, and he hoped she knew that above all else.

Mendez threw on his cover and boots and left the tent to head to Command, dropping the letter at mail call on the way. Excitement about his future—something not only related to his job—overwhelmed him for the first time since he joined the Marine Corps. He knocked on the post outside the tent and was let in right away.

"Sergeant, glad to see you back. I heard from Captain Hoffman you're ready to consider a career change?"

"Yes, sir. I'd like to take you up on the offer to switch MOSs to Intel if it's still on the table, sir."

"Well, I for one, am glad to have you. We've got some paperwork to send through to Pendleton, to your battalion, which may take a week, but welcome to the team, Sergeant."

Mendez tried not to smile too big, look too eager. "That's it? That's easy enough."

The Colonel laughed. "That's it when you're in my position. I don't envy the POG back home who has to process that on a timeline I will be happy with." Mendez lost the urge not to laugh and the Colonel smiled. "It's okay to be happy about this. You've worked hard, you've done more than most have done in a lifetime. And, you'll do more for us here, you can bet on that, Sergeant."

"Thank you, sir. I'm incredibly grateful for this opportunity."

"You got it son, and if I'm not being too forward, good luck with the young lady that's motivating you. She must be special."

Mendez laughed. "She is, sir." They shook hands and as Mendez was leaving, he thought of one last question. "Colonel, what's next? Should I wait to hear from you?"

"Yes, sir, but for now, I'll pass on to Captain Hoffman that you should be on post duty here, relieved of your squad-related responsibilities. I'm also going to put in for you to be promoted to Staff Sergeant until we can get home and transition you to Lieutenant. Congrats, son, you're on the road to becoming the officer you were meant to be."

Mendez smiled and left, not caring about the heat that blasted him on the face or the dust that swirled around him, worming its way in between his clothes. He was done, and it felt so much better than he thought it would. He was going to be able to take care of Sarah in the way she deserved, in the way Kora did, too. He couldn't wait to tell them both. Maybe he could call from Captain Hoffman's sat phone after chow.

He got back to his tent and the second he walked in was thrown hard against the metal post, the breath knocked out of him, a crack coming from somewhere between his head and back.

"What the—?" he asked, his voice raspy, and his back and head throbbing.

"So, you're selling out, are you? For a chick?" The sour breath and stinging words reeked of the man pinning him to the pole.

Kint. *That's it. He's toast now.*

"You've sealed your fate, Kint," Mendez said, standing up tall, towering over the Corporal. "You just assaulted a superior."

"You're not my superior anymore. You're just another butter bar jerk. I tell you what, *sir*, when I'm back home, I'll make sure to check in on that girl of yours in Long Beach. I'm sure she'll want someone to keep her company until you get home. Plus, I read she's got a daughter, too." Mendez's vision went black, and he stumbled. He focused and saw Sarah's letters and books thrown all over his bed. It was all he could do to not knock Kint out, but he needed to do this right so Kint never saw the inside of a uniform ever again. He'd finally lost it.

"You need to back off now, and pack your bags, Kint. I mean it. You're out of this squad, and out of this Corps." Mendez was shaking, and his head was killing him. He was operating on fumes now, trying to keep his wits about him and not do anything stupid. He grabbed Kint's arm and led him out into the light, where he wasn't alone with him, where there could be other witnesses to back-up Mendez.

"What're you gonna do, Mendez? You wanna hit me? Do you?"

The ground shook, and Mendez staggered into Kint.

Mendez so desperately wanted to hit him. There were marines running around, calling out to one another like something was wrong, though, and for a moment, he let go of Kint's lapel, distracted. He bolted, but Mendez didn't care for the first time since he'd met Kint. Something was wrong—he felt it in the air and in his nerves. He grabbed the nearest marine and asked what was going on.

"An explosion in Haqleniah. Bravo Company, second squad got lit up."

"Who's heading in to help?"

"Looks like Bravo, 3 and 4."

That was Mendez's old squad. His current squad, technically. He had no idea what the right thing to do was by the Colonel, only what he knew was the absolute right thing to do by his men.

He sprinted to his footlocker and got his rifle, his Kevlar, and his helmet, which was tender on his head, and ran out, ignoring the throbbing in his back and neck. He saw Kint hop in a humvee that was already moving, and Kint definitely saw him, too. He gave Mendez a twisted grimace, but he didn't have time to care about that jerk right now. He'd handle that situation when they got back.

Another explosion rocked the base, this one closer than the last. The ground shook again, and the marines answered by calling out men to hop into whatever transport they could find. This needed to end now—the insurgents were getting too close to base.

Mendez hopped into the nearest humvee as it rocked forward, shutting the door on him. The men were anxious inside the truck; those that had been through this before were solemn and quiet, the boots who had never seen combat jittery and talkative like sixteen-year-old girls.

Someone in the front hollered back for them to shut up and then the whole truck was quiet as a coffin. Bumping along the road, more explosions rippling out from the bridge, Mendez did something he hadn't done since he was a kid staying with his grandparents.

He prayed, and he saw Sarah's face as he did, smiling and illuminating all the darkest fears in his heart. It was enough for him, giving him the courage he needed when the humvee stopped, and the men shot out like bullets, weapons at the ready, blinded by heat and light and dust.

It was enough for him to know her, to see her in that moment, before he was shoved from behind and his world went black.

Ten

Recall

Sarah got the call on her way home from grocery shopping. Three days' worth of dinners were becoming more and more expensive, even when she reluctantly opted out of organic ingredients. She didn't know how much longer she could feed three people on one salary, now that her mom was no longer working, but she also had no idea how they were supposed to do it any other way.

She didn't recognize the number, but she'd learned by now that Mike's sat phone numbers came up different each time, and to answer any call she got, just in case.

"Hello?" she asked, her voice light and happy. There was a pause, and she smiled. *Mike*. It had been a little while since she'd talked to him, and she had so much to tell him. "Mike?"

She heard sniffles coming from the person on the other line, and she frowned. "Sarah?" It was a woman's voice.

"This is she."

"This is Cindy, Mike Mendez's mother." More sniffles. Sarah slumped to the ground, unable to speak or move. Ice froze her veins, chilling her from the core until her teeth chattered. Something was wrong with Mike. "I'm sorry I haven't called before now, I've been so busy, but I know how much you mean to him, and it's no excuse."

"It's okay, Mrs. Mendez. I understand. Please tell me what's wrong."

"Call me Cindy. He said you have a good head on your shoulders, that you were intuitive. There's been an accident, Sarah." Sarah's heart raced, and her palms went clammy. "He's alive, we know that much, but they told us it was bad."

Sarah breathed in very slowly, her eyes closed, hoping that if she opened them, this would just have been a nightmare. She exhaled and opened her eyes and that's when the tears fell.

"Can I see him?"

"That's why I am calling. They won't fly any non-family out to Germany to see him, but they seemed pretty optimistic that he'd be flown to the states in a few weeks."

Weeks? He needed weeks to even fly?

"Did they say what happened, Cindy?"

"There were some explosions outside their base, and his team went to help. He wasn't even supposed to be there, Sarah." Cindy let out a sob. Sarah was confused.

"Why wasn't he supposed to be there?"

"The man who called us, his Captain, told us they'd just given him a promotion and job change."

The intelligence position. He got it. Sarah couldn't be happy for him, though, not yet. Not until she was sure he would survive and that he could stay in the Marines. She knew that's what he wanted most. God, let him be okay. "Apparently, the Colonel who promoted him told Mike that he was relieved of his position until they could process the paperwork, but Mike wouldn't let his men go alone. What was he thinking?"

"He's the best man I've ever known, Cindy. There's nothing I can imagine him capable of more than being there for his guys." Still, though, Sarah's stomach lurched knowing that his dedication had led to this, to his being flown home. She fought back more tears. She needed to be strong, help his family figure this out.

"He is. And I'm glad he has you. I'm heading to Germany tonight and will call you when I get there to fill you in. I wish you could come with me—I don't want to go alone, and I know he would love to see you. When he was on the stretcher in the medical helicopter..." Cindy let out another sob but recovered. "When he was being flown out after the injury, it was you he kept asking them to call. He loves you, Sarah."

"I love him, too." Sarah frowned. "Wait, why are you going alone? Won't Mike's dad go with you?"

"Oscar? No, unfortunately not. He and Mike had a falling out a few years back when Mike reenlisted, and he's being stubborn. So, help me, if anything happens to my son, and his father isn't there, I will never forgive Oscar." Sarah was shocked. Mike had mentioned that he and his father weren't very close, but he didn't say they hadn't spoken in so long.

"Why aren't they talking? Sorry, I know you probably have so much to do to get ready to go to Germany, I'm just trying to understand what could possibly keep Mike's dad away from him if he's this hurt."

"I agree. I've never understood the fight, on either end, so I've mostly stayed out of it. Oscar wasn't too keen on Mike joining the Marines and not using his degree; he figured if his son wanted to join the service, he should follow in his father's footsteps and join the Army, and it should be in the officer corps. His words almost exactly."

"But isn't Oscar proud of his son? He's amazing at his job, and he's one of the most thoughtful people I've ever met."

"Thank you, Sarah. I agree, but Oscar is a traditionalist. He saw college, then military service, use that degree for a short four years, then a family, and career after that."

"He'd planned Mike's whole life out for him."

"He did. It's an occupational hazard we have as parents. Mike said you have a daughter, right?"

"I do. Kora. She's almost five."

"She sounds adorable from what Mike's told me about her. I hope you don't mind him telling me about you two."

"Not at all, I just feel bad that I didn't know how much the Marines came between him and his father."

"It's not just that, Sarah. I don't want you to think that Oscar is a villain or anything. There were just a few things that he and Mike didn't agree on, and one fight about Mike's first break up with Angela tipped the scales and led to both of them waiting for the other to call and apologize. That was three years ago."

Sarah was still stuck on Cindy's mention of a woman called Angela. She'd felt like she was just starting to really know the man—enough to love him and consider a life with him—but the biggest parts of Mike's life he'd kept from her.

He wanted her to come clean about the hard parts of her life, to trust him, but he hadn't trusted her with the issues with his dad, or about this woman named Angela, who was important enough, apparently, to cause an irreparable rift between him and his dad.

"Cindy, I'm sorry, but I feel out of my league here. I love your son, but there's so much history we haven't gone over together. Who was Angela?" She felt silly asking, like the man she'd fallen in love with had kept her in the dark and now she was out of the shadows, but without any answers.

"Oh, honey, I think that this is a subject you should discuss with Mike. I don't feel comfortable—"

"Cindy, I would love that, but I can't do that right now, right? I need to know what I'm up against. Was I just a way to get over another woman? I'm invested, Cindy, but I can't go in blind. Not with a daughter. Please understand."

"Sarah—"

"Please. Just what you can tell me."

"Okay. Angela was his girlfriend of a few years. They met in college and were together through his first year in the Marines. They broke up when she cheated on him and got back together for about another year after that. I don't know much more, only that their break up really hurt him, but that the way he talks about you tells me he loves you much more than he ever did her. You have to trust him, Sarah. He needs you now, more than ever."

"I'm not going anywhere, Cindy. I just needed to know. Thank you."

"You're the woman he chose, Sarah. He told me he thinks you're the one. Please don't let Angela get in the way. She's his past. You are his future if you want to be."

Sarah felt her heart thump loudly in her chest.

"Thank you, Cindy. That means so much to me. So, when do you fly out? And which airline are you on?"

"Tonight, at six. Delta, I think, why?"

"That's who I fly with. I know who your flight attendants are—Bill and Megan. I'll make sure they take care of you."

"Oh, that's wonderful, thank you. I'll talk to you soon. Think positive thoughts."

"I will. Hug our boy for me. Tell him I'll be there as soon as I can. And, Cindy? He'll be okay. I know he will."

"I know he will, too. Take care, Sarah."

Sarah hung up and pulled over in front of her house. She broke down crying, her chest heaving, and her breaths short and choppy. Her heart felt like it was physically breaking, and on top of everything else, she felt helpless here. She needed to be in Germany, with Mike and his family, helping him heal. She didn't even know the extent of his injuries or how long recovery might be. All she did know was that she was one hundred percent lost without Mike.

Only tiny snippets of the news she'd learned talking to Cindy snuck through her worry over Mike's health. The tumultuous relationship with his father, the ex-girlfriend he'd been with for years—all of it made Sarah uneasy, leaving the unanswered question of why he'd felt the need to hide these things from her.

Didn't he trust her? Didn't he love her?

She wiped her eyes and dried her face, and pulled the car into the driveway. She checked the rearview mirror.

You look awful.

Though her eyes were puffy and red, she knew she had to go inside before her mom and Kora saw her sitting out here, looking pathetic.

When the groceries were put away, and Sarah caught her mom up on what was happening with Mike—they'd both had a good cry together—Sarah put Kora to bed and went into the studio. She stood in the doorway for the longest moment of her life, imagining a world where Mike didn't exist, where she wouldn't get to show him this amazing room that had brought her back to life, where Kora wouldn't get to know a man as her father, where she wouldn't curl up with him at the end of each night for the rest of their lives.

It was a bleak world, one she wasn't ready to accept yet.

So, she sat at her easel and painted. She painted her worries, her heart's greatest desires and deepest fears. She painted through the night, starting over on old canvases that were half finished until her fingertips were sore, but her mind was light again.

When she was done, she knew exactly what she needed to do. She put a small box fan on the paintings, needing them to dry by that afternoon so she could send them off to Mike. There was no way he could look at these and question her feelings for him. They would be her replacement until she could tell him herself.

She only hoped that was sooner rather than later.

When Mendez first opened his eyes, everything was fuzzy. He saw the scene in front of him as if it were underwater, the pale-yellow light around the edges softening everything.

Wires leading from and to machines while they beeped out a symphony of noises.

Stark white walls with one lone poster of a kitten hugging a gorilla in the center of one.

The padded feet of sneakers on tile racing just outside his door.

I'm in a hospital. Not the one in Camp Leatherneck, but also not one in the U.S, at least any U.S. hospital he was familiar with. He heard voices muttering off to the side, but the figures were too far for him to see and the language too guttural for him to understand.

Mendez tried to sit up but was tethered in place.

Though he tried to follow the wires from the monitors to where they were attached to him, he couldn't focus. He squinted, but doing that made his head hurt, and he groaned. The figure closest to the door ran over, and as it got closer, he recognized it immediately.

Mom. Deep inside his chest, his heart lurched. If his mom was here, he must be pretty messed up.

"Mom," he tried to say, but his throat was raw and thick. The words got lost. "Mom. Why am I here?" The words sounded muffled, and his mom's brows bunched together.

"Why can't he talk?" she asked another shape standing by the doorway.

"There was a lot of trauma to his head, including his ears and throat. It'll take some time, but I expect those injuries to heal completely."

"And the rest?" his mom asked.

There's more? What happened? Why was he here, and why couldn't he ask those questions on his own?

"It's too early to tell. Right now, we're worried about keeping his heart rate down and the swelling in his brain needs to decrease before we can fully assess his leg and arm."

"What kind of timeline are we looking at, Doctor? Until we have some answers."

"Give it a couple days, and hopefully we can tell you more. For now, be happy that he woke up. That was the first hurdle we had to cross."

Mike saw his mom wipe tears from her eyes, and then turn to face him. He wanted to sit up, to hug her, to tell her he was okay, but he... couldn't. Confusion swirled the thoughts in his brain, and a constriction in his chest made it hard to breathe all of a sudden.

He gasped for air until a mask was lowered over his mouth. The air came easier, but none of the brain fog dissipated. That was scarier than the rest of the unknowns piling up at his bedside.

"I'm going to have to ask you to step outside, Mrs. Mendez. We need to keep him calm right now." His mom turned to leave and even though he wanted to ask her to stay, tell her she was helping him, no words came.

What did the doctor mean his arm and head were hurt? He couldn't even feel them. He just wanted someone to talk *to* him, not around him.

As the unanswered questions pelted his skull, his vision began to fade, and his back and head started to feel better. *This is nice,* he noted, his last thought before he fell asleep and couldn't hear anything or feel anything anymore.

It seemed like minutes later he woke up, but when he opened his eyes, he could see better than he could the last time. The light around the edges of his vision was still there, but the whole room came into focus now. His vision drifted to a slumped image in the corner of his room.

Mom. Mom is still here. His throat burned and ached like it'd been doused with flames, making words impossible, so he just held out his hand and attempted to smile.

"Hey, baby. How are you?"

He raised his eyebrows. His head didn't hurt as much as before, but he still felt pressure along his entire spine, and now, there was a sharp pain on the right side of his body.

"Yeah, I know, hun. How is your head?" He nodded as much as he could, and his mom smiled. "Good. That's so good, Mike."

"Dad?" he mouthed to his mom.

She shook her head. "No. I'm still trying, though."

He turned his head to the right and tried to lift his hand, but it wouldn't budge. Pain and frustration shot through him in equal doses, and he groaned. Or tried to. Only his pulse registered his agitation, and the machines behind him whined with his attempted exertion.

"Mike, Mike, hun, I need you to calm down or they are going to have to sedate you again. Can you take a couple breaths for me? I'll tell you everything I know if you can just breathe." He nodded, closed his eyes, and inhaled slowly. It brought him back to his training, what he was taught to do.

He took four long, slow breaths, and opened his eyes.

"Okay, Mike, I'm going to tell you some things that are hard to hear, but I need you to listen until I'm done, okay?" Mike nodded. "If you still have questions after I'm done, I'll get the doctor. Sound good?"

He nodded again.

"You were on deployment, you know that much, right?" Mike looked at his mom like she was crazy. "Okay, okay. Jeez." She laughed and squeezed his left hand. "I just wanted to know how much you remember." He let go of her hand and mimed an explosion. "Yes. You were hit by an IED, they called it. A bomb in the ground, hidden from view." He rolled his hand, telling her to move on. "The explosion knocked you unconscious, which is why your head probably hurts."

Mendez shook his head and jabbed at the paper and pen his mom had on her chair. She handed it to him, and he used his left hand to scrawl, "Kint" in almost illegible handwriting.

"Oh, him?" his mom said. Mendez nodded, pointed to his head. "Yes, your Captain said they caught him, that he will be taken back to the States and tried as a traitor. Thank God."

Mendez tried to sit up. *What?*

What was his mom saying? She must have the wrong person. His head was pounding, but he kept trying to sit up. Finally, his mom put her hand on his chest.

"Hun, you can't sit up right now. The pressure in your head is too great. What's wrong?"

He pointed to the name on the paper, tapping it with urgency. He snatched the pen and wrote again.

Are you sure? What did he do?

It took his mom a moment to read his left-hand scribbles, but when she finally got it, she nodded.

"Yes, Mike, we're sure. Your Captain said he threw you into an area they had cordoned off for having bombs in it. I could kill him, I swear. If anything worse had happened to you, I would be going to jail for what I did to him. The Captain was actually on his way here to ask you why this guy Kint might have done something like that, but he got pulled back to base."

The pressure in Mendez's head increased exponentially with this information.

Holy crap. Kint was responsible for this? For him being in this hospital bed? The beeping on the monitor above him went haywire as he rolled this new information over and over in his head. No matter which way he turned it, though, surprise never came. Only regret that he didn't say something, *do* something sooner.

The doctor rushed in. "I told you if he got this agitated, you'd need to leave. It's not good for his blood pressure or immune response necessary for healing."

No! he wanted to shout. *I still need answers.*

"No. I'm staying here." Mendez sighed with relief and the beeping slowed. "I got him to calm down earlier. Something about this," and she held up the pad of paper, "got him upset. Let me help."

"Fine, but if his heart rate spikes, you're out of here." She agreed with a curt nod, and he would have smiled if he was able. He'd never loved her so much as in that moment.

"Mike, hun, you have to write down why this is upsetting you. Take deep breaths. You're safe here, do you understand?"

He nodded, grabbing the pen and paper.

He wrote, "Kint. Hit me. Before bombs. Because jealous. I got job. With Captain. Went to help. Guys blown up. Don't remember any. Thing else. Are you sure 'bout him. Throwing me?"

This took his mom nearly five minutes to decipher, and during that time, Mendez took calming breaths that would keep his heart rate down because he needed answers. But inside, his brain was a whirlwind.

All of this—Kint...the explosion...the intention behind Kint's actions—it was too much to take.

He'd known Kint was dangerous from the first time he met him, but mostly because of his attitude and the way he never tried to bond with the guys, setting him up as an outsider from the start. He never, *never* imagined that Kint would be capable of something like this.

What he'd done was attempted murder.

Mendez was furious. Not with Kint, but with himself. He should have stopped Kint from getting on that convoy, should have pinned him against the wall and called for cuffs after Kint had hit him. He grabbed the pen and paper just as his mom was finishing the last part aloud.

He added, "Anybody else hurt?" She shook her head, and he closed his eyes, breathing in a sigh of relief. He smiled at his mom, nodding.

"Aw, hun, I am so sorry you went through this. He'll be taken care of, and he won't hurt anyone ever again, hopefully. But we are sure about the explosion. So many of your men had the same story. He saw you get out of the humvee and headed right for you. They said it looked like he was looking for you and just you. He pushed you from behind, right into that field." At the part about Kint not hurting anyone anymore, Mendez perked up, grabbing at the paper again.

"Sarah?" he wrote.

"She's fine, hun. She wanted to be here, but we asked her to wait until we knew more. And she sent you these." She pointed to two large boxes in the corner of the room. "She doesn't know about the extent of your injuries yet, though. I'll call her tonight and fill her in now that you are awake."

He pointed to his head, gestured to the machines.

She shook her head. "Yes, your head but the rest of your injuries as well. Maybe now that the doctor is here, maybe he can explain everything else."

Mendez shifted his gaze to the doctor and frowned, pointing to his back.

"Your back looks fine, actually. You might be sore for a few weeks, but there is no permanent damage there. Your head looks like it will be okay as well. Your swelling has gone down, and there seem to be no deficits as of yet. You're really quite lucky that way."

Mendez raised his left hand the inch it would go as if to say, "Yeah, so, then what's the problem?" He was annoyed by the way everyone was dancing around this topic, like he was fragile.

"Tell me," he mouthed to the doctor, who nodded.

"There have been extensive injuries to the right side of your body, Sergeant. The right arm had nerve and tissue damage due to shrapnel, though we hope you will regain some of your original strength, and your right leg absorbed most of the blast." The doctor took a large breath, and his jaw grew tight and serious. Mendez raised his eyebrows, nervous. "There is a good chance, even if we can save the leg, that you'll never walk on it again." Mendez felt like he'd been punched in the gut. "I'm so sorry, son." He patted Mendez on his good arm, an empty gesture.

His breaths came in short gasps, the heat behind his eyes growing with each second his mom and the doctor looked at him like that—like everyone would look at him from this day forward. As if he was less-than, someone to be pitied.

"Mike, hun, if there's anything you need, please let us know. Everyone here is working so hard—"

Mendez turned his head so that he couldn't see his mother or the doctor anymore. He knew everything he needed to know. He might lose his leg, and even if he could keep it, he would never get to stay in the Marines.

Sarah wasn't here, and again, even if she was, he no longer had anything to offer her. He'd lost his chance at a job that would secure his, and her, future. What more could she see in him? He used his good arm to wipe a tear—the only one he would allow to fall—and turned back to them only long enough to find the pen and paper.

Using the pad one last time, he wrote, "Leave. Plz," and didn't turn around to see if they listened or not.

Eleven

Saying Goodbye

It had been three weeks since Cindy had first called Sarah to tell her about Mike's accident. For three weeks, Sarah had only sporadic phone updates to keep her hope afloat. She needed to hear his voice, hear from him how he was feeling, not just doing. Yet, each time she asked to speak to Mike, she was rebuffed in some way. Either he was sleeping, or in the restroom, or the doctors were in the room.

Sarah was growing restless. Mike was out of immediate danger—Cindy told her that him waking up from the medically induced coma was the biggest hurdle they had to cross, and he'd done that, and more, successfully. However, no one seemed to want to tell her what had happened over there, or what Mike's chances of staying in the Corps were.

Desperation clawed at her chest, waiting to get out.

"Tell me he doesn't want me anymore, that I was just something to distract him through his deployment and I'll move on," she told Cindy after Mike was awake a week but wouldn't take her calls.

"I can't tell you what isn't true. Just be patient."

Patience used to be her virtue. But not when Mike's health was on the line. She loved him and love changed the game.

"How is he?" her mom asked last week while she put together a Nutella sandwich for Kora. "Any news?"

"*How is he*?" Sarah cringed at the whiny octave her voice had taken on. "You're asking the wrong person. I have second—maybe third-hand news, but nothing from him. Nothing."

She'd swallowed the sob, but it lodged in her throat and hadn't left since.

When her cell rang the day after that conversation, she'd let a small trickle of hope through the wall she'd erected around her heart.

Maybe it's him.

But it wasn't.

"Sarah, hun. I just wanted to keep you up to speed. Mike's got a long road ahead of him."

As if Sarah didn't know that. But, why was she being kept at arm's length? Why not just let her move on, or bring her into the fray?

"His head?"

"No, the right side of his body sustained the most damage. Docs have been working with it, but—"

"But what? Please, Cindy. You can tell me anything."

"I was hoping he'd be the one to share this with you, but he's not up to it just yet. Sarah, he might lose his leg."

Cindy had gone on to tell Sarah if he kept the leg, he'd likely have a permanently handicapped walk. Sarah didn't care—it wasn't Mike's leg that she'd fallen in love with, it was his heart, and as long as that was still open to her, she wouldn't be going anywhere.

"He's been getting your letters, and though he hasn't said as much, I can tell they're helping. Just hold off on them until we get back to the States so he doesn't miss any in transit."

Sarah agreed, but kept writing them, anyway. Without a place to send them for two weeks, they'd piled up in her art studio, a reminder of the best weeks of her life bookended by the worst.

Though it was frustrating writing for no audience, Sarah was overwhelmingly relieved that Mike was well enough to travel home. So, she wrote and waited, and painted and waited some more.

They were the longest weeks of her life.

She busied herself with Kora, who seemed to sense that something was amiss and was more needy than ever. When Sarah wasn't flying, she and Kora and Luise went on dates to the movies, to the park, and to the beach.

On one such date, Sarah and Luise were sitting on the water's edge watching Kora run from the waves, squealing and laughing like she hadn't a care in the world. Watching her was the lightest Sarah had felt in a month. Luise cleared her throat.

"Sarah? I need to talk to you."

Sarah's eyes didn't leave her daughter. "Sure. Go ahead."

"We need to talk about Mike, hun."

Sarah's jaw clenched, but her eyes didn't waver from Kora, from the rolling surf that calmed her. "What about him?"

"I think you know." When Sarah still didn't respond, her mother persisted. "He hasn't responded to any of your phone calls or your letters. Maybe it's time to move on, let him heal and be with his family."

"Mmmm," Sarah replied.

"Sarah. I wanted this for you more than anything. You deserve happiness, and you and Kora deserve a family. I hoped it would be with Mike as much as you did. But you have to know when the timing isn't right. Things are different now."

"What's different, Mom? I told him I loved him, and I meant it. I didn't say, 'I love you only if you come back okay.' I said, 'I love you.' Period."

"I get that, honey, but sometimes love isn't enough."

"When, Mom? When isn't love enough?" Sarah watched Kora jump and splash in the cold water and could see the little hairs on her legs and arms standing on end when she got close enough to them. She'd blown it again for Kora. They'd been so close to having a real family, and Sarah had invested it all too soon. Now her mom was telling her to fold when she was already all in.

Luise scooted closer to her daughter in the sand, putting her arm around Sarah's shoulders. "I don't have any answers for you, hun. I wish I did. I just don't want to see you crushed again."

"It's a little late for that, Mom. But I'm not going to give up. If I have to break down his door, I will."

"What's your plan, then? If you're going all in, I'll help where I can."

"Watch Kora?"

"Of course. When are you thinking?"

"My classes are on break next week, so I picked up a short LA to San Diego flight. Cindy said they'll be there at least that long, so that's it, that's my plan. Show up and make him tell me to my face that he doesn't love me anymore."

"Sarah, hun, what if that's exactly what he does?" Sarah saw Kora talking to a little boy down by the water, showing him how to jump the waves in just the right way so as to not get his arms wet. He looked at her like she was the strangest but most magical creature he'd ever encountered, and Sarah wished, for even a moment, that no one looked at Kora any other way. That she could somehow do the impossible and save her daughter from the kind of pain that came with loving and losing.

Sarah finally looked at her mom. "I'll walk away if he asks me to. But he has to tell me that."

Luise nodded, and they both sat in silence for another hour watching Kora play. It was such a simple pleasure for Sarah to see her daughter so free and joyful, that even though Mike was never far from her mind, she found that she could push her problems to the back of her thoughts, like she'd been doing for the past five years. She could, and would, get through this, but hoped she didn't have to, that her mom and her own worst fears were wrong, that Mike still loved her.

Loading Kora into the car later that afternoon, Sarah chuckled, smiling for the first time in days. Kora'd fallen asleep on her mom's shoulder on the walk up from the water to the parking lot, tuckered out from her exertions at the beach. Sarah wished she could fall asleep so easily; perhaps if Kora stayed asleep when they got home, she would sneak in a nap as well.

With her mom's help, Sarah laid Kora down in her bed, brushing her feet off as gently as she could manage. Passing the studio, Sarah resisted the urge to paint her afternoon away. She needed to catch up on some sleep first.

"I'm gonna head up to the mailbox, and then crash for a bit, Mom. I'll be right back."

"Okay. Get some rest, hun. I'll make dinner tonight."

"Thanks."

Sarah walked to the end of the driveway, noting that the weather was turning. There was a smell in the air that only came in autumn, the smell of death and decay that signaled it was time to slow down, be still as winter wormed its way in.

Even though the seasons were mild in southern California, Sarah loved fall the best. The leaves changing color, the disappearance of tourists from the beach boardwalks, Kora going back to school, and her excitement at the end of each day as she recounted what she had learned—all of it made Sarah grateful for this moment.

She inhaled deeply at the end of her drive, taking it all in. She collected the mail, sifting through it on her walk back to the house. Two bills for her mom, and what looked like a letter from a doctor's office addressed to Luise. Her mom hadn't had any recent appointments to Sarah's knowledge, so that topped the list of dinner conversations she'd bring up.

There was an envelope from the community college where she was taking her art classes, promising that inside were classes she could take next semester. She talked herself out of getting her hopes up for that, putting it at the bottom of the pile. The next piece of mail stopped her in her tracks on the driveway.

It had the red and blue stripes on the outside of the envelope, and Mike's cursive scrawl on the outside. The address was his base on deployment; the letter was from before his injuries.

Her hands shook as she delicately pried the envelope open, and her knees buckled when she saw his letter, his handwriting as optimistic as his opening, "Dearest Sarah." She sat down on the old pine stump from her childhood, reminiscent of when her father wouldn't let a freak snowstorm in LA bar them from finding a tree for Christmas. He'd promptly gone out to the yard, without so much as a word to her and her mom, cut the tree down, dragged it back by its trunk, and gone on with Christmas as scheduled.

Now, as she sat there, waiting to read Mike's last words to her from his deployment, according to the date—the date of his accident—she felt conflicted. This letter arriving showed a man who would never give her the silent treatment, no matter what came his way. Yes, maybe he needed time to heal, but if he truly loved her the way he said he did, he would at least want to see her.

Maybe he was hurt enough, changed by his experience enough, that he no longer wanted the same things. And sure, she'd respect that if that was his choice.

Then again, maybe he still wanted what he had but was terrified to ask for it. This letter arriving at this juncture in their relationship made her more confused than ever. She read the two-page letter, hoping for clues.

Dearest Sarah,

It's another hot day here, the sun as relentless as the enemy that we fight, and still, I couldn't find a thing to complain about if I tried. I had the best date with you, and knowing that we feel the same, that you love me, too, makes me the happiest man alive. I've been thinking about that movie, and how it ended, nonstop. It made me realize that I never want to get to the end of life and wonder if I did enough to show you how I feel. Plus, that soundtrack was pretty amazing. Sarah, even here in the desert, I want for nothing, except to make it home safe to you, and to Kora, with the hope of showing you how we can make this work.

To help that along a little bit, I am on my way to the Command tent to tell them that I want to take them up on their offer to join the Intel community, with the hopes of one day becoming a commissioned officer. That means that 1) I will finally be using the degree I got, much to my dad's chagrin, and that 2) I will no longer be going on dangerous missions. Overall, it means that I can provide for you and Kora so you can go back to school, stop that flying all over the world to exotic places thing (wink, wink), and go into teaching like you've always wanted.

I'll let you know what they say but given that Captain Hoffman has approached me twice since the first time we talked, I don't anticipate a problem. Thank you for showing me that it wasn't being in the infantry that made me feel like I was contributing, it was using my skills and what I was good at. Now, I can finally do something real to help, something I know I can do well. I love you for helping me discover that.

So, all of this is leading up to a bigger discussion. You know I love you, and you've told me you love me, too, but I want more than that. I want to not just be your boyfriend, or your pen pal. I want to be your husband, and if you will have me, I want you to be my wife. I know this isn't the most romantic proposal, that I need to ask your mother for her permission, and Kora for hers, of course, but this is just me putting the question out there. I also know that this question is only the beginning of a larger conversation about what we want our life to look like, and I want you to know I can't wait to talk more about all of this. Please don't think I am asking this without realizing the weight it carries for you, your mom, and Kora.

The way I figure it is that we only get one shot at being happy in this thing called life, and I want to spend mine with you. So, you'll find what looks like a shoddy piece of rope taped to this letter, and though it is actually a shoddy piece of rope, it's also my attempt at a ring until I can get back and ask you officially. Silly, I know, but symbols mean a lot to me, and this one more than any other.

Sarah, I love you. I know you have a lot to think about after this letter, but I'll call you soon, so hopefully we can talk through it. Give Kora and your mom a hug from me, and know I am thinking of you today and every minute until I get home.

Love,

Mike

Sarah's hands were shaking. In one, she had a letter that held the key to her future, the one she'd only started to dare to want when she met Mike, and in the other sat a tan ring made of what looked like string from military cammies. Both were things she'd have given anything to be holding a month ago, but now she felt like they were small bombs waiting to explode if she breathed in too deeply or felt too much.

She walked back to her house, the ring clenched in her right hand, the letter folded back into its envelope under the pile of other mail, wondering if she should share it with her mom.

When she got to the front door, though, her mom stepped outside, meeting her on the stoop. She beckoned for Sarah to hand over the pile, but the way her mom looked at her, Sarah knew she didn't mean the bills. Sarah kept back the majority of the mail and sat down on the front stair as her mom pulled out the letter from Mike. Sarah could repeat it verbatim in her head, and wondered as she saw her mom's eyes flit over the page what her reactions to each sentence would be. She still held the ring tight in her hand, and when she saw her mom put the letter down, tears in her eyes, she handed it over. Luise turned it over in her hands and smiled.

Sarah exhaled, unsure until that moment whether her mom was upset or thrilled at this new revelation.

"Okay, okay. I admit it. I was wrong."

"About?" Sarah asked.

"About you giving up on him. This," Luise shook the letter, "this is more than just a crush that went awry. You owe him another chance."

"That's what I was saying before."

"Yeah, and now I'm agreeing with you. Just don't get used to it."

Sarah chuckled. "Thanks, Mom, but I'm not sure I agree anymore."

"What do you mean? This is the most beautiful thing I've ever seen."

"Don't get me wrong, when I read it, it was all I could do to not jump in my car, head to San Diego, and say 'yes.' But what if this was him before, and he's changed his mind since the accident? I'd have been fine if he told me to get lost before. But now, knowing he wanted to marry me, to give me everything I've ever wanted? If I got all the way there and he turned me away, I'd be losing more than just a man I fell in love with. I'd be losing everything."

"But what if you go, and you get everything instead? Isn't that worth the risk?"

"I'm not sure it is, Mom. I've tried so hard to give everything I could to Kora, to keep myself afloat. I can keep that up, but a broken heart would make it that much harder to do."

Luise hugged her daughter, and Sarah felt herself warm and soften like dough in her mom's embrace. "Ah, hun, you're gonna be fine no matter what. You're stronger than another goodbye, I know that. But not knowing if you could have had it all, and just didn't try? *That* might kill you."

Sarah sighed.

Her mom was right, darn it. She owed herself, and more than that, she owed Mike. He'd reached out, in the most meaningful way a man could, and despite all the fear building up inside her like a stone wall, she sat and made plans with her mom for how she should best go about showing Mike that no matter what he was going through, she'd made up her mind to not give up on them, on him.

First things first, they decided. She would need to pack, and as she waited for Luise to bring her suitcase from the attic, Sarah slipped the simple threaded ring around her left ring finger, marveling at how right it made everything feel.

Mendez listened to the activity going on outside of his room like he was under six feet of water, holding his breath.

The lungs in his chest burned, his head pulsed with a dull ache.

For weeks now, it was the same pattern—beeps, the pattering of feet, doors creaking open and softly shutting, muffled voices of doctors and family members who didn't want to let the injured men and women inside the hospital rooms know what they were saying.

That, to him, was the biggest injustice of it all—that he was outside it all, treated like an invalid. He wasn't so fragile he'd shatter if anyone brought up what was going on with him to his face. Except that's how everyone seemed to feel.

His mom was part of those speaking in hushed whispers outside the door, pretending to smile when they'd catch him watching through the glass windows.

Sure, he thought, *I'm sure you're just talking to the doc about the weather.*

He'd stopped pretending to read the magazines people had sent him, watch the news the nurses put on his TV. He just wanted to be part of the conversation.

He grew more and more frustrated with each passing day that didn't happen. Granted, he'd fallen into a pretty deep funk the first few times they'd tried to explain his prognosis and treatment plan, but that didn't mean they should stop trying, right?

Forget them. If they won't talk to me about my own injuries, I'm not making small talk so they feel better about whispering behind my back.

The door clicked open and he pretended to be asleep. For the briefest moment, he considered facing whoever just walked in, but how could he when he'd behaved poorly and they'd ostracized him?

Guilt and fury pressed against each other in his chest, tightening it.

His physician in Balboa, Dr. Braeden, hadn't ever seen combat or even practiced outside the confines of San Diego. He kept going on and on to Mendez's mom about the likelihood of him suffering from depression and PTSD and told her—not Mendez himself, of course—that he wanted him to start counseling right away, along with his PT. Helping the brain with what the body was experiencing was the truest way to heal, according to Dr. Braeden.

What a crock, Mike thought. Let *Braden* go over and fight on the front, see his guys get blown to smithereens, get blown up himself, and find out that it was a pissed off corporal responsible for his injuries, not the enemy. Then let him come talk to Mendez about PTSD. Of course, he was angry and depressed. He'd had the whole world in front of him one minute—a dream career, his dream girl, no more combat—and it had all been stripped from him the next.

Whoever came in dropped something on the table next to his bed. He was used to this new version of mail call but looked forward to it less and less. He'd received a few letters from his guys filling him in on Kint's trial, how he'd been kicked out of the Corps, but that it didn't look like he'd do any hard time. Those were more difficult to read than he thought they'd be. He missed his men, but they made him feel like he was still a part of the team. Really, though, even before the accident, he'd abandoned them to sell out to the officer corps. He sure as heck didn't deserve their sympathy.

Most of the letters, however, were from Sarah, and those were impossible to read.

Mendez knew she called his mom almost every day and wrote him just as often. She'd also sent two stunningly tragic pieces of art she'd painted when she found out he'd been hurt.

Those images were seared to his retinas, there even when he closed his eyes at night. More than anything Doc Brayden said, gave him pause, made him think.

Her talents were immeasurable, sure. And, her heart was infinite. She'd go so far if she wanted to, and he so badly wanted to write her back, tell her to keep pursuing teaching art, but also see if she could sell her paintings, too.

He couldn't, though, not now. It wasn't his place anymore, and that almost killed him more than the excruciating pain of his PT each day. He could tell in her letters that she didn't understand the extent of his injuries, that she was writing to him to fulfill an obligation she'd felt. He wished more than anything that he could go back and not send that letter to her asking her to marry him.

That letter, that call into the void telling her he could, and would, provide for her, love her forever, was only partly true, and the most arrogant thing he'd ever done. How could he possibly have thought that he could write such hopeful, misleading words, no matter how true his intentions were? Yes, he would love her forever, there was nothing at this point that could change that, but everything had changed when it came to him being able to support her. What could she possibly want with a gimp who would be phased out of the Marine Corps with nothing but a small monthly stipend for his troubles?

When the door shut, Mendez waited until he heard the footsteps walk down the hall before he opened his eyes. Glancing at his bedside table, he saw that there was indeed a letter from Sarah, which he didn't have the heart to open now, but another, larger manila envelope lay underneath it. He tore it open using his good hand, but his right hand could almost grasp the paper on its own. His strength was returning, but too slowly to please Mendez.

Great, so he could almost hold a piece of paper. Watch out world.

He closed his eyes and took two deep breaths, a calming strategy Dr. Braeden had shown him when he spiraled down a negative trajectory, but that he only used in secret. Truthfully, it worked, but he didn't want Dr. Braeden to know that or he'd be even more insufferable.

When he felt better, Mendez opened his eyes to the paperwork from the large envelope. It looked like a letter on top, but underneath appeared to be a contract of some sort. Probably something to do with his healthcare once he transitioned out of the Corps. He definitely didn't have the stomach for this right now. He'd let his mom handle it, since she seemed to want so desperately to be useful. He put it aside and grabbed Sarah's letter, taking two more calming breaths before opening it.

Dear Mike,

I'm not really sure how to start this letter, since all of them so far have gone unresponded to. I'd like to ask you questions, answer yours, and share what I am doing, but I am not sure that any of that matters anymore. I know it matters to me, and that I get as much value out of sending these letters as I do writing them—something about the freedom in saying what I really feel—but to know that you enjoy receiving them would be nice, too. I've noticed, in the spirit of saying what I mean and feel, that I learned this from Drunk Sarah. She's been a good teacher in that life is too short to let anything go unsaid.

On that note, I love you, and miss you dearly. This one-sided communication is daunting, but I tell myself that you need time, that I need to give it to you, but then trained-by-drunk-Sarah-me gets weak and writes you again.

Your mom tells me you got my paintings, but not what you thought of them. She says you regained speech—for which I am eternally thankful—but that you don't talk much. Why, I wonder? You always had such lovely things to say, and your voice, which I still hear in my head, was like catnip to me. Addicting and soothing at the same time. I've painted almost every day since your injury, and even though it is some of my best work, I can't look at them anymore. They remind me of you, that you are in pain, and it breaks my heart.

So, instead of sending you art I can barely stand, I am sending you work by another, more prolific and talented artist, Kora. She made this of you, and for you, and though it also breaks my heart, it does so in a way I can tolerate. Her honesty is everything.

Your mom also tells me you started physical therapy for your hand and leg? She tells me it is going well, but (and don't share this with her), I think she lies so I stop asking annoyingly detailed questions. I wish you would call so I could pester you instead...

I don't have much more to add, except that I finished another painting class, and the teacher wanted me to share my work at a student and faculty gallery on campus. I'm not sure I can, though. I paint for me, and for you, and someday, for my students.

I love you, still, and always, and hope this finds you well.

Love,

Sarah

"What have you done?" he whispered to the empty space his life had become. Heat and pressure built behind his eyes, but he wouldn't let the tears fall, not if they'd impede his ability to see the artwork that accompanied the letter he wouldn't soon forget.

The watercolor was of a man with a huge, round head that didn't match with the dimensions of the body—him, he supposed. The man wore different color browns and beiges, had a cap sitting atop his head, and brandished a gun-looking weapon. Behind him were smiling people, both in and out of the uniform the man wore, and there was a caption that read, "Mike, my hero."

Mendez looked at it a long time, before folding it back up and putting it in the drawer of the table, where over thirty letters from Sarah sat, all opened, all read, and none of them given a response.

What could he possibly say? He'd hoped if he didn't respond that she would move on with her life, that he could imagine her happy, cared for, and that he'd be okay with that. But now, knowing she suffered, too, he wasn't so sure anymore. Maybe he should call, or at least write her back, tell her she needed to forget him, that he would be fine, but that he couldn't be with her anymore. Each time he thought of that, though, his fingers froze, and he couldn't make the call.

He was a coward, who told himself that he was doing this to protect her, but he knew it was really because he couldn't be the one to hurt her. Let time help her forget.

The door opened, and Mendez was caught, his hands still in the open drawer, as his mom walked in. He sighed.

"I had a feeling you weren't asleep," she said, pulling up the chair beside him.

He shook his head.

"What did she have to say?" His mom pointed to the letter's envelope peeking out of the drawer.

"Not much. Same old."

"She still loves you?"

Mendez nodded, looking away.

"Do you still love her, Mike?"

"We've been through this. Sure, but that isn't enough right now. Let it go."

"I disagree. Love is always enough if you both feel it. It can get you through anything, even this," she told him, pointing to the hospital bed, to his leg that lay atrophied beneath the sheets.

"Like it did with you and Dad?" he asked. He knew this was cruel, but he couldn't help himself. He wanted her to know the hurt he felt coursing within him.

"That's different. We love each other, we just aren't at a point where we can understand each other."

"Yeah, well, same with us, Mom."

"No, honey, it's not. Your father loves me, and whether or not you believe it, he loves you just as much if not more. He just is as stubborn as you are, and is holding tight to the belief that what he is doing is for your own good. Sarah is reaching out, at least."

Mendez scoffed. "Yeah, right." Darn that heat behind his eyes. It was getting harder to keep at bay.

"Mike, you hear me, and you hear me now. Your father has called me every day since your accident to ask how you are. Every day. He cares more about you than you will ever know."

"Oh yeah? Then why isn't he here, Mom?" Mendez wished he didn't sound as whiny as he did.

"He doesn't know how to be, Mike. He's trying to work up the courage, but when you've been avoiding something for as long as he has, for what you think are the right reasons, it's awfully hard to just up and change direction, isn't it?"

Mendez turned to face her and saw her gaze shifting between him and the letters.

He sighed again. "Subtle, Mom."

"Well, I'm past being subtle. You deserve to be happy, Mike, and you have a chance at it here. Don't mess it up. Let me work on your father."

Mendez closed his eyes again, took more than two deep breaths this time. "How do I start, though? I've been so cold. I haven't written any of her letters back. I haven't returned any of her calls. How do I do this and not sound like an idiot? How do I pretend to offer her the world I promised her, when we both know I can't give it to her anymore?"

"Be honest. Tell her why you've been quiet, and ask her to forgive, even if she doesn't understand, though I am sure she will. You'll be surprised how far that will get you. As for the rest, you'll figure it all out. She isn't expecting you to keep your promises about providing for her, just the ones you made about loving her."

Mendez paused before responding, "Has he told you he's sorry?"

"He has, and it did get him a long way, but he knows the most important apology is still to come. Like I said, let me work on him. You concentrate on Sarah."

"Should I call her?"

"You could, though a little birdie texted me to let me know she's getting on the plane to come down here. You could just wait and tell her to her face."

Mendez's brow sweated. "When? When did she leave? Mom, seriously? You let me sit here this whole time without telling me?"

His mom smiled, pulling back the sheets on his bed. "She'll be here in a few hours. You've got time to shower and get in a quick nap. I didn't tell you right away because you weren't ready to hear it. Was I right?"

Mendez frowned at her, though the corners of his mouth turned up. "You know me well."

"That's my job, son. Now hurry up so I can get the nurse in here to clean you up a bit. You stink."

Mendez laughed, for the first time in months, and swung his left leg out of bed, inching his right one closer to the edge so he could get in the wheelchair they provided him for showers and making his way down to PT.

"Thanks, Mom. How about the hair and beard?"

"I like them long. Leave them but comb the hair."

Mendez mimed a salute to her and moved himself to the chair. He didn't think he could sleep a wink, knowing Sarah was on her way down to see him. He was surprised at how quickly he could get excited to see her, even though so much had changed since they last saw each other.

He had work to do to bring her back to trusting him that he was willing to do whatever it took to make her happy, give her a life she deserved, but he was willing to try. But first, before all of that, a shower.

Time to clean up, he thought.

Twelve

The End

The rain battered the window in small pings, so that it sounded like the inside of a tin can being fired on by a BB gun. She sat upright in the uncomfortable hospital chair in the hallway and fixed her scarf for what felt like the millionth time, softening its grip so that it showcased her collarbones. That was the second place on her body he had touched, the first he'd done with the intent to be close to her. He'd run his pointer finger across it, from her right shoulder to the spot below her neck where it dipped into a perfect finger-shaped shelf. He'd left his finger there just long enough for her to blush, and then, embarrassed, pretended to be touching the silver necklace she never took off. Then, he removed his finger entirely and sat on his hands. She'd loved how timid he was around her after all they had shared—especially after coming to her rescue earlier that day, where he'd been anything but shy.

Now, though, she looked at him through the glass doors and barely recognized the tall, broad-shouldered marine that she'd met what seemed like a lifetime ago.

A year. Had it really only been a year? His hair sat damp and limp on his forehead, lower and more disheveled than she'd ever seen it, and the stubble on his face aged him a good ten years. Or maybe it was what he'd been through that had really aged him. He couldn't see her, and she felt like a voyeur watching him comb his hair, smooth out his shirt. She wondered if he'd tell her anything that had happened over there, or if it would be like the stories she saw on TV, where the veterans closed up, shut their families out. She hoped not. Talking to his mom, a small smile played on his lips.

I missed that smile. But she'd never seen it with so much facial hair. It made him look sexy, more capable than the constantly above-board man she knew. He'd wanted to take it slowly, get to know each other, but now, after almost a year, and despite the hospital bed, she wished she would have talked him out of that.

Her cheeks flushed at the thought of his rough facial hair brushing her cheeks when he went to kiss her, where that kiss might lead, after all this time spent imagining it. His mom left the room, and Sarah's gaze shot down at her lap, trying to erase the heat from her cheeks.

"Sarah," his mom exclaimed, coming over and giving her a hug, "it's so nice to finally meet you."

"You, too, Mrs. Mendez."

Mike's mom shook her head. "Call me Cindy. How are you?"

Sarah nodded, but then shook her head. "I'm great," she started, then, "okay, I guess. A little nervous. Is that silly? I mean, I haven't seen him in almost a year."

Cindy smiled. "It's not silly at all. I'd be concerned if you weren't nervous, honestly. But, Sarah, I have to be honest with you. He's not the same as the last time you saw him."

Sarah nodded again. "I know. I don't expect that. I know he's really hurt."

"He is, and I want to prepare you. His leg is in bad shape. They don't think he'll lose it anymore, but it's never going to be completely normal again."

Sarah found herself nodding yet again and willed herself to stop so she didn't look like a deranged puppet, unable to do anything but shake her head up and down.

"Is there anything I can do? To help?"

"Listen to him, be patient with him. He's been through hell, and it took all this time to work up the courage to see you. He's afraid of what you'll think, but be honest with him. It's the only way the two of you can move forward."

"Okay. I can do that. Does he want to see me? I mean, I know I am blindsiding him, not asking him or giving him any warning."

"I think any other way would have given him the chance to chicken out. He's wanted to talk to you but hasn't known how. Like I said, a lot has changed. But, his love for you hasn't. Thank you, by the way, for that. I'm so happy he has you."

Sarah felt the heat in her cheeks again and smiled. "Me, too, Cindy. Me, too."

"I'll be in the cafeteria if you two need anything. It's good to finally have you around."

With that, and a small intimate squeeze of her shoulder, Cindy left Sarah there, searching for any courage she might have forgotten about. *Ugh*. Why was this so hard? There, a hundred feet in front of her was the man she loved. She took one small step and then another, until she got to the door to his room. She knocked, and the same voice she'd fallen in love with answered.

"Come in."

Opening the door, her hands trembled, but she steadied them, waving a sad little wave when she got in the room.

"Sorry," she said. "Lame. I just don't know what to do that isn't jumping you and kissing you until your face falls off."

He laughed, shaking his head. "I've missed you, Sarah. So much. Come here."

She went over to the bed, her hands trembling. She brushed her fingers across his forehead, which felt clammy, unnatural, and ran them until they reached the top of his beard, which was softer than she'd pictured. She shivered, and her hand, still resting on his cheek, twitched. He stirred beneath her, and she moved back toward the chair, watching him watch her.

Why did this feel strange, awkward, when she was the most comfortable she'd ever been the night they'd met and the months of writing back and forth since? This was all she'd waited for, to have him home safely, to start the life they'd talked about together, finally. She knew it would look different now, but it didn't make her want it any less.

She wished his mother would come back so she didn't feel so out of place. She also wished she'd visited sooner, but now that she was here, she could see why his mom had advised against it. All the wires and tubes and periodic beeping that chimed every few minutes weren't helping her nerves. She couldn't imagine what the room must have looked like two months ago when he'd first arrived. What he must have looked like.

His eyes betrayed any other changes that tried to hide her from the man she knew and loved. They were the same soft brown, shining from behind dark circles and the otherwise pale skin that spoke of his time in the hospital. They blinked slowly, moving up and down her body, taking her in, and her heartbeat matched pace, beating audibly in the otherwise silent, austere room. She clenched and unclenched her hands, wringing them nervously. A thin, fragile-white hand reached up from under the blankets and reached for hers, and it took her almost a full minute to realize it was his hand. She gasped, and her hand went to her mouth, covering her surprise. His hand retreated back under the blanket.

Her hand dropped from her mouth, but she did not reach for him again. She smiled, but too slowly. He saw her fear, she could see the change on his face, and he frowned. She shook her head, realizing her mistake a fraction of a second too late.

"It's good to see you," she tried, but her voice caught in her throat. She was so nervous and couldn't shake it off. The furrow on his brow deepened. "I'm sorry it took me so long to get here. Did your parents tell you I tried to come sooner? Did you get my letters?" She was rapid-firing questions at him like a machine gun at a target.

She needed to calm down. They would be fine; she would be fine. She breathed in deep, tried to let it out slowly. She tried not to look down at his hand, at his body, but at the same time, she wanted to see him, all of him, let him know it was okay, that things were different, but that she still loved him.

He nodded to the bedside table to his left, where she saw a pile of letters, opened but placed back in their envelopes. Still, he hadn't spoken a word since she'd stepped into the room. It had been over two months since she'd heard that lilt in his voice, the one that made each sentence sound like it was a question, an invitation, and she wanted more of it, all of it.

Her idle hands felt like anvils at the end of her arms, dead weights that were dangerous to anyone close to her when she was this nervous.

She moved closer, fidgeting with her scarf again. She reached for his hand, at the edge of the blanket, and felt him flinch beneath her fingertips.

"I'm sorry. I don't know how to do this. It's not at all like I imagined," she said, pulling her hand away again.

"No," he said, the sudden sound of his voice jarring to her, gravelly like sandpaper. It was commanding, what she imagined he sounded like to his marines. She shivered again. "I'm sure it's nothing like you thought it would be. I'm sure I'm not anything you thought I'd be." He looked at her with an intensity she didn't remember, but then, how long had she really looked at him last time? Ten hours? Most of that had been spent nervously looking into her lap, or all around them as she'd flailed her hands and talked at a speed faster than she did with him now.

He'd always unnerved her, but it had never been a liability like it was now.

"That's not what I meant, Michael." Why had she used his full name? It sounded stupid, coming from her, made her sound desperate, maternal. This was going so badly.

"What *did* you mean, Sarah Jean?" He used her full name back, and this time it was her turn to flinch. He knew she hated that name.

"I just meant that I'm nervous. It's been a year since I've seen you, and months since we've talked on the phone. I hoped it would be different. Less..."

"Less what?" He threw the words at her like daggers. "Less like me crippled in a hospital bed? Less talking to a guy that used to be strong, that you can barely stand to look at now? Less what, Sarah?" She was shaking now, and her hands fell to her waist. Her right hand fingered the thin, braided rope tied to her left ring finger, twisting it around and around, the way he was twisting her words.

She dared to look him in the eyes, meet his gaze with the love she felt pouring out of her for this man, who was so clearly broken, battered. She'd give anything to put him back together.

"Yes, to all of that. But not like you think. I wish you weren't here, that you could have come home with your friends, that I could have picked you up and had your first meal be anything other than hospital food. I wish there was something I could do for you, to help you."

At this, his face changed. A smile spread across his face, but his brow didn't unfurl. It gave the effect of making him look sinister. A chill rippled down her spine.

"Help me? *Help* me?" *Oh, no.* She shook her head, her eyes wide, trying in vain to stop him from saying what was about to come next. He went on, ignoring her silent pleas. "Do I look like I need *help* from *you*?" He was shouting now, his hands waving the tubes at her maniacally.

Tears fell down her cheeks and still, she shook her head at him.

"That's not what I meant, you know that," she whispered. Her breaths came shallow now, and her whole body tensed. She was losing him. What had previously seemed impossible, was now happening before her eyes. "You know me," she added.

"I don't know you. And you sure as heck don't know me or what I've been through. You never did or you wouldn't be here right now."

"Stop it, just stop it. You know that isn't true. Help me understand what happened to you, I want to know. You're the only one who knows me, Mike." She was crying harder now, begging.

"I doubt it. There's probably some guy here waiting in the wings for you to leave me so he can take you dancing like I can't anymore." He pointed to his right leg under the sheet, visibly thinner than the left.

"Now you're just being cruel. How could you possibly say that? I'm on your side here, Mike. I'm not the enemy."

"What side is that, exactly, Sarah?"

"The side that is here for you, to make good on all the things we promised each other. Remember? They're still right there for me." She touched the space on her chest where her heart lay beneath her skin, beating furiously.

"Who says they are there for me, *this* me, sitting here right now? I'm not the same person you fell for."

"I know that, but what will it take you to see that doesn't matter to me, that I'm not going anywhere? Your mom told me you were excited to see me. Please."

"What if I want you to go? What if I want to forget about the whole thing?"

She stared hard at him, searching for anything that might be hidden beneath the rock-hard exterior he'd built up around himself in a matter of seconds.

"Was the whole year a lie, then?" she asked when she was met with silence.

"It wasn't a lie. It was a distraction. For both of us. You got to play military girlfriend, and I got to forget about the desert for a few hours a week. We both got what we wanted. Leave it at that, will you?"

She held up her left hand, pointed at the rope ring tied to her finger. "That's baloney, Mike. What about this? Was this a distraction? I got your letter, you know. I want all of that. Still."

He winced, and she knew she had wounded him. Good. At least something was breaking through the armor he'd put up between him and her.

"Maybe. I don't know what that was. A lapse in judgment, maybe. A desert mirage." She scowled at him. Who was this man, and what had he done with the one she'd sent to war a year ago?

"Get out, Sarah. Just leave me alone."

"Why? Why should I leave? Give me one good reason why I should give you anything you want right now?" The tears fell so quickly she could barely see through them.

"Because I don't love you, and I don't want you here." She cried out, a short sob that escaped from somewhere deep within her. Some place she reserved for only her deepest hurts. It was the only thing he could have said to change her mind, to make her leave, not matter how much it killed her to do it.

"I'll go, but you'll change your mind, you'll see. And guess what, I'll be there waiting when you do, because I'm not a quitter, Mike. I'm *not* going to give up on you. Tell your mom I tried, that I'm sorry I didn't say goodbye."

"Go!" he yelled, and she could see tears forming in the corners of his eyes as well. It broke her heart more than the words he'd said.

"Take this, then. I only want it back when you're ready to see the promise through." She took off the ring and set it on the edge of his bed. She knew she'd wounded him again, but she was past caring. She was frantic now, her world unraveling quicker than she could gather the string to stop it from fraying.

She grabbed her coat from the back of the chair and ran out as fast as she could, unwilling to let him see another of her tears fall. The torrent of tears fell when she got to the elevator, and as she went to push the button, the doors opened and his mother appeared.

Sarah pushed past her, shaking her head and waving her hands, staving off any questions. The look of shock on his mother's face matched what she felt, but she didn't have the heart to rehash what she barely had made it through once.

She needed to be as far away from anything that reminded her of the perfect life, with the perfect man for her, that had all disappeared as fast as she'd found it.

When his mother got to his hospital room, he was stoic, any evidence of sadness wiped away. He was good at that. A trained marine was hard to kill.

"What did you do?" she hissed. Then, when he didn't answer, "What did you say to her?"

The look on his face wavered so slightly she couldn't have seen it or she would have pounced on that crack in the veneer. He turned away to face the dark, rain-streaked window. Outside, cars pulled into the parking lot, turned off their engines, and then too much time would pass before the driver and any other occupants would come out. He knew they were bolstering their courage to come in, to face different realities than the ones they'd been given by crummy circumstances.

He pictured Sarah doing the same thing before she came in, and his confidence almost wavered.

"What I had to do to save her."

"Bull. You did it to save yourself. I didn't raise a coward, Michael Mendez."

"Mom, please. Can you let this go?" Mendez was on the verge of tears and didn't want that mortification on top of the rest today. Watching Sarah leave was the hardest thing he'd done, including all his rehab, and finding out that Kint was out in the world, a civilian, but free from jail, despite trying his best to kill him.

"No. You were so excited to see her. What could have happened to change all that in a matter of minutes? She was sobbing, Michael." She used his full name twice in one visit. It made him feel young, like the dumb kid he'd been when his mom'd had to use it every day.

"You should have seen the way she looked at me, Mom. Like I was a monster."

"I'm sure she didn't, and you didn't even give her time. I was horrified when I first saw you, at what they had done to you. I barely recognized you, Mike, despite having given birth to you, and you only gave her five minutes to react before you shoved her away. You were incredibly unfair."

"How do you know, Mom? You weren't here."

"Because I talk to her every day, I bring you her letters, and I see you read them when you don't think anyone is watching. I know you love her, that she's the one you've been waiting for." He kept his eyes on the window.

"I've never loved anything more, which is why I had to make her leave."

"I don't get it, Mike. Explain it to me." His mom, the most stubborn woman he knew, had her arms crossed across her chest and the same furrowed brow he wore. Their similarities were what pulled them together and similarly pushed them apart over the years.

"This," he gestured down the length of the battered frame beneath the thin hospital blanket, "isn't the man she fell in love with. The man she met a year ago died in the desert. Leave it alone, Mom. She'll be better off without me, you'll see."

"I hope you know what you're doing, Mike. God help both of you if you don't."

His mom walked out, but rather than softly letting the door close behind her as she usually did, she slammed it in anger instead. The noise reverberated in his head, creating a dull ache.

He didn't know what he was doing. Truthfully, he'd just reacted, and though he knew his mom was right, that he'd been quick to judge Sarah and her intentions, there was nothing, *nothing*, he could do now to change that. He'd let her walk away, and in the process, made darn sure she wouldn't be back.

Mike closed his eyes and pictured Sarah on the day he'd met her, her hair longer then, pulled back in a high ponytail, and a smile that showed each of her flawless, white teeth, including the small gap one that brought out his own smile.

All he could hope, all he could pray, was that she found a way to get back to that carefree smile again, now that she wouldn't have the burden of him to lug around the rest of her life.

He let that image, and the morphine drip, lull him back to sleep, where he could relive the happiest months of his life over and over, without having to wake up and find her gone.

Thirteen

Life Without

Summer was gone for good now, the leaves all turned overnight into brilliant shades of red and gold, reminding Sarah of the crowd at USC ballgames. There was a chill in the air as well, one that seemed to reach right under her long sleeves and give her goosebumps. Even in southern California there were typically four seasons, but this autumn seemed to come out of nowhere, and resembled the start of winter more than anything else.

Sarah's teeth chattered as she adjusted the thermostat. They would have to live with sixty-five degrees during the day and sixty-eight at night. They were rarely all around during the day anyway, but still. Sarah figured they would only have to do this another week until her training hours at the bar were done, and she could tend bar full time. The money would be enough to offset the bills they had piling up that she just couldn't get ahead of no matter how hard she tried.

Flying just wasn't enough. She'd talked to her mom earlier in the month about canceling this semester's art classes, but her mom had stood firm. She would stay in school no matter what, and if Luise had to, she would go back to work, but that wouldn't work. The pain in Luise's arm had meant she was at risk of another clot, possibly another stroke, and she was advised to seek medical disability, to stop working outside the home.

Now, though, Sarah wished she'd just dropped out and not told her mom. She needed more time to study than flying and bartending would allow, and those were both needs, not wants. As long as she was enrolled, though, she would study and try her best. She didn't know how to give up. Besides, what else did she have to fill her down time now that she had a Mike-sized hole in her life?

With the heat turned down, Sarah grabbed another comforter and settled in on the oversized chair in the studio with her *Lesson Planning in Art Class* textbook. The chair was the only piece of furniture she used these days, and Sarah still cringed when she came in the room and saw the sheet over the easel, untouched now for over a month. Painting was just too hard.

She felt stuck, unable to see past her hurt to translate it to the canvas. She imagined it was what writers called "Writer's Block," but hadn't been able to find any remedy for it. Google searches had suggested writing—or what she read as painting—every day, even if she didn't feel like it. She'd done that once or twice, but it felt indulgent, wasting the expensive paints on meaningless drivel. Now, she wondered if she would be able to conjure up enough of something, *anything*, to pass her oils class in two months.

She read and reread the same paragraph at least four times before she gave up and put the book down for the night. She still had an hour and a half until she had to get ready for her third-to-last training shift at Collins Pub, enough for a short run to clear her mind.

Grabbing shoes, a hoodie, and her beanie, she headed out, pausing only to gather the courage to open the door to the almost freezing temperature outside. She slid her shoes on without untying them, zipped up the hoodie, and jogged from the front door. There was no point walking to warm up anymore; she would have to walk a marathon before she was warm enough to feel comfortable.

The cool air hit her face and formed tears in the corners of her eyes that had been otherwise dry since she'd gotten home a month ago, cried all of the tears her body could produce into her mom's shoulder, and vowed not to waste a single tear on Mike after that.

Yet, Mike was still there, just under her skin, at the edge of her thoughts, and the corner of her vision. At this point, she didn't think there was anything that would rid her of him except time, which she desperately wished would hurry up so she didn't feel this empty all the time.

Her lungs filled with the cool air, and she welcomed the tears that ran down her cheeks, a product of her body's mechanics rather than emotions. Her neighbor, an older woman who, similarly to her mother, had suffered a stroke and moved in with her son and his family, waved to her as she rounded the corner, picking up speed. She waved back, and through the window, saw the son and his wife in the kitchen together, making dinner. Sarah pushed harder, wanting to sprint away from what she saw, what she felt, and the secret wish she still had that a life like that was possible for her.

Sarah ran until her legs threatened to give out underneath her, until she felt the pulse in her wrists pounding with exertion. She ran through her streets, weaving in and out, glimpsing the Pacific Ocean from the tops of hills and watching it disappear as quickly as she sped down the other sides. She got lost in the miles, and would have been late, if it weren't for her phone buzzing in her hand. She'd forgotten she'd even brought it but looking at the screen realized she'd missed three texts from her mom. She slowed down, moving to the corner of the sidewalk.

A car slowed down, too, pulling over across the street, but the glare on the glass from the sun setting wouldn't let her see in. She didn't recognize it, but a warning pricked all five of her senses. There was something suspicious about the way it stopped in the middle of the neighborhood the same time she did.

Her phone buzzed again, and she forgot about the car and the sky.

Just got home with the Bug. Spaghetti for dinner before you leave?

You got a package. I put it on the bed for you. When will you be back? Starting the water now.

The third, most recent, read: *Where are you? All OK? Call me.*

Crap. She'd forgotten in her haste to get out of the house to leave a note for her mom and Kora, who were probably both worried. She knew she'd been freaking her daughter out, that she'd been more quiet than usual, but she didn't know what else to do. She worked, she slept, she studied, she worked some more. Kora was the only joy in her life right now, but the worry of providing for her was getting to Sarah.

She dialed her mom's number.

Luise picked up on the first ring. "Where the heck are you? I've been worried sick, and dinner's on the table."

"I'm sorry," Sarah said, out of breath. "I took off for a quick run and lost track of time. I'm on my way back now. Is Kora okay?"

"She is. I put a movie on for her. Leave a note next time, please? I hate worrying about you."

"I'm really sorry, Mom. I will. I gotta go so I can get back in time to eat and change. Do you mind if I leave you with the dishes?"

"Of course not. I wish you didn't have to work at that skeevy bar, but if it means worrying less about money, I'll take dishes every night to help ease your mind. Just know when I finally get discovered, you'll be doing the cooking and dishes. I'll be too famous for you."

Sarah smiled and noted that the car across the street had left. Weird. "Okay, Mom. I don't think singing in your shower is going to get you found by an agent. But, hey, I really gotta go. I'll see you in ten." Her mom always knew just what to say to change her mood, usually for the better.

She ran fast this time, not to get away from anything, but to get home to her family. Her body felt fluid now, listening to her mind that told it to run all out, to pause only enough to check for traffic, and to forget, at least for now, about Mike.

When she got home, Kora ran up to her. "Momma! I thought you left already and I wouldn't get to show you my picture."

"No, Bug, I'm sorry, I just went for a run. Show me what you have." Sarah went to her bathroom and began stripping off her clothes, not bothering with the shades or the door to the hallway, in too much of a rush to get showered and to dinner before work.

"Time to eat, Sare-Bear," her mom shouted from the kitchen.

"Showering first, but I'll be quick!" Sarah called back as she turned the water on as hot as it could get. She was warm from the run, but her body reacted now to the cold house.

"Look, Momma, I did this at school today. It's for that nice man who gave me the flowers." Sarah cringed, thankful her back was to Kora and that she couldn't see the hurt those words caused. "Can you send it to him?"

"No, honey, I can't. He's moved somewhere else, and I don't know how to reach him." Sarah thought how true those words were, on so many levels, and how sad that made her. She had no idea how his healing was going, if he'd relearned to walk. She didn't know if he'd met someone new, or if he was still angry at her for the last time they'd met. It was all the unknowns stacked up against the others that made forgetting him impossible. Maybe if she had answers, she could finally move on.

Kora was still outside the bathroom going on about how she should use the computer to look up where he lived, because that worked when Nana needed the man to come and fix their phone the other day. Sarah smiled weakly at the innocence her daughter radiated. She hoped Kora would forget about Mike soon, but until then, her adoration was sweet and seemingly harmless. Sarah was able to fend her off and jump in the shower by promising she'd try Google later.

Her shower was quick, and Sarah pulled her hair back into her usual ponytail, limiting her makeup to just mascara. Other women who worked the bar or floor came dolled up like they were trying out for a production of Grease, but Sarah didn't want that kind of attention. She wanted to do her job and go home. Period.

"Nana says that the package you got is from Mike's mom. Maybe she will know where he is!" Kora yelled as soon as Sarah walked in the kitchen. Sarah glared at Luise.

"Is that true?" she asked her mom. Luise nodded, looking down at her spaghetti, and told Kora to shush and eat her food, that it was almost time for bed. "Why didn't you say anything?"

"When would I have? It must have come while you were gone, and you just sprinted to the bathroom. I think it's time you stopped taking your break up out on us, young lady. We haven't done anything wrong."

"Young lady? Mom, I'm not fifteen."

"Then stop acting like it. You're moping around like he was the only thing that mattered to you, and Kora and I are left here picking up the pieces. I won't have it. Now, come sit and eat."

Sarah's eyes were misty. She knew that every word her mother said was true, and it killed her, but she had to know what was in the package from Cindy. "I'm not hungry," she said, and walked out of the room. She'd apologize to her mom tomorrow and start making it up to Kora right away.

"I'm not saving you a plate!" Luise yelled after her. Sarah sighed. She wasn't being fair, she knew it, but maybe this was the closure she needed. She had to see. She grabbed the box, struggling under its weight, and her jacket, and headed out into the cold, shutting the door behind her. In her car, she tore open the box and saw all the books she had lent Mike in nice, neat piles. So, this was it. She was getting all her stuff back. It was officially over. On the side of the box she saw the edge of a full sheet of paper and pulled it out. It was a handwritten note from Cindy.

Dear Sarah,

I am writing you this because, sadly, my son lacks the courage. I know he still loves you, that he has a million things he'd like to tell you, starting with an apology for the way he acted at the hospital, but like his father, his tough skin gets in the way of that a whole lot. I'm not going to speak for him, though, so I'll keep this to the package I sent.

I've returned the books you lent Mike, even though a few of them look pretty good. I'll have to check them out at our public library. I've actually heard a lot of good things about Barbara Kingsolver. It seems he finished the books, though, and he didn't seem to be too upset that I offered to mail them back to you. In fact, he seemed intrigued, but made me promise just to send a post-it note, not a whole letter. He must know me.

Anyway, I know we might not talk much going forward, though I'd like to, but Mike is still my son, and I have to respect that for whatever silly reason, he hasn't contacted you. I just hope this finds you well, and I hope you can remember your time with Mike in a good light. You meant the world to him, and a big part of me suspects you still do. He's just hurting, mentally and physically, and we have to give him time to heal.

I hope this isn't the last time I talk to you, but if it is, you take care of that darling little girl of yours, and thank you for loving my son. I believe it is that love that brought him home from the desert and I'll always be grateful to you for that.

All My Best,

Cindy Mendez

P.S. If you're in the mood for something different, you should check out The Nightingale by Kristin Hannah. It's a good story told well.

Sarah opened the top book, *The Poisonwood Bible*, and aimlessly flipped through it, wondering how Cindy knew Mike had read them all. Did he talk to her about them? Sarah felt a pang of jealousy imagining Mike having the conversations she wanted to have with him with someone else, even just his mom. She stopped when she saw blue pen in the margins, and opened it to a page covered with it. It was Mike's writing. He'd underlined and made notes like she had, many of them contradicting or responding to her comments.

She flipped through slower now, noticing that almost every page was covered in blue scrawl. She tossed the book in the back of the car and grabbed the next, flipping through it, too. It was the same thing in each of the books Cindy had sent back, which was more than twelve. He'd read and responded to all the books she'd sent him, while he worked on getting a better job, went on missions for insane amounts of hours, while he kept in touch with her. And now she was left with an assault of the senses. The books smelled like the desert, and she had thousands of pages of Mike's words to pore over. Sarah read the note from Cindy again, going back and forth between wanting to laugh and wanting to cry.

Her phone dinged, and she looked at it absently. It was just her alarm telling her she had fifteen minutes until her shift started. Shoot. She'd be late for work if she didn't leave now. She started the car, distracted by the books in her backseat and backed out. With her mind back on Mike, and how soon she could get to those books, she barely noticed the car from earlier parked across the street, its lights dimmed, but the engine running.

She registered when it pulled out after her, staying close enough to follow her, but far enough away to not be seen, all the way until she got to the parking lot at Collins Bar.

But she couldn't be bothered. Not with Mike on her mind.

Mendez grunted as he moved his left foot forward. Even though it was technically his good leg, moving it meant putting all his weight on the right, which still had a long way to go until it could support more than a few pounds comfortably. He switched his posture on the PT bars and inched his right forward next. Just four steps in and he was winded like he'd just run a first class PFT.

This is for the birds, he thought, but then just as quickly recovered and added, *I'm lucky to be alive.*

That trite addendum to his "spiraled negativity," as Dr. Braeden called it, was designed to take him out of his own pity and make him "more aware of his blessings." The first few times the doc had made him do it, it felt forced, and he almost laughed at the absurdity of the mantra.

Once, Mike had added—out loud unfortunately—that, "yes, I'm lucky to be alive. No thanks to Kint, the slimeball, who's now free out there in the world because there wasn't enough evidence to convict him of a potential crime committed overseas on a combat deployment, where, let's face it, the laws are different."

"All of this," he'd continued, his voice raised so that other doctors had come in by this time to make sure he was okay, "means that I've been medically discharged from the Marines and am no longer able to take care of Sarah and her daughter. Which, of course," he yelled, "means I lost the only thing in life that ever mattered to me. So sure," he cackled at Dr. Braeden, whose face went pale and brow furrowed beyond any normal measure of frustration, "I'm lucky to be alive. Whoopee."

His lengthy addition to Doc's mantra made it so he had ten weeks of mandatory psych visits to "monitor his depression." He'd thrown his crutch at the door when Doc had peeked his head in to tell him that good news.

At some point in those ten weeks though, he'd started repeating the words "I am lucky to be alive," without any hint of sarcasm or anger. Sometime after that, he started telling himself that without the negative thoughts that usually triggered it.

Finally, he realized he meant it. He was alive, he was getting stronger every day, and he had time to think about what he wanted his next step to be without worrying about money or bullets being fired at him from all directions.

As he got to the end of the PT bars, the therapist clapped her hands.

"Whoop! That's it!"

He exhaled and looked up, wishing it was Sarah there clapping for him instead. He knew she'd be legitimately proud of him, not just performing as part of her duties. He wondered where she was, what she was doing, if he'd ever run into her. His new PT office was only five miles from her house, and his new home not much further than that. He felt her every time he came down here, the past week especially.

Silly, he knew, but it was the same feeling he'd had when he first met her—that instant connection.

Now, it pulled at him, and he wished he knew why.

"Great work, Sergeant! Record time today."

"Yeah, I'm hoping I can still make those Olympic Trials," he quipped, patting himself on the back with his good arm. He felt better today than he had the day before, and without a doubt better than two months ago when he'd started PT.

"You joke, but honestly, I have it on good authority that no one here expected you to keep your leg, and when you did, all bets were against you ever putting weight on it again. You're doing better than any of us professionals thought you would. So, yeah, who knows what you'll be capable of if you keep this up. Smile. You have a lot to be proud of."

Mendez flashed her a cheesy smile, but then laughed heartily.

"He sure does. And I can see he still has his way with the ladies," a voice boomed from behind Mendez. He turned around, keeping his balance on the bars with his hands, which were almost equal now in their strength. The therapist, old enough to be his mother, laughed and fake-fanned herself.

"Captain Hoffman," Mendez said, his eyes bright. He held out his right hand, bracing himself with the left. The Captain shook his hand vigorously, and Mike felt how much strength he still had to gain. That man was still a beast.

"Looking good there, Sergeant. You're making some good progress."

Mendez gestured to his therapist. "That's what she tells me, but man do I feel weak standing next to you," he joked.

"I get that a lot," Captain Hoffman said, slapping Mendez on the shoulder. Mendez was pleasantly surprised that he didn't budge from where he was standing. The Captain noticed, giving him a thumbs up.

"When did you guys get back?" Mendez felt his heart speed up when he mentioned his men. He'd stopped getting letters a few weeks back, which clued him in to their imminent return, but this was the first contact he'd had with anyone since.

"Four days ago. I would have been here sooner, but we had all the on-boarding paperwork to do, and those bright guys we left behind somehow screwed up the housing for the junior marines."

Mendez laughed again. "Per usual, sir."

"Yep. But, I'm here now. Let the new eager-beaver Lieutenant take over for a couple days and watch him regret his decision to not join his daddy's law firm." They both laughed. Mendez felt lighter than he had in months. He'd forgotten what it felt like to be around his fellow marines, what joy it gave him back to laugh freely, joke instead of discuss treatment plans. But it all came back in an instant.

"So, not to sound ungrateful for your visit, but why are you here, sir?"

"I see you're all business, as usual, Sergeant. Well, aside from missing your handsome mug around our squad, I came to see why I never heard back from you about the paperwork I sent over. You give up that easy on your goal?"

Mendez looked at Captain Hoffman, confused. "I'm not sure what paperwork you mean, sir. And what goal?"

"Intel, son. You got the job, and just because you disobeyed orders and got blown up," at this he slapped Mendez's shoulder again, "doesn't mean you're still not the man for the position."

Mendez winced at the joke but still had no idea what the Captain meant. "Ouch, sir. Too soon. And, um, sir, they discharged me. I'm not active anymore."

"I know. I filed that paperwork to get you out. There's no way you're running a PFT again, son, not competitively at least, so the

Marines are a no-go. I'm sorry about that, but it doesn't mean your career is." Captain Hoffman picked at some tape on the bar.

"Okay, I'm getting that, sir, but I'm afraid I still have no idea what you're talking about with the paperwork."

"I sent over a full-size envelope with an offer for you to come aboard as a civilian contractor. It had a letter of intent, outlining the pay and training and benefits, which, if I'm being honest, are a heckuva lot better than what you would've had in the Corps, even as an officer. Under that was a contract that you just had to sign and send back. Since it's been awhile, I thought I'd touch base. You'd be an idiot if you ignored it, and since I know you're not an idiot..." Hoffman shrugged his shoulders.

Mendez's brain rapid fired through memories of his mail drops from the past few months. "Was it a manila envelope, sir? About three months ago?"

"Sure was. Glad the explosion didn't rock your brain too much."

"Sir, I gotta be honest. I wasn't in a place to read more paperwork when that came in. I have no idea where it is now." Panic settled low in his stomach, making him queasy. Dang it. Where had he put that envelope? Had he given it to his mom?

"Haha, I figured as much. I'm sorry I didn't give you the heads up it was coming your way last time. We were in the suck, right in the middle of it, and comms were down. I had the POGs back here ship it off. I'm surprised it made it to you, honestly."

"No worries, sir." When Captain Hoffman only offered him a shrug, Mendez tried to put off the idea that he might have a job offer, despite his injuries. A job he'd love to do. "Anyway, how are the men? They all make it back?"

"They did. It was a messy couple of months, though. The guys' heads were all out of whack with what Kint did to you, that one of their own could do something so heinous, but I got 'em on track pretty quick. Jameson got sent home early with shrapnel to his face, but he was an ugly schmuck anyway, so he'll be fine."

"Seriously, though, sir, what happened with Kint? No one back here seems to know anything. Do I need to talk to anyone? Is there anything we can do to get him put away? I just don't trust that he's out there somewhere. He seriously wanted me dead, sir. I'm pretty sure he's pissed I'm not."

"I'm sure he is. Unfortunately, there's nothing we can do on the civilian end. What he did was overseas, so he's responsible to the Uniform Code of Military Justice. But you let me handle it, okay?"

Mendez nodded, but unease took flight in his chest.

"So, what do you think, son? You interested in coming to work for me?"

Mendez smiled, some of the unease settling with the shift in conversation.

"I am, but, sir, I've got so much PT left. I mean, I can't even live alone yet. When's it start?"

"Whenever you're ready. It's a civilian job, so we can play with the dates a bit. I can get you started with the training a few hours a week if you're interested. Mostly reading and some paperwork. Always more paperwork. It is a government job, huh?" The two men laughed.

"I'm interested, sir, and can start now if you need me, but I don't know if I can deploy again any time soon. Look at me." Mendez waved his right hand down his side, to his leg that was still half the size of the left.

"Who said anything about taking you anywhere with us? No way, son. We don't want that kind of liability. You're sticking around here."

"No deployments? What about PCS orders? I can't move for the next couple years at least, as long as I still have PT orders."

"No moving, either. I mean it. You're stuck here."

Mendez was grinning so much it hurt his cheeks. "Geez, Captain, better pay, better benefits, no imminent danger, and no moving every three years? Why does anyone join the Corps in the first place?"

"Easy now, son. Don't you go giving away our trade secrets. I've got the paperwork if you're convinced. Do you want to run it by your little lady?"

Mendez moved toward his wheelchair. "She's not around anymore, sir. I'll sign today."

"Wanna talk about it?" Captain Hoffman asked, but Mendez shrugged him off. "What'd you do wrong?" Mendez didn't want to go here today, not when he'd just been so happy.

"I had nothing to offer her, sir. I gave her an out."

"She want that out you gave her?" Mendez shrugged. "Did you think to ask her what *she* wanted?"

The necrotic black spot in Mendez's chest where his guilt and shame had been growing now pulsed with renewed energy.

"No, sir."

"Well, it's never too late," Hoffman said, pulling a packet of paperwork out of a bag that Mendez hadn't seen him come in with. "You're a good kid, Mendez. I know she saw that, and if you're honest with her, I think you've got quite a bit to offer her now. Check it out." He handed the paperwork to Mendez, who choked when he saw the pay. It was more than double what he was making as a sergeant in the Marines, with the chance for a raise every three months the first year, every six after that.

"Woooo." He whistled. "That's not bad, sir."

"No, not bad at all. But very much deserved." Hoffman stuck out his hand again, this time with a pen, and Mendez wasted no time signing the paperwork, looking over each page of the contract, getting more and more excited with each line he read.

He wished, now more than ever, that Sarah was here, that he could see her face when he told her to quit the airlines, to go back to school full time and teach after that. He could finally give her a life where she was supported, but there was still the issue of his leg.

Glancing down at it, he had a moment where he saw the possibility of a full recovery, of running to Sarah, picking her up, and spinning her around before kissing her and never stopping. It seemed so far-fetched, but seeing her at the end of it, after a huge apology from him, lit something inside of him that had been extinguished until now. Captain Hoffman saw him looking at his atrophied muscles, scars still bright pink and tender.

"She'll see past the injury, son. You're more than just that leg, you know."

Mendez nodded. "I've made a lot of mistakes, sir."

"We all do. And, somehow, we all end up okay in the end. Can I give you one more piece of advice?"

Mendez looked up. "Yes, sir."

"Make a gesture she can't say no to."

"Sir?" Mendez looked at him, biting his lip in confusion.

"A grand gesture. Make it all up to her, show her what she fell in love with in the first place. And, son, this time, ask her what *she* wants."

Mendez smiled. "Yes, sir. I think I can do that."

Captain Hoffman shook his hand again and patted him strongly on the shoulder. "I'll make sure your squad has some time off to come up here and see you, son. Good luck, and I'll talk to you next week about your training schedule."

"Thank you, sir," Mendez said, his voice wavering. "For everything."

Captain Hoffman nodded and left him in the therapy room, alone with his thoughts. The therapist came in after a few minutes, all smiles.

"That seemed like a good visit. I haven't seen a real smile on you yet. It suits you."

Mendez nodded.

"Are you ready to do some more hard work?"

Mendez thought of everything Captain Hoffman had told him, specifically about Sarah. He knew what he had to do, and now, finally, he had the courage to do it. He only hoped it wasn't too late.

"I am. I really am."

Fourteen

Hurt

Sarah's feet throbbed. She needed to find a pair of black shoes with heels that weren't torture devices, but just couldn't justify spending more money when the purpose of this job was so that she could catch up on bills.

The printer behind her chimed to life, spitting out three separate orders for table service, all with at least one blended drink. She groaned. Between air travelers requesting mai tais, and this new gig in a bar so close to the beach, she would give anything to escape to the mountains and never see a fruity, fancy drink again.

"Hey, sugar. I've been here ten minutes already," a man whined behind her. He wore a floral print top that was at least two sizes too small and a straw hat sat atop his bald head. Sarah wondered who thought people in Long Beach looked like that when they made their packing choices for vacation.

"I'll be right with you, sir," she told him, putting on the best flight attendant smile she had in her repertoire. Her training shift had quickly turned into her first solo shift when the young bartender had called in with a sick child. Sarah didn't mind it, but she was exhausted with the table service turning over every hour. She looked at the tickets and prioritized, making the mixed drinks first so the blended drinks didn't separate. She'd learned that the hard way her first week.

When each of the pina coladas, mai tais, and blended margaritas were made, she came back to the man at the bar, whose scowl had only intensified.

"Hi, sir. Sorry for the wait. What can I get you this evening?" He rolled his eyes at her, and she resisted the urge to tell him waiting for a drink was a first world problem. Did he know that there were Americans getting shot at overseas?

"A Miami Vice. And a little quicker than you made the last one, eh?"

"I'm sorry, I don't know that one." She hated telling people that, but so many times they looked up drinks online, and the names weren't universal. She had a list going in her till of drink translations she'd amassed so far.

"Hello? How long have you been doing this? It's half a pina colada, half a strawberry daiquiri. With fruit, okay?" His voice was nasally and strained.

"Ah, no problem," she said, even though those were the worst, and she called them Lava Flows. Two blenders for one inexpensive drink, but Sarah smiled and made small talk with him while she worked.

Once she got him going, she couldn't shut him up. He told her his name was Ari, that he was there from the midwest, that he'd never been to the beach before, and slowly, she began to feel sorry for him. His wife had left him for a lawyer, the same lawyer she'd used for their divorce, and this was his first trip alone. In fact, it was his first trip past Colorado ever.

"There's a lot to see in southern California. How long are you here for, Ari?"

"I leave tomorrow. To be honest, it's been nice to see the water, but it's not really my pace here."

Sarah chuckled. "I understand that. Someone is always going somewhere, changing something, or fixing something."

"Exactly. How long have you been here?" Ari actually smiled. If he got rid of the shirt, maybe worked on his first impression, he would be the kind of guy she'd want to set her mom up with. He wasn't unattractive, especially when he smiled.

She recounted the abridged story of how she came to be at the bar, that she'd been born in LA, raised a couple miles from there, and was raising her daughter in her childhood home now. She left out the parts about her mom's stroke and Mike, feeling like as nice as Ari was, there was no reason to burden him with her past.

To that end, the less clients knew about her, the safer she was, and therefore the safer Kora was.

Ari stayed two more hours, switching to gin and tonics at her suggestion, liking them more than the sweetness of the blended drinks. She appreciated his company and how fast his stories made the time pass. Before she knew it, it was eight o'clock. She was halfway through her shift.

Her phone rang, and she snuck a look at it. Her mom and daughter's faces popped up on the screen with "Momma" above it. She sent it to voicemail. She was due for a break soon and would call them back. She owed her mom an apology but hadn't come up with what to say yet.

Not to mention the fact that she had a stack of books in the back of her car that she hadn't told her about yet. Sarah didn't know how to broach that subject, since Mike was such a point of contention between them right now.

Her mom's opinion was no secret.

Forget him, move on, get back to life.

What was her life without the possibility of love, though? Working two jobs, taking care of her daughter—and at times, her mom—going to school... There wasn't much of a life left after all of that. Besides, Sarah still felt the connection to Mike in the way she had when she'd first literally bumped into him in the airport. Even after Hank had died, Sarah hadn't felt as strongly as she did now. It was maddening, trying to decide what the right thing to do was.

"You there, hun?" She looked up and saw Ari waving at her.

"Sorry, Ari. I just spaced out a bit. Can I get you anything else before I head to my break?"

"No, I'm good. Thank you for tonight. You're the first nice person I've met here."

"Aww, I'm sorry to hear that, but I'm glad you're having a good time on your last night. You take care of yourself, Ari, and come see me if you find yourself out west again."

Sarah took her phone and left her apron under the counter, out of reach. By the bathrooms, she dialed her mom's number, breathing quickly. She was nervous, thinking about how to fix the aftereffects of her tantrum earlier. Outside, Sarah sat on the stoop, stretching her feet, her shoes off, finally. Luise picked up on the third ring.

"You missed Kora. She was a hot mess, not unlike her mother, so I put her down to bed fifteen minutes ago."

"Mom," Sarah started, but Luise cut her off.

"I know. Me, too. I just want you happy, and I know you thought Mike was the one, but at least entertain the idea that..."

Sarah heard the door open behind her and turned around. All of the servers were needed on the floor in order for her to get a break, and she wasn't remotely ready to put her heels back on. The floodlight put the person's face in shadow, but Sarah could tell it was a male, which meant at least all her servers were still on the floor, and a customer was lost. She stood up, turning toward the door.

"Just a sec, Mom," Sarah said, putting the phone down at her waist. "Sorry, sir, but the main exit is on the other side of the building." She pointed back to where the man had come from.

"Well, isn't that sweet. The selfish little woman still telling people what to do. We're a bit bossy, aren't we?"

Sarah's breath caught in her throat. She *knew* the nasally voice but couldn't place from where. Did he know her? She moved to the right to avoid the glare, but the man put both his hands on her arms, locking her in place. Her breathing grew shallower and more erratic. Her heart rate spiked, and her stomach flipped.

"Get off," she tried, but the words stuck in her throat.

He tightened his grip.

"Let me go. Now." She wished she sounded more confident. That he wasn't blocking her exit. That the front of the building wasn't halfway down the alley and back up another street.

But wishing wasn't an option. Getting out of there by any means possible was.

"I don't think so, Sarah." Oh, no. He knew her name. Something in the way he said it, jogged her distant memory, but she still couldn't see his face, cast in shadow as it was. "I think you and I need to talk." He took one hand off her arm to reach for her phone and she took the opportunity to wrangle free of his grasp and run.

She heard him yell, "Witch!" and take off after her. Her heart thumped against her chest in fear the closer his footsteps got.

Her legs were tired from her earlier run, but she sprinted as fast as she could down the narrow back alley, her bare feet throbbing. She yelped with pain when she landed on broken glass, but she didn't let up. Her chest burned but nothing worse than the fear building in the pit of her stomach.

The man's heavy footsteps were almost on her now. He was a strong runner, but she knew her capabilities. Her one singular thought was escaping, and she thrust herself forward, tossing garbage cans and empty boxes in her wake behind her.

She was almost to the edge of the alley, steps away from streetlights that would have shined a public light on what was happening, when she was yanked backwards by her hair, almost knocking her on her back. She screamed for help, her lungs on fire from the exertion. But she kept screaming, even as the man behind her got ahold of her arm and swung her around. It was only when she could finally see his face, perfectly framed by the nearby streetlights, that she was stunned into silence.

It was the man from the plane where she'd met Mike. *Kint*. The one who had threatened her. She trembled, the fear building from deep within her. She remembered viscerally how frightening Kint was, how he had been the first customer she'd ever believed could cause her harm.

And, he was here. How? How had he tracked her down?

"Ha. I guess you aren't as self-involved as I thought. You remember me." He squeezed her arms tighter now, and she whimpered in pain. "The problem is, you and that jerk, Mendez are responsible for making it so I don't have a job anymore. Do you have any idea—*any idea*—how hard I worked to get into the Marines? Now, you two ruined it. So, I did what I had to do and took care of your boyfriend as well as I could. Now, it's your turn."

His breath was hot and moist on her cheeks and she gagged.

The mention of Mike, of the harm this maniac had caused him, made Sarah see red. If he was going to hurt her, too, she wasn't going down without a fight.

"No thanks to you, he's still alive, and stronger than ever," she spat. She had no idea if this was true, but she had to give Kint the impression that she and Mike still spoke.

"Oooh, I can see why you caught his attention. I like a little spunk. And yes, I may have been a little careless with his 'accident,' not planning it well enough, but only because he got too close to turning me in. I couldn't risk that. I had to act fast."

"A lot of good it did you. He'll recover and find you, and you won't get away so easily next time." Tears streamed down Sarah's face, blurring her vision.

"That's not in the plan, unfortunately. What I have in store for you will take care of him, too. He'll be crushed when he finds out about you, and that's good enough for me. So, I'm going to need you to come with me."

"No! Get off of me! Help!" Sarah screamed. She thrashed against him and saw the frustration on his face as she halted his progress toward the open street. She was winning, making her want to fight harder.

Facing the alley, she saw someone else hurrying down the alley toward them.

No, she thought. *Please don't let him have help. I can't overcome two.* She desperately clawed, hit, and kicked Kint, who grew more and more agitated. As the person got closer, she saw through her wet eyelashes the familiar floral print from earlier.

Part of her rejoiced that help was on the way, but she felt defeated knowing it was Ari, a tourist who hadn't so much as raised his voice in his life.

She shook her head, mouthing *no, no, no.*

She didn't want another person to get hurt, but she was too late. Ari got close to them, swinging an empty trash can at them both. It hit her shoulder, knocking her sideways, but did its job in releasing Kint's grasp on her.

She toppled backwards as Ari grunted and swung at her assailant until he and Kint were out on the open street. She heard Ari yell for help, everything happening slowly around her until she landed, her head and back cracking against the brick wall behind her.

She slid down the wall, her phone clattering to the damp, dirty ground beside her. As her vision faded, she heard a small, frantic voice coming from the speaker, and her unlikely hero still screaming for help.

Somewhere in the distance, sirens blared, but before she could tell if they were getting closer, if she was safe, the pinprick of her vision disappeared to blackness and her mind went blank.

Mendez finished reading through the second of five manuals he needed to complete by the end of the month, set down the book and blue pen he used to take notes on the material, and shook out a cramp building in his right hand. He was so close to full use of the hand, but noticed a big difference in the amount of time it took to wear out his strength. It didn't help that he'd been writing pages and pages of notes on the new job materials.

He had to admit, though, it made him feel so good to work again. He hadn't realized how stir crazy he was going with only his mom and the slightly neurotic Dr. Braeden. The visit from Captain Hoffman had brought him more than just a future, it had brought him back from the dead.

Now, though, he had other work to get done, work that he was looking forward to undertaking. He got up and walked slowly and carefully down the hallway to his bedroom to change his clothes, happy that he could lift his right leg enough to dress himself. Even Dr. Braeden was surprised by the mobility Mendez had gained in the past three weeks.

Pleased with his choice of flannel and fitted jeans, he moved to the bathroom.

The mirror reflected a man who more closely resembled the one who'd left on the deployment. His right leg was almost the size of his left and was getting more agile each day. The color was back in his cheeks now that he was back home and could sit outside and read, or walk the driveway to get his mail. He'd kept the longer hair and stubble but maintained it more than he was able to in the hospital.

What would Sarah think if he kissed her with the longer hair around his mouth? To heck with it, he thought. He'd shave for her, without a question. His stomach flipped, thinking about kissing her again. He knew he was getting ahead of himself, that he had a lot of building back to do, but he was willing to try.

Happy with how he looked, he grabbed a bag by the door and headed to his car. He went to set the bag in the back seat when a car pulled in. A black Subaru that looked like his folks'.

Was his mom supposed to come by? He thought he was meeting her at the hospital later that afternoon for his PT session. He waved, smiling until the glare on the windshield faded beneath the shade of the palm tree in his front yard, revealing that it definitely wasn't his mother.

The car stopped and the door opened. Mendez stood there, frozen.

"Hey, Dad."

A breeze worked through Mike's beard, proof this wasn't a dream.

"Hey, Mike." His dad ran a hand through hair that had thinned since the last time Mike saw him. It was peppered with more gray, too. "I'm sorry I didn't call first. I honestly wasn't sure you'd answer. Did I catch you at a bad time?" His father, Oscar, nodded to the bag in Mendez's hands.

"No. Well, yeah, but I have a minute. Come in."

"Thanks," his dad replied. A static electricity seemed to pulse between them, charged enough to singe them if they got too close. Oscar moved around Mendez, his hands in his pockets. Mendez led the way into the dining room and gestured for his dad to sit.

"Sure. Thanks, again."

"Um, wow. I wish I had some small talk built up, but it's been a bit too long for me to pull that off. What brings you by, Dad?"

His dad bit the corner of his lip, his smile tucked up half an inch higher on the right. Their smile was the only physical feature they had in common. Mendez was otherwise a more masculine clone of his mother. Emotionally, too. He always figured that's why his dad gave him so much grief. Because he was too sensitive, or something cliched like that.

Mendez always resented that notion, not because it meant his dad saw him as weak, but because it meant his mother was as well. There wasn't a stronger woman he knew, besides Sarah.

"You look good, son. How's your leg?"

"It's okay, better than they thought." He leaned forward, his elbows resting on his knees. "Is that why you're here, to ask about my leg?"

Mendez didn't want to get agitated, especially not before he went to Sarah's, but really? His leg? After all this time, all that had happened to him?

Oscar stood up and paced the room. "I know I'm not doing this right, son. I get that. But, I'm here, I'm making the effort. Can you cut me a little slack?"

Mendez put his head in his hands, letting out a silent scream. "Dad, listen to me. I get that you're here, that you think showing up and saying sorry—if you're even saying that—just fixes everything, but it doesn't, okay? I've been deployed three times, blown up on the last one, I broke up with Angela after years of toxic dating, I met a girl I fell in love with, someone who made me a better man, lost her, have been in months of physical therapy just to walk again, and you think showing up will be enough to make up for the fact that you weren't there for any of it?"

Mendez took two breaths, but neither of them calmed him, and he didn't even try to recite the mantra about how happy he was to be alive right now. He would have laughed at himself. "Do you have any idea how much I needed you? I've gone over and over how all of this might have been different if you'd have just been there for me to talk to. But you weren't. You were stubborn, and I'm sitting here a gimp and there's nothing either of us can do to fix that."

His dad came over and put a hand on Mendez's shoulder, but Mendez shrugged it off. His father put it back on, his other hand on his son's other shoulder as well. Mendez was shaking, and he hated that his body still reacted to his father's touch, relaxing under it. He wanted to be mad, to throw punches, to scream at the top of his lungs at the time they had lost, but he felt his breathing regulate, his pulse slow, and his anger subside.

"Son, I get you. You aren't telling me anything I haven't been telling myself for months now, kicking myself for letting it allow our relationship get this messed up. I thought I knew what I was doing, that I was teaching you a lesson that your choices have consequences, but whether or not I was right," Mendez looked up at his father, his lips pursed, and his brow furrowed, "and I wasn't, geez, give me a chance to finish a sentence." Mendez chuckled, despite himself. His dad laughed, too, a lighthearted sound that was almost unfamiliar to Mendez. He didn't know the last time he'd heard his dad laugh, and that realization made him sadder than he could ever be upset.

Oscar continued, "I wasn't right, about any of it. Not in keeping my distance, or the reason I did. Your mom told me about your new job, and son, I'm so proud of you. The thing is, I've been proud of you the whole time. I just didn't want you to turn out like me, a vet with nothing else to show for his life. You had, well *have*, so much potential, and I just didn't want to see you squander it."

"I didn't, Dad."

"I know that, son. I'm just sorry it's taken hindsight to make me see that. Haven't you ever made a mistake and realized it too late?"

"I have." Mendez was fighting back tears thinking about Sarah, how he'd done the same thing to her, not giving her the benefit of the doubt that she could make her own choices about what was best for her. He'd pushed her away the same way he'd been pushed away by his dad.

He hoped it wasn't too late, that he could still reach her.

"Someday, when you're a father, I hope you learn from my mistakes, son. Don't let your arrogance get in the way of loving someone, especially your children, as they find their way through life. You turned out okay in spite of me, but still, I wish I'd been there."

Mendez felt the dust and debris around the space he'd reserved for his father in his heart begin to crumble and fall away. But he was running out of time.

"Dad, I love you, and even though I can't believe I'm saying this, I forgive you. I could forgive you almost anything. And, I'm so glad you are here, but I can't stay. I'll come by for dinner tonight if that's okay, but I've got some place I have to be right now." He stood up with the help of his father, who smiled.

"You bet. Go get her, son." Mendez smiled back and crossed both his fingers.

"Love you, Dad," he said, embracing Oscar tightly.

"Love you, too, son. Always have and always will."

Mendez got as close to a run as he could to get to his car, threw the bag in, and drove off toward Sarah's house, feeling like finally, everything was coming together. His career and his relationship with his father were back on track, and all he needed now was the love of his life to make him the happiest man on the planet.

The drive to Sarah's was shorter than he expected. All this time and she'd been within fifteen minutes of his new home. Another pang of regret shot through him, almost rendering him immobile, but he pushed it down, telling himself that each moment he waited was another moment wasted.

He got a card and bouquet of fake daisies out of the bag and ran through his speech in his head about how these daisies wouldn't fade, like his love for her wouldn't. Cheesy, he knew, but it was just the start. He recited it under his breath as he walked from the drive up to her door, and mustered all the confidence he could to knock.

He waited for thirty seconds, then knocked again. When there still wasn't a response, he peeked in the side window. The lights were off, and the place was in complete disarray. It looked like they had been in the middle of making a snack and had been pulled away suddenly. Everything he knew about Sarah told him she never would have left food on the dining room table, from what he could tell, for days. There was a browned, half-eaten banana, grapes that he could tell from here were shriveled, and a broken loaf of bread in the middle of it all.

Toys that had to be Kora's were scattered across the living room floor, and one of them caught his eye. It was a doll, laying on her side, and the head was a foot away from the body, as if it had been kicked or stepped on and left behind.

Something was definitely wrong. Neither Sarah nor Luise would ever leave that. He pulled out his cell and called Sarah, not giving a damn if it was uncalled for after all this time. It went straight to voicemail.

He hung up, not sure what to say, unable to give a voice to his growing fear.

Mendez tried Luise's number, but the same thing happened. Straight to voicemail.

C'mon... His pulse thumped against his neck; his jaw tight with stress. This wasn't right. He got back in his car, unsure of where he was going or what he could do. He felt helpless and was spiraling out of control when the phone buzzed on the seat beside him.

He picked it up without even looking at the number. "Sarah?"

"No, I'm sorry. Is this Sergeant Michael Mendez?"

He pulled the phone away from his ear and looked. It was the physical therapy's office.

Dang it.

"This is." He didn't mean to sound gruff, but his therapy was the furthest from his mind right then.

"Dr. Braeden would like you to come in at your earliest convenience to fill out your insurance paperwork before today's appointment."

"My what?" Mendez had no idea what she meant.

"You are being transferred from United Healthcare to Blue Cross Blue Shield of California. The changes need to take place in our system before we can see you today. Are you available to come in right away?"

Mendez's brain could barely keep up with her. *Insurance.* Something was wrong with Sarah, he knew it in some indescribable way, the way he knew right away she would change his life. And this lady wanted him to think about his insurance?

"Fine." He hung up the phone, his body mechanically steering toward the hospital, glad at least to have a destination. He thought of calling his mom, but decided against it until he had more news.

Fifteen minutes later, he pulled into the hospital parking lot, almost forgetting why he was there. He walked through the lobby in a trance until a little girl ran by him, brushing against his leg. She looked up at him, a scowl on her face like he'd gotten in her way.

"Sorry," he said, unnerved by her for a reason he couldn't place. He turned around and watched her, wondering why she looked so familiar.

Someone collided with him while he was distracted, and he uttered another, weaker, "Sorry," without turning to see who it was.

He was completely consumed by trying to figure out how he knew the little girl.

"It's okay. Sorry about my granddaughter, she's a little stir crazy."

Mendez froze, then turned around to face a voice he knew, and as he did, everything clicked into place.

"Luise?" he asked. It was like looking at a barely-older Sarah. The little girl who'd ran past him was Kora, in the flesh. He marveled at how similar the three women looked. Without waiting for a response from Luise, who seemed thoroughly confused at how this stranger knew her name, he hugged her, squeezing her tight, even though she pushed against him. Finally, he backed away from her, and instead of anger, he saw the confusion lift.

"Mike?" she asked. He nodded, tears streaming down his face. "I'm so glad you're here. How did you find out?"

Mendez looked at her quizzically, turning to confusion. "Find out what? What do you mean? What happened?"

"Wait, if you don't know, why are you here?"

"I do my PT therapy for my leg here. Luise, please, what's going on? I just went to your house and it looked like a bomb went off. I tried to call you both, but it went to voicemail. I've been going out of my mind."

"We had to leave when we got the call. I haven't even thought about the mess we left behind. Oh gosh, I have to get back there at some point, but... Oh, Mike. Sarah's hurt. Badly." Her voice broke and Mendez reached for her hand, squeezing it.

"What happened?"

She wiped at her cheeks, which were damp with tears. He reached in his jacket pocket and pulled out a handkerchief which she used right away.

"Thank you. It was that man, that marine. He found her," she cried, and dissolved into a new flood of tears. Alarms went off, but he ignored them as she continued, "When she tried to get away, she hit her head. She's been in a coma ever since. The doctors don't know if she'll wake up at all." Kora was attached to her grandma's leg and looked as if the world had greatly disappointed her. He'd never seen a child so sad.

All Mendez heard were the words "Marine... hit her head... coma." His bad leg was trembling. *Kint*? Had he really found her? He'd had plenty of chances to copy down her address in Afghanistan, but Mendez never thought he was capable...

No, it couldn't be. But either way, the worst had happened. Sarah might never wake up. He was too late.

"Luise, please, I know you don't owe me anything, that I royally screwed up, but I was trying to find her today, to apologize. I'm sorry it took me so long."

Luise nodded. "Oh, hun. She loves you so much. What you must have been through with that evil man. I only hope Sarah gets the chance to see you, to know you're back. She never did get over you, you know."

"Me neither. But, Luise, I need to know, what evil man are you talking about? Please, please tell me everything."

Luise gave Kora a coloring book, then gestured for them to sit. Only when she was sure Kora was otherwise engaged, did she fill Mike in.

Sarah took a second job at the bar, but what followed were the details of Kint stalking Sarah, of following her to work, of attacking her outside the back entrance, how a tourist visiting the bar was the one who'd saved her, but had suffered a laceration on his cheek as a result, how she heard everything through the phone, had run to her neighbor's to use their phone to call 911.

It was too much. And, it was his fault.

Mike felt the blood drain from his face, from his body. He felt empty, his insides replaced by a fire that wanted to consume everything and torch it, starting with Kint. His fists were clenched so hard, he drew blood. He squeezed his eyes shut and a tear fell from each.

"I'm sorry. I know this is a lot. Do you want me to continue?" she asked him.

He nodded, knowing that if he'd only come back sooner, none of this would have happened. Sarah wouldn't have had to find work at the bar, Kint wouldn't have gotten close enough to touch her, and she would be there, taking him to PT, planning their lives together.

He deserved to hear every gory detail. He deserved to be punished for abandoning her.

"What happened to him? Can he still hurt her?"

Luise shook her head. "Thank God, no." She went on about how Kint had gotten away, how that had been the longest night of her life, sitting in the hospital, wondering if Sarah would ever wake up, and also if Kint would be back to try to finish the job. They'd stationed police at her door, and at the entrance to the hospital, but by some twist of fate, he'd been picked up by highway patrol for a broken taillight. They had the APB with his picture on it, and he'd been booked immediately, held without bail.

"And Sarah?"

"She's stable. But she hasn't been improving the way they'd hoped. The doctors expected her to be awake by now. Mike, we're trying to be optimistic, but they told us to prepare ourselves for if she doesn't wake up."

Mendez shook his head violently. "No. No, I refuse to believe that she won't. I mean, I found you, against all the odds. I came back and I found you guys. It has to be for a reason. I got a job, I can take care of her, of you and Kora. It can't all be for nothing, it just can't." He was openly crying now, and Kora came over to him.

"You're my mommy's friend," she declared. He nodded. "It's going to be okay, Mike. My momma is a fighter, Nana said. Want to draw her a picture with me?"

He forced a smile. "I'd love to, Kora. It's nice to meet you by the way." He looked at Luise. "You, too."

"It's a pleasure, Mike. I wish it was under better circumstances, but I'm inclined to believe you. There has to be a reason why we're meeting now. I believe in miracles."

"I'm starting to," Mendez admitted. He was nervous to ask the next question, unsure whether he wanted the answer to be yes or no, knowing both would be just as difficult.

"Can I see her?"

Luise smiled weakly. "Sure. Let's go see our girl."

Mendez followed behind them, sending the same prayer into the ether he'd said on deployment.

Please, please, please bring me back to her. Bring her back to me.

He got on the elevator to the ICU and as the doors closed behind him, he felt like maybe he'd been heard.

Fifteen

Believing in Miracles

Dear Sarah,

Hey there, Sare-Bear. I've decided I'm going to keep this journal so you know every single detail about what's happened since you've been asleep. I'll read it to you each day, but I'm still not sure if you can hear me (neither do the doctors), so I'll give it to you when you get up, too. I keep saying "when" you get up, and I think the doctors have stopped correcting me to "if" because they don't particularly like the looks I give them. I know the odds are against you, Sare-Bear, but they always have been, haven't they? And you've always found a way to come out on top.

I guess, since it's my journal, and because we are always more honest when we think we have something to lose, it's time for me to say how truly sorry I am. My job as your mother is always going to be, foremost, to keep you safe. I'm afraid I haven't been doing a good job of that, and the guilt, rightly so, is killing me. But sadly, it's hurting you, too. I don't mean keeping you safe from something like this, a freak lunatic with a death wish (because if I see him, I'll kill him), but the situation I put you in to even be at the bar that night.

If I were the mother you needed, I would be stronger, able to work, or at least not be the burden I am to you financially. Now, I know that you are going to argue when you read this, that I help with Kora, but that's my other job, anyway—to love on my granddaughter every chance I get. It doesn't count as carte blanche for the stress I've put on you to care for me, too, and again, for all of that, I am sorry.

Keeping with the theme of forgiveness (that I am seeking from you, Sare-Bear), I also want to say how sorry I am for not believing in your love for Mike. As fate would have it, he found us in the hospital two days after your accident, after going to the house to find you and us not being there. He saw what a wreck the house was, which will forever be mortifying, and knew something was wrong. I swear that man has a sixth sense when it comes to you, baby girl. Anyway, I filled him in on what happened, and after he saw you (don't worry, I combed your hair before I let him come in), and sobbed for a few minutes, he took my keys, drove to the house, and cleaned it top to bottom.

Then, to add to his awesomeness, he hadn't been gone more than a couple hours and he came back with fresh clothes and food for Kora and me. Baby girl, Sare-Bear, I wish you could see the way this man has shown up for us, for you. Every day he brings textbooks and sits by your bedside, reading to you, to himself, then talking to you, talking to himself. He brushes your hair (I know, I'm sorry, but one day I found him telling you about his new job, just brushing your hair like it was the most natural thing in the world, and I let him keep going. It's kind of adorable.), takes Kora to gymnastics so I can be with you, and at night, he sits here, in the hospital room, playing Kora at checkers. She's actually gotten pretty good. I worry your winning streak might be over when you wake up. Most of all, he talks to me, hun. Tells me about all the things that went through his mind when he got hurt, when you went to see him, and every minute after. I hope you can find it in your heart to forgive him, because, Sare-Bear, there's nothing like this man out there. Believe me, I've looked.

Well, this is just the start, hun. I know it might seem overwhelming, like everything is happening without you being around for it, but I promise you, we are all here for you. I hope this is the only letter I have to write and read to you, that some time tonight I get the phone call that you've woken up, but either way, I'll talk to you tomorrow.

Love you,
Mom

Dearest Sarah,

It's day eight of your "nap," as Kora calls it. She wants to know why you still have to nap, when she doesn't have to anymore. She's so smart the way she knows something bigger than her is going on, that something sinister happened to you, but it's the small stuff that trips her up, makes her forget about that and make up imaginary reasons for your coma. Sometimes, she thinks you just worked too much, that you needed to catch up on your sleep, other times she wonders if you got tired of being a momma, but I'm quick to correct her on that one. I tell her nothing made you happier than being her mother. Still, though, she's doing okay, all things considering.

She's really taken to Mike, which I guess isn't that surprising, since we all kinda fell for him in our own ways. She brings him her writing and reading homework, and, though I wish you didn't have to hear this from a letter, she can read Go Dog Go and Red Fish Blue Fish all by herself now. I know. Your little hellion, who wouldn't take any lessons from you on reading, math, or otherwise (read: cleaning her room and putting the cap on her toothpaste), is now a full-fledged reader. Turns out she just needed a handsome former marine to teach her. Now that I think of it, that's a pretty brilliant business plan, don't you think?

Speaking of handsome marines, just in case he cuts it, let me tell you about Mike's beard and long hair. I know you aren't really a fan of facial hair, but, baby girl, he's quite a looker. He's had about ten nurses hit on him while he's here, thinking he's your brother or something. Luckily, if I'm not there to set them straight, Kora is, and you should see it. She tells the nurses not to talk to him that way, that he's her daddy and loves her momma, and Mike just stands there, grinning, not saying a word, just smiling. I get such a simple pleasure when he doesn't correct her. The look on their faces when they realize they're flirting with a man who's in love with a woman in a coma—priceless. I will say, on those days, we get some better coffee delivered to the room.

Oh, Sarah, I wish you were here, like really here, to talk to me, to laugh with me about these silly antics. Sure, they make us laugh, but really, after it's all said and done, I just want you, hun. I hope you're in there somewhere. The docs came by today and told us even if you do wake up, that they can't guarantee you'll be the same. I told them I don't care, that I want you, however you come back to me.

I'll talk to you soon, hun.

All my love, Mom

Dear Sare-Bear,

We are in week three of you being in the hospital, and last night, something amazing happened. Well, according to the doctors it was usual, but you squeezed my hand when I was reading you my letter. They tried to tell Mike and me that your body was just twitching, that it had nothing to do with whether or not you heard us, but Sarah, here's the amazing part—you were unresponsive until I told you I wished you could hear me. Then, two soft squeezes. Mike and I didn't care about the doctors' pessimistic rambling about brain waves and muscle memory. We just held each other and cried together by your bedside, laughing at the idea that maybe, just maybe, there's hope you'll come out of this.

Mike went out today and wouldn't tell me where he was going, but he asked to take Kora. I know how protective you are over her, hun, but I trust him completely. They were gone for almost two hours, and even though, I'll admit, I was starting to get nervous, they strolled back in, laughing and playing "what animal am I?" He was so into it, Sarah, using his arm as an elephant trunk, and Kora was totally eating it up. She was giggling so hard she wet her pants, which only made all of us laugh harder as she shuffled to the bathroom. It was the first time there has been genuine laughter in the house (or hospital room) since you got hurt, and it felt good. We were less guilty this time, thinking you could hear us, and that you were cracking up at Kora's hilarious impression of a penguin also. It was so good for her to get away, Sare-Bear. She was a kid again, and I am so grateful to Mike for giving that to her. I've been trying, but I've just been so sad, hun. It's hard for me to see out of this.

Anyway, when I asked where they went, Kora went on like Mike had taken her on a weekend getaway. They'd gone to the park, she told me, then ice cream, and the library, where she got to pick out three books (she was more excited about this, even more than ice cream, which tells me maybe we should shift our priorities, haha), then finally, she told Mike to show me what else they'd gotten, and he produced a beautiful bouquet of daisies for your hospital room, plus peanut butter and jelly sandwiches with the crusts cut off. When I offered to pay him for all the stuff he bought us and Kora, he told me to jump in a lake, that he never wanted to hear that from me again. Basically, he wins. At everything. Then, he kicked me out, told me to head home, take a bath, have some wine, and come back later. So, here I am, in the tub, wishing you were the one being pampered instead. I know you have so much to look forward to, with school, and Kora, and now this man in your life. And bubble baths. You have so many bubble baths ahead of you, Sare-Bear, which should be enough to wake you up.

Okay, enough of my rambling. Just know I'm not giving up on you, and neither is anyone here. We're all pulling for you, more so each and every day that passes. You are my baby girl, my Sare-Bear, my love. I hope you are having fabulous dreams, but not so good you don't want to wake up.

Love you always,
Mom

Hey there, Sare-Bear,

So, I have some good news to start off this letter! The doctor did a scan today to make sure you are still *"you"* in there. Basically, he wanted to check and see that things are firing the way they should be, and that you are going to be the sassy, strong-willed woman you were before the accident when you wake up. The most interesting part of the doc's visit was his use of the word *"when"* to talk about you coming out of this. I don't know if I am just wearing off on him, or if he actually believes it, too, but Mike noticed it as well and gave me the biggest smile. His hopes have never waned, Sarah.

This is my thirtieth journal entry to you, hun, and I wish I had more to report on your health than just the scans, that I could tell you how you are showing signs of healing, but the fact that you are still stable has to be enough for now. But you know me and my impatience. When it comes to you, I'm even worse. I snapped a little at the charge nurse the other day when she came in to change your lines. She put her tray on your chest like you were a table, and I lost my mind. "You do know there is a person, a living, breathing, loving, child of mine, under that tray? You think you can treat her like that, and not a countertop?" I asked her. She looked shocked, then embarrassed, and Kora frowned at me after the nurse left in tears.

"You don't treat people like that, Nana. Remember you told me 'integrity?'" Your little girl is so smart, hun. Which, in this case, isn't all it's cracked up to be. Seriously, though, she misses you something fierce, and I just wish you could hear the stories she tells you. The other day, she told you all the things she learned in school and how Mike taught her to do "the right math." She showed you on a napkin, just like if you were awake, holding it up to your face. Mike saw the tears building up in my eyes and distracted her with ice cream.

Other than that, she is doing well. I can't tell you how much she has gained in one month in terms of reading. She's ahead of everyone in her class, and at her conference, her teacher told me she's moved Kora to the first-grade class next door for reading and writing time. Mike is 100% responsible for this. He reads to her every night before I take her home to bed, and always makes her read the last two pages of the book.

Speaking of Mike, I know how I've told you all about how great he is to me and to Kora, but I can't say enough about how much he is there for you. When he gets off work, he picks Kora up and brings her here, and then he does the movement exercises the physical therapist recommends we do with your legs to keep the blood flowing. He talks to you the whole time, mostly about these books he's reading based off your suggestions—nothing I understand, but it's pretty incredible that he's still this invested. I asked him about it yesterday, I couldn't help it. I told him there was a chance that you might not wake up, and wondered why he didn't just move on, especially since you two hadn't even had any real time together. I told him no one would judge him if he left. He looked me in the eyes with the saddest expression I've ever seen, Sarah, and told me there has never been anyone for him but you, and even if the worst-case scenario happened—which he won't even discuss, he told me—that this would still be true. He told me he gave up too easily last time and it almost ruined him, and look what it had done to you. He told me he thinks you two are better together, and even though you're still asleep, I couldn't agree more.

    I picture all the things you will be able to do when you wake up, Sarah. I just need you to hear them, to want them. I know life was hard before, that being asleep might be easier, but I promise you that everything is different now. Mike has said one hundred times to you that there is no way you are going back to the bar, or to flying. It's school, then teaching for you, painting and spending time with Kora in between. On the flying note, I am inclined to agree with him. Not one of them has stopped by to see how you are, Sare-Bear, not one. Just a letter telling you how many sick days you have accrued, after which you will be docked pay. You deserve so much more than that.

    That's all I have for now, love. I want you to know how much I love you, how much I wish you could hear all of this, and that it would be enough for you to come back to us. We all need you, hun, so please, please, please keep me from writing you another letter. I will as long as it takes, but I'd rather have you live your life than me tell you about it. I will talk to you soon, Sare-Bear, one way or another. Hugs from all of us.

    Love you always,

    Mom

P.S. In case you needed another reason to wake up, there is a new Ryan Gosling movie coming out next week. Mom and daughter date night? We have a babysitter now... ;) If he isn't worth waking up for, I'm not sure what is, baby girl. I'll save a seat for you.

Mendez went through the gates of Miramar Naval Air Station and waved to the marine on duty. The kid looked young and fresh-faced. Mendez wondered if he'd ever been to combat before. He remembered when he was first in as a private, looking forward to anything he could learn, every new place he would go.

Man, how that had changed. It only took one push to the desert to make Mendez rethink all that youthful optimism. What had taken its place, though, was a sense of pride that nothing he ever did after that would be as meaningful.

Per usual, he was wrong, though, especially with the recent turn of events in his life. His job was more fulfilling—but also more challenging and demanding—than anything he'd done in the Marine Corps, and that thrilled him to no end.

At the end of each day, he came home to Luise's place, which was its own kind of fulfillment. He'd recently rented out his own home so he could tag team the care of the house and of Sarah with Luise.

And, that was the thing. He'd always assumed it would be his job that would give him the most, add the most to his life. But it wasn't that way at all. Sure, he loved what he did more than ever, but he also couldn't imagine his life without the three Murphy women. They gave him more hope, more laughter, more love than any job could.

Still, it was bittersweet, this new addition to his life, since it came at the cost of losing the one thing that made it all worth it—Sarah.

Her injury had rocked him at first, made him seriously consider why he had survived the blast in Afghanistan, but then, slowly, he'd come around to realizing that Sarah's coma, though tragic, was only a hiccup. He knew, without a doubt, that she would come out of it, and that he was going to spend the rest of his life loving her. If anyone had heard him admit that aloud, he'd have sounded crazy, he knew, because there was no evidence that she would either come out of her coma or love him like she once had.

He didn't care at all about any of that, though. He believed in her, in them, and that was enough for him. He allowed himself to daydream about things they would do when she got better as he drove to meet Beverly, a real estate agent he'd known for years through his mother. She'd called him at work and told him to come that afternoon to a house he'd fallen in love with. It was a weird call; she was uncharacteristically vague about why she was calling, and he was nervous.

From the moment Luise had mentioned needing a bigger space so Kora and Sarah wouldn't need to share a room when she woke up, Mendez had started seriously looking, picking up where he'd left off in Afghanistan. He hadn't told anyone yet, especially Luise, but he'd found the perfect home for them, the four of them, if they would have him. If Sarah would have him.

He did worry, in the back recesses of his mind that he tried not to perseverate on, that he'd gotten this close to Kora and Luise, and Sarah would reject him like he had her, and then he'd lose three of the most important things in his life in one fell swoop. He didn't know how he would handle that.

So, instead of letting his mind wander down the "negative spiral" he'd all but forgotten about, he imagined going grocery shopping with the three of them, picking out a bottle of wine for him and Sarah to share that evening, letting Kora sneak a bag of M&Ms into the cart with a smile and a wink. He thought of them getting home, unloading the groceries, him putting his hand on her hip, maybe sneaking a kiss on her forehead as they passed each other with the ingredients they would use to make dinner together. He let himself get as far as grabbing her in the middle of chopping vegetables to slow dance with her in the kitchen, Kora and Luise watching, smiles all around. It hurt his chest, he wanted all of that so badly, but luckily, he pulled up to the house before he got too wrapped up in the future.

Each time he'd seen the house, he was overwhelmed by its perfection for Sarah and her family. The living room and dining room had been recently renovated to be one large room, and the family that was selling it had one wall of the living room installed with built in bookshelves. He knew Sarah would melt when she saw that, and he could see her meticulously taking them out of the boxes in her small garage, lining them up, and making sure they all could be seen.

Beverly met him outside, a huge smile on her face. Her cheeks were rosy and when she greeted him, she sounded and looked so much like his grandmother, it only endeared him to her more. Her voice sounded like she had smoked the past fifty years, and he bet that wasn't far from the truth.

"Well, hello there, Michael," she boomed, opening her arms for a hug. He embraced her warmly. She was the only one besides his grandmother who could get away with calling him by his full name.

"Beverly. Thanks so much for meeting me today. I hope it's good news," he said, and winked at her.

"Why the heck else would I take you away from that lovely lady of yours?" she teased. "How's she doin' by the way?"

"She's good. Stable. The docs just did a test and it looks like her brain activity is strong, so that's a plus."

"Oh, honey, that's terrific. You give her a hug from me, you hear?"

"I always do."

"Okay, enough of this chit chat, let's talk business." Mendez nodded and laughed. Beverly was usually the hardest person to keep on task. She usually wanted to know how he'd been, what he'd been up to, how Kora was doing in school, anything but talk "business." She must have something big to tell him.

"You're the boss. What's up?" He was genuinely curious about why she'd wanted to meet here, and not at the office.

"Do you want to go inside? We can talk there."

"I don't know, should we? I've already seen the house and know it's perfect."

"Well, I hate to break it to you, mister, but there are a few details that have changed that we need to go over."

Dang it. He'd worried about holding off on pulling the trigger on this place, but he'd hoped Sarah would have woken up by now to help make the decision. As it was, Luise didn't even know he was looking for, let alone found, a place. Maybe that was all better now, not to have their hopes up, since it looked like things had changed.

"Lead the way, then," he said, trying to not to sound as downtrodden as he felt.

She headed up the walkway, and as she unlocked the door, Mendez felt his heart sink. He really loved this house, and though he knew there were plenty of others out there, this one was the perfect fit. It was even two blocks away from Kora's school. He could walk her there in the mornings before work.

Beverly went into the kitchen, and Mendez followed, trying not to look around and remember all the small quirks he'd fallen for with the house. There was a stack of papers on the counter, and a small bag on top of them. It looked like keys were inside. Maybe she was going to show him other properties after this? But then why meet here?

"Here's the deal, Michael. It turns out the seller took the house off the market." Mendez's face dropped.

"Any idea why? It seemed like they were really ready to get out of here."

"That's true, I agree, but—" The doorbell rang, cutting Beverly off. "Ah, he's here. I just thought since you were so invested in the house the seller should tell you directly."

Mendez started to protest. "That's not really necessary, Beverly—" The door opened, and Mendez's brows lifted in surprise. His old Colonel walked through the door with his wife.

"Sergeant Mendez, how are you, son?" He held out his hand and shook Mendez's firmly.

"I'm terrific, sir, thank you for asking. How have you been since you got back stateside?"

"Good, good. The wife here's got me busy with packing and house hunting in Lejune, so that's why I haven't checked in with you. I'm real sorry about that. This is Maggie, by the way."

"Pleasure, ma'am. Not at all, sir. It wasn't expected in the least. So you're PCSing?"

"Yep, they saw fit to promote me to a one-star, can you believe that? Proof our leadership in Washington's got its head on backwards."

Mendez chuckled.

"No way, sir. No one deserves it more."

"Son, I appreciate you saying that, but it's you we've got to thank. What you did for your men, going out on that mission when you didn't have to—I've rarely met men who exhibited such courage. Thank you."

"It was my job, sir. Though the friendly fire I could have done without." They both laughed again, and the Colonel slapped him on the shoulder.

"Glad you've still got your sense of humor, Sergeant. Anyway, I've got to talk to you about this house. Would you care to sit?" He motioned to the couch in the living room, and Mendez walked over there, his limp barely visible.

"I've got to say, though sir, I'm a little confused. You didn't have to come all the way down here just to let me know the house is off the market. I'm sorry you had to go through the trouble when you're so busy."

"No, it's my pleasure." Pleasure? That didn't make sense. "Beverly, do you need to do anything first?" the Colonel asked. She shook her head, trying unsuccessfully to hide a conspiratorial smile. Mendez knew that look from every time they got to a house, he knew she liked more than the others. Something was up.

"Alright, you two," he said, addressing the Colonel and Beverly, leaving Maggie, who had been quiet in the back, out of it, "You both look like you're plotting something. No offense, sir, but I'm on to you."

The Colonel's smiled broadened. "You see, Maggie, I told you he was bright." His wife nodded in agreement, smiling demurely. "Well, son, here's the deal. This lovely lady here," he put his arm around Beverly, "was hired to sell our house, and she got to talking, as I am sure you can imagine, and went on and on in one of our meetings about a young marine who'd been injured in Afghanistan, and how much he loved our house, et cetera, et cetera. After a bit, I realized she was talking about you. I knew your story like the back of my hand, and I know now isn't the time, son, but I am deeply sorry for all that happened to you over there. You need to know that we as a command blame ourselves for not seeing his deficits and handling him sooner."

"Thank you, sir, and I agreed with you in the beginning, about me not seeing his issues earlier, but if I've learned one thing from all this, it's that I can't live in the past. Plus, with one big exception, things have been going pretty well for me since. I am one of the lucky ones, sir. I know that much."

"Well said, Sergeant. We also heard about what happened to your girlfriend on account of Kint. There are no words, son. My wife and I were devastated."

"Again, thank you. That's been the toughest part, sir. Getting hurt over there is part of the gig, but that he could want to hurt me over here by hurting her? I've struggled a whole heckuva lot with that. What I've done to her and her family."

"I understand, believe me. What we do over there always seems to find a way back to haunt us back home, and oftentimes it's those we love the most that suffer our demons. What happened to her was heinous, but degrees of it would have happened, anyway."

Mendez nodded. He knew exactly what the Colonel was talking about. He'd hurt Sarah all on his own before Kint was even a concern to her. There was healing that needed to be done across the board, it seemed.

"Well, if there's anything I can do, please let me know. But for now, let's talk about the house," the Colonel said.

"Yes, sir."

"When we found out it was you that had the most interest in the house, we took it off the market, son. But, may I ask why you didn't make an offer? The VA loan will more than cover what we are asking."

"It will, sir, but I was just waiting, I guess. To see if Sarah woke up."

"Okay. That makes sense. But my wife and I want to make you an offer, son. One that will hopefully help you and us at the same time. We," he grabbed his wife's hand, "would like to lower the price thirty percent if you buy the house by the end of the week."

Mendez looked back and forth between the Colonel and his wife, staring in disbelief. Thirty percent?

"That's incredibly generous, sir, but how does that help you?"

This time it was the Colonel's wife, Maggie, who spoke. "This is the home we raised our children in. It is where our youngest learned to ride a bike, and our oldest got married out back. We have the most cherished memories from here, and Mike, we would love to know we were leaving the home to someone who would build the same life within its walls. From what I hear, you're not only an incredibly deserving individual and service member, but you will make those memories. *That's* how you help us." She hugged him, and he felt his body shake with sobs. He didn't think he was undeserving, but all of this—the job, the house, Luise and Kora—all of it was too much.

"Thank you," he said, his voice breaking and muffled. "I don't really know what to say. This is unbelievable."

"Well, it comes with a catch. You'll make our lives a heckuva lot easier if you say yes, and you're willing to move in this week."

Mendez laughed, wiping his eyes. "How could I say no? You've got a deal, sir," he said, and shook the Colonel's hand. The Colonel broke free and embraced Mendez.

"Okay, then. Let's sign some paperwork."

"One hitch, sir. I haven't been officially approved for the loan."

"That's not a problem, Michael. When the Colonel and his wife approached me with their offer, I filed the loan paperwork you gave me. You're all set, hun." She winked at him again and he got the distinct impression she was enjoying this very much.

Mendez shook his head in disbelief.

"You guys. You have no idea how much this all means to me, what it will mean to Sarah and her family."

"That's what we're counting on, son," the Colonel said.

The four of them laughed, and the Colonel and his wife told stories from their time in the home. Tears were shed, and after an hour or so of catching up and paperwork, the Colonel handed Mendez the keys.

"You take care, son, and if you get the chance, send me some photos from time to time of your family. I'd love to see you grow in this place like we did. I hope it's good to you."

"I'm sure it will be, sir. And thank you, again. This is pretty amazing."

"Thank you, son. Your bravery won't be forgotten. Semper Fi."

"Semper Fi."

The Colonel and his wife left, waving until their car was out of sight. Mendez walked over to Beverly and hugged her tight.

"You're a sneaky one, aren't you?" he teased.

"I've got a few tricks still left up my sleeve, Michael. I'm not dead yet." She giggled like she'd shed forty years off her age.

"Thank you, Beverly. I don't mind your tricks when they end up like this," he said, waving his arm back toward the house.

It was his. His and Sarah's. Now, he just had to get back to work and bide his time until four when he could leave and pick up Kora from school. He couldn't wait to tell her and Luise to start packing.

Beverly and Mendez stood there in the front yard talking about his ideas for the home, her back to her normal chatty nature. They fantasized about who would get what room, and where to put Sarah's studio, when his phone buzzed. He pulled it out of his pocket, smiling when he saw Luise's number on the screen.

"Hey there, Luise! How's our girl doing?" he asked.

"Mike. How fast can you get here? She's awake."

Mendez stood there, the phone still to his ear, his other hand balled up in a fist up against his lips, pressing against them tight. The tears from before fell again, this time accompanied with bubbles of laughter.

Finally, he remembered Luise was still on the line. "How is she?"

He could tell by the hiccups that came through the receiver that Luise was crying, too. "She's perfect. She's asking for you."

"I'm on my way." Mendez hung up the phone and ran to Beverly, scooping her up and twirling her around, despite her squeals. "She's awake, Beverly. She's awake!"

Beverly started crying as well, dabbing at her eyes with a tissue she pulled from her purse. "Well, this is one kind of day, isn't it, Michael?"

"It is, Bev. It really is."

"Now, go! You're wasting time, precious." He smiled, kissed her on her cheek, and started a full sprint to his car. He was almost there, when he heard her yelling behind him. "Your keys, hun! Don't forget your keys!"

He ran back to get them, kissed her again on the cheek, and took off, his body on full alert like it always was before a mission that was uncertain. He couldn't let himself believe Sarah was going to turn him away, but still, his nerves were on rapid fire, making his hands and legs shake as he drove. He took ten deep breaths and they didn't make a dent in his excitement.

No matter what happened to him, Sarah was awake, and she was okay. It was all he'd ever really wanted.

When he got to the hospital parking lot, he whipped into a spot, scaring a small, gray-haired lady who was getting out of her car. She waved a cane at him, and he had to try not to giggle, instead mouthing "Sorry!" to her, which didn't change her scowl. He only paused to grab a small bag from his glove compartment, which he put in his pocket as he ran. He waved at the old lady on his sprint toward the front doors of the Emergency Room.

"She's awake!" he yelled.

He took the stairs two at a time, unwilling to wait the painful amount of time for the elevator to show up and patiently take him to his floor. He didn't stop until he got to her room, where he came to a dead halt. His breathing and heart rate were out of control, but his leg fared okay. No amount of time spent trying to calm them outside her room was going to change anything, so he took one last deep breath and opened her door.

Sarah was there, sitting up in bed, a team of doctors and nurses attending to her, fluffing the pillows on her bed, pulling at tubes and adjusting her fluids. It looked like a princess being made up for court.

In the middle of it all, Sarah looked at peace, her pursed lips set in a smile. Kora was draped over her lap, Mendez saw, meaning Luise had probably gone to get her early from school. Sarah ran a hand through Kora's hair methodically, like she hadn't skipped a beat. Luise stood tall by her daughter's side, not flinching at the movement and buzzing around her from the staff. She was resolute, holding her daughter's other hand, much the way she'd spent the past month.

He stood in the doorway, taking it all in, tears silently falling onto his cheeks. Suddenly, Sarah saw him, and her face lit up the way it had the first day he'd known her, on the airplane, when she'd seen him on the plane before the marines took off for Germany.

This, *this* was what he'd spent almost a year and a half waiting to see. That smile, the way her eyes crinkled into her cheeks when she was happy. Never mind the ominous backdrop that told of a darker story, all of his longing was met in that moment.

She beckoned him with her free hand. "Come here," she mouthed, and he felt his body moving toward her automatically, the way it had since the start. The doctors and nurses parted around him like water, keeping busy but making room for him beside her. He reached out for her, and his other hand reached for Luise.

"Hi," was all he could get out under tears. He squeezed her hand and she squeezed back.

"Hi, you. We have to stop meeting like this, you know."

He laughed, and it did the trick of, at least temporarily, stopping his tears.

"So true. Welcome back, Sarah. You have no idea how much we've missed you."

"I do, though. I heard it all. My mom's letters, your stories, Kora's mini math lessons." They all laughed at that one, and Kora chimed in.

"That's not funny. I was teaching her," Kora said, nestling back in her mom's lap. She looked so natural there.

"I know, Bug. I loved it, all of it," she said, looking at Mendez. "Can we have a minute, please?" she asked the room. The commotion and melee stopped abruptly until her doctor spoke up from the corner.

"There's so much we have to do to make sure you're okay and stable, Sarah. I don't think that's a good idea."

"Will any of it make a difference if we wait ten minutes?" she asked. The doctor looked at Mendez, then at her.

"You've got ten minutes. Not a minute more." She nodded, and he cleared out the medical team. Luise picked up Kora off the bed.

"C'mon, hun. Let's give your mom and Mike a few minutes to talk. How does ice cream sound?" Those, as usual, were the magic words, and Kora, who'd started by violently shaking her head at the request to leave her mom, brightened at the mention of her favorite treat, and followed her grandma out of the room. Mendez watched Kora drag Luise down the hallway.

"So," Sarah said when they were finally alone.

"So," Mendez replied. "You could really hear everything we said?"

"I think so. I'm sure I missed some of it, but I caught so much. It was weird, like I was hearing it in a dream. I thought I was, until my mom told me those things had all really happened. It was so bizarre."

"I can't imagine what you went through. Sarah, I'm so sorry for everything. I really screwed up—-"

"No. Don't do that." She cut him off, waving her hand. "We both made mistakes. I don't want to go there, Mike; I want to move forward."

He nodded. "Okay, but we're gonna go there someday."

"Fair enough," she said, and looked down at her lap. "Mike, I do want to thank you for everything you did for my family while I was sick. You saved the day, really. I don't know what my mom would have done without you. But I want you to know there is no obligation to stay just because—"

"Nope." This time he waved her off. "We are *never* going there. I didn't do any of it—-not a single thing—because I felt obligated to. I love you, Sarah, and I'm sorry it took so long for me to come back, but I never stopped loving you."

She put her head in her hands and wept. He continued, his voice wavering, "I understand if you don't love me back, especially after all that happened to you because of me, but you need to know how I felt."

She looked up at him, her face wet with tears. "I love you, too, Mike. I have since the beginning, and even when you sent me away, that didn't change. Please know that."

"I do," he said, his chest thumping wildly.

"And about Kint, Sarah, I don't know where to start with that, except to say that I should have been there. I'm sorry. So very sorry." He kissed her cheek. "He's gone, though. For good. They caught and tried him for attempted murder and he's being held without parole."

"It's okay, Mike. I'm okay, and you're here now, so that's all that matters. I am glad to hear Kint won't be back, though."

"Not for a long time, if ever. He's got a laundry list of smaller offenses they're trying him for, too."

"Thank God."

"So, now what? Where do we go from here? What do you want, Sarah? Because I know where I stand." He was taking Captain Hoffman's advice, asking her what she wanted this time around, not making any more assumptions.

"I want you, Mike. If the offer still stands, I'd like to ask for that rope ring back." She looked nervous, smiling and biting her lip, and the color had come back tenfold to her cheeks.

He looked at her, his face serious, his smile gone. "Actually, that offer is no longer on the table."

Her face fell, her smile faded along with his, and she looked down at her lap.

"Oh, I know. Sorry. Um—"

She was quiet for a few moments, and he watched her, patiently waiting for her to look up at him. When she finally looked up, he was there, bent on one knee, a bag by his side, and a small box open in front of her.

She gasped. Inside was a round, halo-encrusted diamond ring.

"Sarah, I did this all wrong the first time. All of it. If you would do me the honor of becoming my wife, I promise to spend the rest of my life making it up to you and more. Sarah Jean Murphy, will you marry me?"

Sarah was crying again, but she was smiling, too. She playfully smacked his shoulder. "I don't know what to say," she sobbed.

"Say yes, Momma," Kora yelled from the doorway.

Mendez and Sarah laughed. Luise was there, wiping her eyes as well.

"You think I should?" Sarah asked Kora, who had run back into her lap by this point.

"Yes! I love him, and I know you love him because you're smiling like you do when you eat ice cream."

"I am, aren't I? Well, you heard the girl, Mike. I'd love to marry you." Kora and Luise whooped, and Luise came in to join them in a family hug. Mendez slipped the ring on her finger, a perfect fit.

"I helped him pick it out, Momma!" Kora squealed.

"You did?" Luise and Sarah asked at the same time.

Mendez nodded.

"She did. This was her favorite, and she has pretty good taste, if I might add."

"When did you two sneak off to do this?" Luise asked.

"Last week, after the library. I had to buy her two scoops of ice cream to bribe her not to say anything."

Luise laughed. "I'm so happy," she eked out, her face hidden in Sarah's shoulder.

"Me, too," Kora added, followed by a "Me, too" from Sarah and Mendez. Mendez pulled away from the women, clearing his throat.

"Hold on, ladies," he said. "I have another surprise for you. All of you." All of them, Kora included, looked at him, their eyes wide. He marveled at how similar they all looked, three clones, mere decades separating them from looking like sisters. Mendez pulled the set of house keys from his pocket.

"I've been looking for a home for us all to go home to, if this went the way it did today, the way I hoped it would, and I found the perfect one." He went on to explain the unusual circumstances surrounding his purchase of the Colonel's home, from the initial interest, to discovering how perfect it was, to being shocked by the Colonel's incredibly generous offer. The women screamed when he told them the home was theirs, all of theirs, as of that afternoon.

"Can I have my own room back?" Kora asked. The women all looked at Mendez.

"Not only can you have your own room, Kora, but you get a playroom. Also, your mom gets to keep her studio. And Luise, there's a heckuva mother-in-law suite attached for you, so you can have privacy or be a part of the craziness, whatever you feel like."

"Mike, you are too good to be true," Sarah said, as Kora didn't waste a minute rattling a million miles a minute to her grandmother about what she wanted her new room to look like. Mendez took Sarah's hand.

"I love you, Sarah Jean. And don't think you're getting out of this without following your dreams to teach."

She laughed.

"Oh, I fully plan on it. And I love you, too, Michael Mendez." He bent down and cupped Sarah's cheeks in his hands, and kissed her, wanting to seal this moment in his memory forever. This would always be the best moment of his life, when he realized he had everything in the world he needed to make him happy.

"Eww, gross," Kora said. Mike pulled away from the kiss, laughing, but kept his forehead against Sarah's.

As the four of them gawked over Sarah's ring, and talked about the house, about moving, and what their future looked like, the doctor came back with the full medical team behind him.

"How are we in here?"

"We're great," Sarah said. "Never better."

"It's my job to make sure you stay that way, so I'm going to need everyone to step out for a bit so we can run some tests. Okey dokey?"

"That's fine," she said.

Mendez wanted to protest, but Sarah shrugged him off.

"We have the rest of our lives together, Mendez," she said. "We have forever."

"We do, Murphy. We do. I'll see you soon, then." He started to follow Luise and Kora out of the room, but turned back, kissing Sarah fiercely on the mouth again.

"I love you, Sarah."

"I love you, too. So much."

Mendez released her and walked out of the hospital room, scooping up Kora in his arms and tickling her. He walked with his new family down the hall, feeling like, finally, he could say that things were going to work out. He held Kora's hand, listening to her continue to talk about her new room, and for the first time in a long time, didn't want for anything.

He was a man fulfilled.

Acknowledgements

Thank you first and foremost to my readers. This book was the first romance I imagined when I knew I wanted to write in this genre. Imagining an epistolary romance was a challenge since it's not a common format, but it felt important to tell this story.

I couldn't have done that without Anna, Kate, Stacy, Erica, and Samantha--best friends who champion my writing. You all are the reason my work has seen outside my imagination. Thank you for the cups of coffee and glasses of wine that went into talking about Sarah and Mike's story.

Thank you to my Comfy Cozy Books editor, Cindy, who has helped my career in immeasurable ways and is another champion who believes in everything I do. That is so rare and so appreciated.

A giant thank you to my parents, who buy a copy of every book I write even if they know I saved an author copy for them. They're my biggest fans and I feel lucky to call them mine.

Lastly, most importantly, to Isabel. I love you with my whole heart (my whole lifetime, and more). Thank you for giving me the time to write, to dream up stories on our walks, and for being the best dang daughter a woman could ask for. You're the reason for everything.

Made in the USA
Columbia, SC
26 June 2024